Talented Horsewoman

Talented Horsewoman

L.C. Evans

Draumr Publishing, LLC
Maryland

Talented Horsewoman

Copyright © 2008 by L.C. Evans.
All rights reserved. No part of this book may be reproduced, stored in a retrieval system, or transmitted in any form or by any means without the prior written permission of the publishers, except by a reviewer who may quote brief passages in a review to be printed in a newspaper, magazine, or journal.

Any resemblance to actual people and events is purely coincidental. This is a work of fiction.

ISBN: 978-1-933157-25-2
PUBLISHED BY DRAUMR PUBLISHING, LLC
www.draumrpublishing.com
Columbia, Maryland

Printed in the United States of America

DEDICATION

To my husband Bob, who always believes in me.

Chapter 1

If only. Those two little words were to haunt me for weeks. If only I hadn't put off getting my hair trimmed, I wouldn't have had to spend so much time trying to tame what had become an unruly mop of brown curls. If only I hadn't paused to answer the phone, I wouldn't have wasted ten minutes on a telemarketer who repeated my name—Leigh McRae—twice in every sentence, as if that would prompt me to buy the magazines she was selling.

I finally cut her off and, still feeling no sense of urgency, sauntered out to my truck. Later I would wonder why I'd given in to a demon caffeine habit that had dictated I stop for coffee at Bo's Diner, and then linger stuffing my face with a jelly donut.

It wasn't until I'd licked the last bit of sugar from my fingers that I finally considered I'd be late for my appointment with Rita Cameron if I didn't hurry. I drove a few miles over the limit until I came to a construction zone, where I lost all the minutes I'd gained.

Cursing under my breath, I inched my way past a mile of traffic cones, then sped the rest of the way down a country road to whip the truck into Rita's driveway. I bounced through a pothole, rounded a bend, and let out a muffled shriek when I registered a horse barreling toward me. In a microsecond I hit the brakes and jammed the shift lever into park, barely avoiding a nasty collision.

A sorrel filly streaked toward the truck at dazzling speed before sliding to a stop that left grooves in the dirt. Without pause she rolled on her hocks and changed direction, racing back toward the barn. After a quick circuit of the corral, she finally slowed from a gallop to a prance, flying her flame-red tail like a banner and holding her head as high as the prow of a sailing ship.

My breath whooshed out. The one horse stampede was over. Another second or two and the filly I knew as Sandstone Tinker Star would likely head for the patch of Bermuda grass near the hay barn and settle down to grazing—easy for me to catch her and put her back in her stall. But before I could act, a screaming woman brandishing a flimsy pine branch flashed into view from the left, and Tinker turned on the afterburners.

I leaped out of the truck and hit the ground running, my arms whirling like plane propellers. "Stop screaming and waving that stick around. You're scaring her."

The branch-wielding woman showed no signs of having heard and, as Tinker raced past, she planted her legs wide apart and landed a solid blow on the filly's rump. Without missing a beat, Tinker fired with both hind legs, barely missing the woman's head. The filly's tail swished and she swerved toward the training arena.

By then I'd had time to conclude that the horse-chasing woman was Millie Destin, Rita's neighbor from across the road. If she wasn't careful, she was going to end up getting kicked or worse.

I turned to follow Tinker's movement, hoping she wouldn't head back toward Millie. As I tracked the galloping form past the barn, a bundle of rags on the ground hardly merited my attention—until an instant later when I realized the bundle wasn't rags. With a jolt somewhere in the center of my chest, I forgot all about the horse and stumbled forward a few steps.

"Oh, my God, it's Rita," Millie sang out, echoing my thoughts. She scurried over to grab my arm, her fingers digging in like pincers until I peeled her loose. I glanced sideways and noted her complexion was the color of an undercooked biscuit.

We moved closer and I saw that the figure was indeed Rita Cameron. Holding on to each other for support, Millie and I stared down at Rita. She lay on her stomach, her face pressed against the concrete that formed a parking pad in front of the hay barn. Blood had pooled around her head.

I dropped to my knees to feel for a pulse in her neck. Nothing. I knew it might be dangerous to move her if she were still alive, but she wasn't breathing. CPR might be her only chance, so with Millie's help I rolled her over. Then I wished I hadn't. Rita's blue eyes were wide open and had taken on the blankness of dolls' eyes. Her blood-caked face was tinged purple.

"She's dead, ain't she?" Millie stuck her hands in the pockets of her baggy overalls. She screwed up her mouth in an attempt at a smile as if we were simply discussing last night's rain, but I couldn't miss the wobble in her voice.

I nodded. I'd never seen a dead person up close, but there wasn't a shade of doubt. Living people have light in their eyes.

"Must of fell out of the hay loft." Millie bobbed her head to reinforce her conclusion.

I swallowed hard, barely able to take in that Rita was gone. "Looks that way."

A soft whicker drew my attention back to Rita's filly. After ending her race at the edge of the woods, she'd ambled back as far as the training arena gate where she stopped and watched us, her head lowered and her ears flicking back and forth. For the first time I saw a bright smear of crimson on her right shoulder.

"We better call someone," Millie said.

"Yeah." I scurried across the driveway to the stable, kicking up pale clouds of dust that didn't even have time to settle on my jeans. With shaking fingers I punched in 911 on the phone in Rita's office.

The authorities summoned, I walked back with a lead and snapped it onto Tinker's halter. Maybe I should have stayed with Rita, but I couldn't bring myself to look at her again and, after all, help was on the way. I led the filly into the stable and inspected her shoulder. A ten-inch long ragged gash ran from her chest at an angle toward her withers. Not deep, but still nasty looking.

"Barbed wire," I said out loud. But Rita didn't have a foot of barbed wire on her property.

By this time Millie had left the arena to join me. "Horse got cut over at my place." She jerked her thumb to indicate. "Galloped too close to my front fence."

Rita had told me a few days ago that Tinker had managed to flip open the latch on her stall and she was going to have to get a clip for the latch to keep the filly from getting loose again. I glanced at the stall door. It looked like Rita hadn't gotten around to the chore.

I put Tinker in the wash rack, using cross-ties to hold her. Then I hunted in Rita's feed room until I found a tube of antibiotic ointment. I washed the wound, then layered on a generous amount of ointment.

I rejoined Millie in the yard and we waited—me still fighting back nausea and leaning against my truck with my arms wrapped around myself, Millie pacing in front of me, occasionally shaking her head. It was a beautiful March day, warmer than normal even for a Florida spring, and the sun was dazzling. The sky was as blue as I'd ever seen it, the color of Texas bluebonnets, without a wisp of a cloud anywhere. Still I shivered as if I were outside without a jacket in the middle of December.

"I didn't know Rita was around," Millie said, crossing her arms over her chest. "That horse—the one running loose—trotted into my yard right before you showed up. He trampled half my plants before I managed to chase him back across the road."

But first she'd chased Tinker close enough to a barbed wire fence to rip her shoulder open. And then she'd almost gotten herself kicked in the head.

"You didn't see Rita when you got here?" Of course she hadn't. We'd spotted the body at the same time.

"Lawd, no. I was too busy trying to run that animal back into the barn. I was planning to give Rita a piece of my mind, too. Hey, ain't I seen you around here?"

"I'm Leigh McRae, a friend of Rita's from the horse club."

"That's it. I don't have horses myself. Prefer hogs. But Rita never liked my hogs and I reckon they didn't like her. Hogs are smart as people, you know."

I gritted my teeth. Why was she talking about hogs when all I could think about was Rita with half her skull crushed?

A siren screamed in the distance, and I turned to peer toward the road. But because of the bend in the marl-surfaced driveway, as well as a line of Brazilian pepper trees along the fence, I couldn't see the road from where we stood. Moments later the siren stopped, and a rattle of broken shell and loose dirt got louder as an ambulance and a car from the sheriff's department appeared around the bend.

I peeled myself away from the truck to intercept the two deputies heading for the stables. "Over there," I said, pointing toward the larger barn where Rita stored her hay. They reversed direction.

I experienced an odd sense, I guess I'd call it surreal, as I watched the scene unfold in front of me. The ambulance crew, a man and two women, rushed up carrying cases of medical equipment. They snapped on rubber gloves and positioned themselves around Rita; one of the women whipped out a stethoscope.

A black Jeep Wagoneer slid to a stop behind my truck and a plump woman wearing a platinum blonde wig eased out from behind the steering wheel. Paris Winslow. She used to be Olive Winslow before she gave herself an upgrade to a classier name. Real estate saleswoman and part-time newspaper reporter for the *Del Canto Star*.

I winced when I saw her lime green polyester pantsuit. In a moment of even more bad taste, she'd accessorized with neon pink shoes, pink purse, and pink plastic beads that matched her lipstick. She leaned inside her car and exchanged the purse for a gadget-encrusted camera, a mini tape recorder, and a notebook. Neither the paramedics nor the deputies objected when she started snapping pictures. Her husband was the county sheriff, Dude Winslow.

The dust had barely settled on Paris's Wagoneer before a generic, county-issued car rolled up and parked alongside the ambulance. If people kept showing up, we'd soon have the population of a small town milling around Rita's barn.

A man wearing a navy blue sports jacket, white shirt, and dark tie emerged from the county car. A black woman in a navy pantsuit got out from the passenger side. After briefly checking out the scene next to the riding arena and consulting with the paramedics, the woman led Millie to the shade of an oak tree. The man—thin and with a severely receding hairline—strode over to me and said, "Hey, darlin'. I'm Art Frazier, detective with the sheriff's department. Mind answering a few questions?"

I felt my back stiffen and the surreal feeling evaporated. How would he like it if I called him darlin' or maybe honeypot? "I'm Leigh McRae. Millie Destin and I found Rita Cameron dead next to the arena."

"You seem a little shook up. Want to sit down?" Detective Frazier flipped open a notepad and drew a pen out of his shirt pocket.

"I'm fine," I said. It was a lie. I was still trembling and probably even paler than Millie's biscuit color by now, maybe as pale as the white Del Canto, Florida Horse Club shirt I'd put on this morning. I took a deep breath just as a random breeze from the east floated the sour smell of Millie's hog farm into my personal space.

"What time did you find the body?"

"Right before I made the call to 911—about nine. I came over to pick up a load of hay we'd split. The first thing I noticed was a horse running loose." I pointed toward the barn as if Frazier could see through walls. "Millie was chasing the horse with a branch. When she galloped between the arena and the hay barn I turned to watch, and that's when I saw Rita."

"A loose horse? Could it have run her down or kicked her?" Unlike mine, his voice was flat, completely lacking in tell-tale trembles.

"No." I shook my head. "A horse won't deliberately run into something—or someone. And that filly is gentle."

I'd bred and raised Tinker myself. Last week I'd sold her to Rita, and if there was a sweeter filly in the state, I didn't know about it.

"So you don't think the horse hurt Ms. Cameron?"

"Millie and I thought Rita must have fallen out of the loft. She knew I was coming to pick up my share of the hay and she was most likely up there getting a head start, throwing the bales down for me to pick up."

"Looks that way." Detective Frazier shook his head. "She should have waited for help. Lot safer to do a job like that with a spotter. Especially at her age. How old was she, about sixty?"

"Fifty-nine. Rita always said the good Lord would come for her when it was time."

"Reckon he showed up with a one way ticket this morning. Religious lady, was she?"

I nodded. "She once told me she'd read the Bible cover to cover five times."

"Religion's a nice thing, real comforting, but it can't protect your skull if you don't take precautions." Frazier nodded sagely.

I didn't know what precautions could prevent gravity from pulling someone to the ground really fast if they fell out of a loft twenty feet in the air. I was sick over Rita's death and I wanted to go back and check on Tinker. I glanced at my watch.

Detective Frazier jotted in his notebook. Finally he snapped it shut and squinted at me. "I can see this is a real upsetting time for you, Ms. McRae. I'll contact you again if I have any more questions."

"Sure." I didn't expect to hear from him again. I supposed there would have to be an autopsy, but from what I'd seen and what Frazier had said, it seemed clear that Rita had fallen from the loft and landed on her head. Nothing but a tragic accident. Except…something about the scene didn't seem quite right, but I couldn't think what was wrong.

Chapter 2

The deputies' green and white car was blocking my truck—an aged, midnight blue Chevy pickup—so I couldn't leave. Millie didn't have that problem. She'd trudged back up the driveway a minute ago while I was completing my interview with Frazier. I expected she needed to get her hogs fed and watered before it got any hotter.

But I wouldn't be alone. Paris Winslow had finished snapping about a million pictures of the arena and the two barns, inside and out. Now she whipped out her tape recorder and sailed in my direction.

"Leigh, thought I recognized you." She ought to. She used to work in my ex-husband's real estate office until she got tired of taking orders from a man who could have been poster boy of the year for control freaks. "Would you give me an interview about the tragedy?"

"Fine, as long as you don't take my picture." I didn't relish the thought of myself—sporting barn clothes and with my messy hair—staring foolishly out from the front page of tomorrow's paper.

"I promise, though I don't know why you'd object. You look fantastic and I love your new hairstyle—sort of gypsy-out-in-the-wind. God, I always wished I'd been born with the genes to grow up tall and willowy. What are you, about five-nine? Size eight? I guess I'm stuck with short and stocky." She gestured at her body and made a face.

I shook my head. Paris had nothing to complain about. She was an attractive and dynamic woman, despite the unusual taste in clothing style.

We moved over a few feet to stand in the shade cast by the barn. I briefly recounted the story and she stopped me a couple of times to mouth comments into her tape recorder. She referred to Frazier as "Del Canto detective." Rita was "wealthy woman" and "local horse trainer." I was both "talented horsewoman" and "equine enthusiast." I wondered if she'd cross the road when she was done and interview Millie. Probably not. She'd have to call her "hysterical hogwoman."

"That's it then?" Paris asked when I got to the part about the paramedics arriving.

I nodded and she turned off her recorder before finishing up with a cheery, "Thanks so much, Leigh. You look wilted. Let me know if there's anything I can do to help you cope." She rushed to her car and sped away without waiting to see if I needed her help coping.

The nausea I'd felt earlier had returned and I massaged my stomach as I went to check on Tinker. Then I watched the detectives for a few minutes, wishing they'd hurry.

They measured the height from the loft floor to where Rita lay. Frazier squatted to get a closer look, before pointing out something on an arena fence post and taking a sample. I knew what it was; I'd seen the red splotch earlier. But the blood was high on the outside of the fence, nowhere near Rita, and most likely came from Tinker's shoulder.

The woman detective, presumably Frazier's partner, climbed the ladder and busied herself inspecting every square inch of the loft and taking pictures. No one was going to accuse her of failing to document an accident scene.

I wandered into the barn, dodging a saddle and bridle lying in the aisle, and sat at the desk in Rita's office. By now my head was screaming "impending stress headache," and I needed to get out of the sun before it cooked me.

The top of Rita's desk was dust free, but cluttered with scraps of paper, horse show fliers, paper clips, and pencils. A box of horse magazines took up one corner. A black notebook lay open in front of me.

I picked up the notebook and saw she'd neatly listed her horses and the kinds and amounts of feed each received. I swiveled the desk chair and looked at the paneled wall to my left. Framed photos of Rita with some of her show winners nearly covered the entire surface. A calendar featuring a picture of a spring foal hung by the window. The days leading up to today were neatly X'd out. For today's date Rita had written in pencil, "Jared," and underlined the word. Underneath she'd written "Leigh M. picking up hay." For tomorrow she'd scrawled, "hair salon."

A tear rolled down my cheek. Rita wouldn't be keeping any more appointments at the Cut 'n Curl.

Despite our nearly twenty-four year age difference, we'd been friends linked by circumstance and our mutual love of horses. But now I understood I didn't really know her. I didn't know if she read poetry or if she liked seafood. I didn't know if she'd gone to college or if she'd dreamed of traveling to Rome someday or if she wished she lived in Wyoming. Didn't know how she felt about the new city park that had cost so much taxpayer money. I wondered if it was normal to feel guilty for not finding out what Rita was really like while she was alive. And for not being on time to prevent her fatal accident.

Rita had saved my life once. As a teen, I'd been attending a horse club pool party where I'd slipped on the wet deck, knocking myself out and falling like a rock into the deep end. Rita saw me go under and she dove in, pulling me to safety almost before my unconscious body could suck in a breath. Fair was fair. How come I couldn't have returned the favor? How come I couldn't do one single stupid thing for her?

I leaned back in the chair and closed my eyes, then opened them immediately at the sound of yet another vehicle bumping down the driveway. I glanced out the window and saw a silver

Ford Ranger pickup slow at the bend. The driver hesitated as if he were going to make a u-turn.

Frazier waved both hands overhead and hurried across the grass to intercept. He pointed to the stable, then said something I couldn't make out.

The stranger jumped out of his truck, heading my way at a fast walk. Before I went back to studying the walls so he wouldn't see I'd been spying, I noted his medium height and muscular "I-work-out" kind of build.

Footsteps tapped across the concrete, then the man stopped in the office doorway. He was close enough now for me to see his squarish, Brad Pitt jawline, periwinkle blue eyes, and dark chestnut hair with reddish highlights.

Confusion flickered across his face when he glanced up and saw me. I guess Frazier hadn't told him there was someone in the stable.

I jumped to my feet and held out my hand. "Hi, I'm Leigh McRae." I felt as though I should add something, but didn't think "talented horsewoman" or "equine enthusiast" would be quite the thing.

"Jared Beaumont." He shook my hand. He had a solid grip, though his hand was damp. Understandable in the heat. "Mind if I wait here with you? The detectives want to ask me some questions."

He must be the "Jared" on the calendar, the appointment Rita would never keep. "No problem. But I guess you can't tell them much more than I can. Still, they're cops, they've got a job to do, and they like to ask questions."

"That's what I hear." He ran his hands through his hair, glanced sideways at the wall calendar as if it held the answers to whatever the cops needed to know, then sat heavily on the desk. "What a shock."

"Are you a close friend of Rita's?" I was sure I'd never met him.

"Uh, no, we aren't—weren't—well acquainted. I'm new in town, took a computer consultant job at the hospital, and was planning to buy a couple of horses. Had an appointment to come out and see Mrs. Cameron about what she has for sale. And you?

I mean, did you know her well?"

"We were in the horse club together. I had the day off from work and came here for a load of hay. A neighbor and I discovered her body."

He studied me intently and I got the impression he was waiting for me to elaborate. I'd want to talk about all this later, but not now, not while I was still struggling with disbelief. And not with a stranger.

Detective Frazier appeared at the door. "We'll notify Ms. Cameron's kin. Ms. Destin told us she had a sister. Anyone else you can think of who ought to know right away?"

I started to say there was nothing, but then I remembered the horses needed looking after. "She had a hired hand. Someone has to feed the horses." I dragged myself to my feet and picked up the phone book on Rita's desk. "Rita told me he was off today, but I can call him."

"Appreciate it."

Frazier hovered in the doorway while I dialed Doug Reilly, Rita's barn help. Doug was good with horses, but it was common knowledge that the defining moment of his life occurred when he tasted cheap wine for the first time. If he'd already drunk up his last paycheck, he'd likely be sober enough to come by and look after Rita's animals.

There was no answer from Reilly, and not even an answering machine to take a message. I copied his number onto the back of a crumpled Walgreens receipt I found in the pocket of my jeans. I told Frazier I'd call Doug again later.

The police would notify Rita's sister, Maggie, but Maggie wouldn't be able to take care of the horses. Maggie was strictly a dog and cat person. She owned a pet grooming shop east of town—Fancy Felines and Dapper Dogs.

Meanwhile, there was still the problem of Tinker. I couldn't leave her in the wash rack with the hot sun beating down while she waited for Doug to show up.

I addressed Frazier. "Is it okay if I put away the filly? The one in cross-ties?"

Frazier looked startled. "Good idea. We're done taking pictures of the accident scene and we're almost ready to clear out."

Jared Beaumont wandered out of the office, trailing behind Frazier and me. I glanced at him and he shot me a friendly smile. I turned my attention to Tinker and put my hand on her halter.

To me, she looked distressed. I wondered if there were some way she sensed Rita was dead. The skin on her left shoulder quivered as she shook off a fly, then she put her muzzle up to my face and exhaled gently.

"Yeah, I know, baby. Tough day, isn't it?"

I led Tinker down the aisle, opened her stall door, and put her inside. While I was taking another look at her shoulder, Jared picked up the saddle and bridle I'd seen earlier. He waited in front of the tack room door until I came over and opened it. He hung the bridle on the closest peg near the door where sunlight streamed in through the window, catching the silver accents on the browband.

It was one of Rita's show bridles. Now why would she use a show bridle just to take a few turns around the arena? Especially since the saddle it had been paired with was a battered one she only used at home or on trail rides. I remembered her show saddle was top-grade, well-oiled leather that matched the bridle.

I glanced around, completing a mental inventory of the tack as quickly as I could. Frazier had consulted his watch twice in the last minute. Rita's show saddle rested in its usual place, on a rack under the window. But her work bridle lay in pieces next to a can of leather oil on an old card table. Someone had been oiling the bridle and hadn't finished. That explained the show bridle being used. Rita had probably been in a hurry. Didn't sound like her, though. But then, neither did getting herself killed falling out of a hayloft.

Before I left the tackroom, I grabbed a metal snap off a bench and went back to attach it to Tinker's stall latch so she couldn't turn herself loose again. The other detective came into the barn and escorted Jared outside. The interview wouldn't take long. He'd know even less about the accident than I did.

I went back to the office and tried Doug Reilly's number again, but got no answer. When I came out of the barn, Jared was leaving, and a few minutes later the detectives pulled out. I jumped in my truck and followed as slowly as I could, giving Frazier and his partner time to pull in at the driveway across the road. I figured they were going to ask Millie a few more questions, or maybe check out the yard damage she'd complained about earlier to save themselves a trip.

Busy morning, Sheriff Winslow. We investigated a fatal hayloft accident and the ruination of a lawn before we headed over to the Burgers 'n Such.

I turned toward town, sparing only a quick glance in the direction of Millie's doublewide trailer home set back about fifty feet from the road. Rita had said more than once that if Millie spent as much time working as she did spying on her, she'd be a millionaire. I didn't see how Millie could do much spying with the thick growth of Brazilian pepper trees lining Rita's fence and her driveway. The only view she could possibly have was across the width of the driveway, and then only as far as the bend where the road curved up to the stable.

The road stretched in front of me, an asphalt line so straight it could have been laid out against a giant ruler. Heat waves danced above the pavement, shimmering into a mirage that promised water it would never deliver. I shook my head and glanced in the rear view mirror at the empty truck bed that should have been filled with bales of sweet smelling alfalfa.

Whitney, my eleven-year-old daughter, would be heartbroken when she found out about Rita. Rita had been her trainer ever since she'd started riding. We'd bought Whitney's new show horse, Sonny Joe, from Rita, trading Tinker as part of the payment. I slapped the steering wheel hard with my right hand. If only.

Chapter 3

I mashed the gas pedal toward the floor, speeding the rest of the way home. Palmettos whizzed by in a green blur until I forced myself to slow before I had to turn in at my driveway.

My headache had backed off right after I left Rita's, shifting to a barely noticeable twinge. Then it clunked down hard, becoming a throbbing pain that arced from the back of my neck to my forehead.

I pulled up beside the barn. Later I'd back the truck into the shed. Unlike the animals, the Chevy could wait for attention.

I checked on Sonny Joe, setting him up with a flake of fresh hay. I ran the automatic waterer to be sure it was working, turned on a fan, and looked in on the other horses.

Lena, excited by my arrival, limped back and forth in her stall, nickering non-stop. She was the equine equivalent of the Type A personality. Lena had ripped a tendon in her right foreleg in a freak accident at a show earlier in the year. She'd been in her rented stall waiting for her class when she'd managed to catch her hoof in a loose board. Horses generally panic when their feet or legs are trapped, and Lena was wound tighter than most. She'd damaged the leg beyond repair before the stall board finally popped off, freeing her.

My other horse, Belle, was an old bay broodmare I'd had for years. She was Lena's mother, and normally I'd have had one of her foals coming along that I could have used for Lena's replacement. Tinker should have been that foal, but at two years old, she'd grown too tall for Whitney. My daughter had inherited my mother's petite frame and Tinker promised to mature at more than sixteen-and-a-half hands. Since a hand is four inches, that kind of height would leave Whitney looking like a flea on top of a mountain. Hence the decision to trade Tinker for Sonny Joe, who was not only a comfortable fifteen hands, but was a solidly trained and kid broke three-year-old of rare quality.

Belle had missed last year. Now she was heavy in foal to a top sire, but of course it would be at least two years before Whitney could ride the new foal, even assuming it was good enough for shows. And assuming I felt like showing. Rita's loss was still heavy on my mind, and right now I felt like I'd never know joy again. I gave Belle a pat on the neck, then trudged out of the barn with my hand clamped to my forehead.

There was a hole hidden under the thick grass beside the driveway. Of course, I stepped in it, as I'd done a dozen times before. I didn't fall, but I jolted my headache. One day, I was going to fill in that hole before I really got hurt.

I slipped into the house by way of the back door. After swallowing three extra strength aspirin, I poured myself a glass of iced tea before plopping down on a chair next to the phone. The red message light signaled, but first I had to try again to reach Doug Reilly about Rita's animals. My shoulders suddenly tightened. All unbidden, my fingers started dialing Adam's number instead of Doug's, until I remembered that Adam was no longer part of my life, not since our breakup.

I allowed five rings. Before I could put the receiver down, someone picked up.

"Hello."

I recognized the sleepy drawl. "Doug, this is Leigh McRae."

"Who?"

"I bought Sonny Joe from Rita."

"The blood bay gelding. Traded that tall sorrel filly."

I pictured a light bulb flickering faintly over Doug's head.

"That's right, Doug. I thought you were going up to Starke to visit your girlfriend's brother in prison today."

"Nah. Darryl got out on early parole coupla weeks ago. But Rita already gave me the day off, so I didn't tell her." He snickered. "Tina and me spent last night in Sarasota at a little place called Buddy's Motel, but don't you tell Rita. She'd throw her Bible at me."

"I'm afraid I have bad news." A vein in the front of my head throbbed painfully with every heartbeat. "Rita died this morning. Apparently she fell out of the hayloft and fractured her skull."

Silence for a few extra long seconds. Then a nasal, "That right?"

I shook my head, and immediately wished I hadn't. Doug wasn't showing much sorrow over Rita's death, but then they'd had a love-hate relationship going for years. "The police are contacting her sister Maggie, but someone has to look after the animals."

"Reckon I can handle feeding the horses and the barn cats till somebody shows up. Don't have a key to the house, though, so I can't feed her inside animals."

"Inside animals?"

"Guinea pigs—three of them. And a tank full of fish." He snickered again. "Be funny if nobody showed up and all the water evaporated out of the tank."

Yeah, hysterical. "Right now, Doug, I'm more concerned about Rita's death than I am over contemplating a bunch of mummified goldfish. Since you don't have a key, I'll see that someone else takes care of Rita's fish and guinea pigs." I hung up. Doug was a jerk. Rita wouldn't have given him a key to her house if flames were shooting out of the roof and he was the only one willing to run inside to save her most precious possessions.

But I'd been over to borrow a show saddle once and I'd seen Rita hide a spare key in a birdfeeder by her back door. I told her what I'd seen, and her response was to plant her hands on her hips and say, "Well then, if somebody robs me without breaking in, I'll know who did it, won't I?" She'd left the key right where it was, and I supposed it was still there. If not, I'd have to tell Maggie there were animals in the house.

I checked my messages and found a breathless, rambling stream of consciousness from my cousin Samantha—Sammi—boiling down to the fact that she needed to see me, like yesterday. Despite my headache, which showed no signs of easing up, I started building a green salad. I didn't bother to return Sammi's call. Chances were good that whatever had prompted her message would resolve itself before I could track her down by phone. If not, she'd certainly let me know.

I was in the middle of slicing a tomato when a familiar, older model, black Buick rattled up the driveway and coughed to a stop near the garage. Sammi hadn't wasted any time.

I watched her get out of the car. Like me, Sammi had inherited her height from her father. Our fathers were brothers and we referred to them—along with my brother Chad—as the Hollister men. At six feet tall, Sammi had three inches on me, though. I was fortunate enough to get my mother's slender figure, but Sammi was solidly built like a Hollister man…weighing close to two hundred pounds.

She flung herself across the yard in the direction of the house, her waist length hair flying loose behind her like a silk, golden cape. At least she hadn't brought along Jeeves, her Old English Sheepdog, known for his world class drooling and shedding.

She'd dressed as if she were ready to conduct a séance. Her loose, purple crepe top flowed down over her arms to her wrists, and her matching skirt reached almost to the tops of her shoes. That much material could have made drapes for my entire house, but the outfit suited her, somehow managing to impart an air of grace she didn't normally have.

She let herself in through the sliding glass door in the kitchen, then stopped short when she saw me. "Leigh, your eyes are as red as those tomatoes. Tension headache, right?" She took the knife out of my hand. "Let me do that before you cut off something important. You should be resting in bed."

"I can't." I knew by now to refrain from shaking my head, which would invariably aggravate the throbbing in my temples. "Wait until we sit down and I'll tell you about it."

"I already heard," she said in her husky, ex-smoker's voice.

"You heard about Rita Cameron?"

"Lead story on the radio. I figured I better detour on over here and offer you a shoulder to lean on. They didn't identify the victim, but of course everyone knows who it is; you know the gossip line in Del Canto. I stopped at the grocery and the head cashier—she's Paris Winslow's aunt—told me it was Rita and that you found her. Is it true she's dead?"

"I'm afraid so. Sorry I didn't return your call earlier, but this has been one hell of a morning."

"I hear ya, hon." Sammi finished slicing the tomato and arranged the pieces neatly on top of the salad. With a final dash of artistry, she dropped five black olives in the center of the bowl before squirting a dollop of French dressing on top.

"Lunch, Sammi?"

"I'd confuse my body if I ate this early, but you go ahead."

A queasy feeling rose suddenly in my stomach, and I knew food would only make me sick. "Let's skip it then." I waved at her to follow me down the hall.

We settled ourselves in the living room, me draped sideways in my faithful recliner and Sammi taking up most of the love seat. She pushed her hair out of her face two or three times, then finally gave up, letting it slide down over her eyes. Sammi had a long face, a long straight nose, and almond shaped brown eyes, so with her hair parted in the middle she reminded me of an Afghan hound.

"So Rita was dead when you found her?" She sounded half out of breath.

"Isn't that what it said on the radio?"

"Yep. Horrible, isn't it? One minute she's tossing hay bales around and the next she's on her way to a slab at the morgue." Without warning Sammi hauled herself to her feet and strode over to peer out through the front curtains. As suddenly as she'd gotten up she was back in her seat, perched on the edge of the cushion and swinging the gold chain of her necklace in front of her like a tiny lasso. "The police are sure it was a freak accident?"

"I think so. I mean, I wasn't there watching in helpless fascination as she fell. Millie Destin, Rita's neighbor, was there before I was and she didn't see it happen, either. Then there was a guy, Jared Beaumont I think he said his name was, who got there after me, so he knows less than I do." I didn't mention that I had nagging doubts about Rita's death because Sammi would expect me to know exactly what was bothering me, and I didn't have a clue. "Are you okay, Sammi?"

"*Excuse me.* Why wouldn't I be okay?"

"You left an urgent message saying you needed to see me, so I assume you're not here out of idle curiosity."

She gave a soulful sigh. "It's Ray, my new boyfriend." She twisted the gold chain so tightly I thought it would snap. "There have been all these burglaries lately on the north side of town and the police have been over to practically accuse Ray just because he has a record."

A line about usual suspects ran through my mind, but I pressed my lips together. She was bringing this problem on herself. Ray not only had a prison record, he was also recently separated from a wife who'd made it clear she wanted him back. Sammi deserved so much better.

She abruptly shifted position, skewing herself sideways in the chair. She grabbed the gold colored purse that she'd tossed on the floor. Her hands tensed, fiddling with the purse strap, folding and unfolding it.

"Did I tell you I finished the course I was taking, and I got a new job as a home health aide?"

"Sammi, that's super." I was genuinely glad. Sammi had a caring quality about her that made her perfectly suited to look after the sick and elderly. And, oddly enough, she had a talent for solving other people's problems, a way of seeing clearly and getting right to the point. I suppose all of us had a little of that quality—the ability to see what's wrong with other people without noticing our own faults. But Sammi sorted things out, getting busy pouring herbal tea and dispensing sympathy almost before you knew you were hurting.

"I know you're not going to like this, Leigh, but you'll find out eventually. Ray's going to marry me as soon as his divorce is final."

I made a face. "You're right, I don't like it."

"You'll get used to the idea same way I did when you married

Kenneth. Only I can't have the police sniffing around over every little thing that goes missing in Del Canto. I might lose my job if my boss thinks I can't be trusted, and I'm a nervous wreck over it. That's why I came to see you."

"Me?"

"You can have Kenneth ask Kendra to tell them to back off Ray. They'll listen to a lawyer."

Kendra was my ex-husband's twin sister, as well as my ex-divorce attorney. Yeah, I know. But I was young and trusting at the time, too cocky to listen to advice from my family, including Sammi. Of course, they were right when they said it was a terrible idea to save money by using the same attorney as my husband, particularly when that attorney was his sister.

"Kenneth and I are divorced, remember? And Kendra likes me about as much as she likes the guy who stole her car last month and wrecked it in Fort Myers Beach. Besides, she's not a criminal attorney."

"I had a feeling you'd turn me down." Sammi assumed the expression of a wronged orphan.

"Sorry," I said. "It's only..." I bit back what I was going to say about her getting hurt if she didn't dump Ray.

She stood and flashed me her best attempt at a winning smile. "Think about it, okay? One more thing, Leigh. I'm working tomorrow for a retired lady. She's my first patient, but I'm supposed to take Jeeves to Maggie's for a grooming." Overdone smile here to foretell what was coming next in my future.

I escorted her to the door. "And you want me to take him, right?"

"Would you, hon? I really hate to cancel again; I mean his fur is *completely* overgrown and I had to cancel this morning because of Ray..."

"Of course I will. What time?"

"Three. Drop him off at Maggie's and I'll pick him up after work. You have the key, right?"

I fished my keyring out of my pocket and held it up, jangling it for effect. Sammi's oversized house key dangled next to mine. "I'll get him there...unless Maggie takes the day off because of Rita." I didn't think she would. I'd heard enough gossip to know the sisters didn't care for each other, and Maggie wouldn't close her shop unless she were on her deathbed.

    Sammi was already climbing into her car. She acknowledged with a thumbs up, then gunned the Buick down the driveway. I stayed outside until she was long gone and the glare from the sun made my vision go blurry. In a few hours Whitney would come home from school expecting to go to Rita's for a riding lesson.

Chapter 4

It was impossible to rest. The phone had rung six times but when I saw the caller ID, I let the machine pick up. I finally crawled off the couch and played back my messages—two hang-ups and four from Kenneth. He sounded more exasperated each time he said, "Call me as soon as possible." I supposed he'd heard the news, but I didn't have any illusions he was calling to offer sympathy.

I trudged back to the barn to turn the mares out, and Kenneth arrived as I was shutting the stall doors. He skidded his SUV to a stop in front of the barn, jumping out without checking first to see if I'd failed to clean up any piles of manure that might trip him up and ruin his shoes. I hung up Lena's halter, then met him in the barn entryway.

"Why didn't you return my calls? I canceled a golf game with an important client to come out to check on you." He inserted himself so far into my personal space I had trouble focusing without crossing my eyes.

"Check on me? Why?"

"Because Paris Winslow called about a listing and told me

what happened, that's why." He launched into an account of how shocked he was to hear about all the blood and gore spattered around at Rita's. He carried on like I'd deliberately found Rita's body simply to mess up his golf game. His face gradually turned a nasty shade of red with bluish overtones, and he stuck his jaw out so far I was afraid it would break off.

Ah, Paris. Newspaper reporter, slash real estate saleswoman, slash biggest gossip in the county.

When he finished his tirade, Kenneth leaned even closer and curled his lip in a sneer. "You weren't up in the loft, too, were you?"

"Nah, I've been scared of heights ever since I took the dizzying fall from prosperity to near poverty post divorce."

He drew back, scowling. "There's no need to be sarcastic. I'm concerned for your safety because you're up to your rear end in this horse thing."

I put my hand over my mouth to stifle a laugh. I could have made an off color remark, but decided to be a lady. "What are you saying?" I asked primly.

"I'm saying, I've realized that being around horses can be dangerous, even fatal. I'm saying my daughter needs protection. Because the fact is, at least fifty percent of kids who ride get seriously hurt around horses."

I sputtered for a good five seconds before I could get any coherent words out. "Let me get this straight. A woman is killed falling out of a hayloft, so that means horses are the next best thing to a loaded 357 Magnum? God, Kenneth, you are starting to annoy me. I'll put your statement in the number one spot on my man logic list."

Man logic was what happened when men forgot that women had brains. This resulted in men making such statements as: "I got a speeding ticket. But no big deal. Seventy-two percent of the world population is ticketed in any given year." Brainy women knew to ask where the man got his facts and figures, because making up facts and figures to excuse their sorry behavior and win arguments was a masculine specialty.

Kenneth backed away so he'd have room to shake his finger in my face. "I'm not going to listen to a bunch of insults. I've made up my mind. I want you to sell the horses before it's too late. If one of Whitney's friends gets hurt, they could sue."

"I'll take that risk."

"I won't. Remember, I still own half this property and I'm not going to lose it because of your stupidity."

"Stupidity? Sure, Kenneth, your ex-wife has the brain of a hamster. She thinks there's no connection between falling out of buildings and getting hurt by horses."

So he was worried about his share in my home—the share he still owned thanks to his darling sister Kendra. She'd made sure in the divorce to leave Kenneth's name on the property instead of dividing things up cleanly. Said something about how I couldn't afford to buy him out, so she'd worked out the best solution. Now I couldn't even build a doghouse without his permission. And I couldn't count the number of times he'd called to tell me it was time to mow the lawn or paint the fence.

"Stop being childish." So much eye rolling here, I was tempted to tell him his face would stay that way if he didn't cut it out.

"It's bad luck Rita got killed." I'd started trembling from rage, so I took a deep breath, which didn't help. Even a tranquilizer wouldn't have helped. "We're not selling so much as a saddle."

"What's this *we*?" Kenneth's eyes had darkened from gray to almost black. "Once again you've proven you can't do anything right." He whirled and stomped out of the barn.

I glared after him. Why the sudden urge to sell the horses? Well, he couldn't make me. But a troubling thought scuttled around in a front corner of my mind. I'd paid for Sonny Joe by trading Tinker and a chunk of cash. Cash provided by Kenneth. I shook the thought away. The sale arrangements didn't mean a thing.

After a long time spent contemplating the barn wall, I ended up back in the living room wishing I could have thought of a clever comeback before he left. I knew the signs. Kenneth had lost a sale or had a bad day at the office. Rita's death—no real connection, but Kenneth didn't need one—gave him the excuse to come over and use me for his emotional punching bag. If I were lucky, a client dripping with money would show up this afternoon and buy the priciest listing in his inventory, and Kenneth's mood would brighten up. He had his nerve harassing me while I was still reeling from Rita's death.

At least he was gone before Whitney got home. The school bus had barely braked to a stop before Whitney jumped off. Gold-colored ponytail bouncing behind her, she raced up the driveway, slinging her bookbag to the ground under a hibiscus bush as she flew by.

I slipped out the door and met her before she got to the barn. "Whitney, I have to tell you something. I'm afraid it's bad news."

She stopped in front of me and her face twisted. "Mom?" she squeaked. "What happened?"

"Rita's dead. She fell out of her hayloft this morning."

"Rita?" She burst into tears. "Rita can't be dead."

Whitney and Rita had been fond of each other. Rita had told me a million times my daughter was "a fine little horsewoman." She'd even called Kenneth and convinced him to fork over his share for Sonny Joe after Whitney had fallen in love with the colt.

We stood together in the driveway with our arms around each other. I told her about Rita's accident, leaving out the gruesome details. She gradually stopped sobbing, and her brow furrowed into a solid line.

"Can I see Sonny?"

She didn't wait for an answer, and I followed as she raced into the barn. She climbed halfway up the stall door to wrap her arms around her horse's neck. "Poor, poor Rita," she said over and over, her shoulders shaking with sobs.

I put my arms around her and then I cried, too…hot tears that burned my eyes.

Eventually, after we both seemed to have run dry, she untangled Sonny's forelock and brushed out his mane with her fingers. Finally finished, she jumped from the top of the stall door.

"Be careful," I said. "Haven't I told you a million times you're going to get hurt doing that?"

"Now it's a million and one." She flounced over to a bale of hay, plopping belly down on top like a seal landing on a rock. Her bottom lip quivered.

I thought it best to give her some processing time, so I went back to the house, barely missing the hole near the driveway. Time for another round of aspirin and another caffeine fix.

An hour or so later, the back door slammed. Slow, deliberate footsteps echoed on the ceramic tile hallway leading to Whitney's room.

"Honey?"

The footsteps stopped. "What?"

"Don't you want to eat?"

"I'm not hungry. I probably won't be hungry ever again. Rita was going to take me to the Fort Myers Horse Club show tomorrow."

I hauled myself out of Greenie, my beloved and ragged old recliner that even my mother couldn't persuade me to get rid of. "Sweetie, I know how disappointed you are."

She stamped her foot. "I'm not disappointed. Don't you understand?"

I did understand. My words had come out all wrong. I sighed deeply. "I suppose you'd rather be alone to grieve right now, wouldn't you?"

"I guess so. But since I'm not going to be able to take Sonny to the show, I want to spend the weekend with Dad the way I was supposed to. And Doreen." She made a face.

Kenneth's impending wife, Doreen—he addressed her as "Sweet Thing"—was ten years younger than I. My hair was an ordinary shade of brown and my eyes were an ordinary shade of blue. I'd been told I was attractive and had a nice body. But if Kenneth had met Doreen while we were still married, he'd have kicked himself for settling.

Doreen had long, chocolate-colored hair, chocolate-colored eyes, and the face and figure of a model. And she was someone Kenneth could order around to his heart's content. When I first met her, I described her to Sammi as the type who would name a Rottweiler "Fluffy."

"Mom?" Whitney grabbed my arm and shook it to bring me back to the present.

"I'll call him," I said. "If you're sure."

"If I don't go now, I'll have to go next weekend. I'm a child of divorce, remember?"

I rolled my eyes. She was only eleven—eleven and a quarter,

she'd say if anyone asked—but already she was showing signs of becoming a contrary teen.

Kenneth was sure to be at his real estate office, so I put in a call and got his secretary, Mona. He'd hired her after our divorce, so I didn't know anything about her except that she had big hair—dyed Goth black—and she thought Kenneth was way more important than he really was.

"Mr. McRae is with a new client. He really shouldn't be disturbed when he's with a client. Ever."

"You'll have to forgive my rotten manners. This is his ex-wife and I need to speak with him about his daughter. Now."

Hostility vibes traveled over the wires in my direction, but I knew the part about his daughter would work. The line clicked and Kenneth's voice greeted me with a gruff, "Hello."

"It's Leigh. Due to Rita's death, Whitney has changed her mind and wants to come this weekend instead of next."

"No problem."

"I'll drop Whitney by the office later." I was moving the receiver toward its cradle when I heard his voice still on the line, barking my name. I reapplied the phone to my ear, gritting my teeth so hard they ached.

"I have something else to talk to you about. It's important, so I'd appreciate it if you'd make time for me this afternoon. Doreen can pick up Whitney at the office after you bring her, and you and I will have our discussion." His mood had improved remarkably since his visit, and I chalked that up to the new client.

"Can't you tell me now?"

"Don't be ridiculous. My client is thinking of signing a contract on a new home in Foxhall Estates."

"Of course. I wouldn't dream of interfering with the expansion of Foxhall Estates. I'll see you when I bring Whitney."

Kenneth's real estate firm was housed in one half of a building that used to be the Montgomery Mansion, but was now McRae Real Estate, and Reich, Hesseman, McRae, Reich, and Jones, Attorneys at Law. Very convenient for the McRae twins, Kenneth and Kendra, to get together to think up new ways to make my life miserable.

The inside of the mansion was dark and heavily paneled in walnut, and always smelled of lemon polish. Oil paintings of the Montgomery ancestors were crammed onto every available wall, eliminating any need to hang tacky wall calendars or prints of owl-eyed waifs holding flowers.

Big-haired Mona ushered us inside as if she were granting access to the Pope. After she left, I turned to Whitney and told her I would disown her if she ever wore her hair two feet high. The remark brought a fleeting smile to her face, the first since I'd told her about Rita.

Doreen bounced in wearing a loose purple, orange, and white top over matching shorts. The whole outfit was plastered with hundreds of tiny beads and rhinestones, and lines of silver glitter, a look that Whitney and I privately referred to as "over-dazzled."

"Hello, Leigh," she said in her tiny voice, flashing me a dimpled smile.

"Hello, Doreen." I returned the smile. "Sorry to spring this on you."

"No problem. We'll rent a movie and make popcorn, won't we, Whitney?"

Whitney shrugged. You would have thought Doreen had promised to take her shopping at a snake pit.

Kenneth made his entrance, announcing to Doreen that he and I had important business to transact. Somehow he made this sound as if the two of us were planning an afternoon of love making in the nearest motel. He greeted Whitney with a hug and a kiss, then he wasted a few minutes issuing orders to "Sweet Thing" about what he wanted for supper. Doreen flashed her dimples and promised to go home and cook.

I refrained from making unkind remarks about a "doormat woman." Given my own track record with Kenneth, I didn't have one bit of room to throw stones, or even the smallest of pebbles. With a final wave to Whitney, I strode outside without waiting to see if Kenneth was following.

He caught up to me at my Honda. I used the pickup only to haul feed, hay, and pull a trailer. Most of the time it huddled alone in its shed while I tooled around town in the car.

"Your car or mine?" I asked.

"Yours is fine. I'll direct you." He ran his hands through his hair, carefully arranging the front to cover a newly receding hairline.

"Direct me where?" I slid into my Honda, and Kenneth hesitated only briefly before folding himself into the passenger seat.

He fumbled with the seat adjustment and slid the seat back to make room for his long legs. "Turn right out of the parking lot and then left onto Hansen Avenue. It's about a mile."

"I know where Hansen is." And I was starting to get a sneaking suspicion about where we were going. My suspicions were validated when we arrived on Hansen and he directed me into the driveway of a model home next to a sign that said Hansen Haven—New Homes at Affordable Prices.

I pulled in, turned off the ignition, and shifted sideways to face him. "I get it. You and Doreen are moving again." He and Doreen had recently moved to a Victorian mansion near the waterfront. The Victorian, even before the renovations, probably cost five times the price of the model home. "Nice choice, but a little under your price range, wouldn't you say?"

"You know, Leigh, I might have stayed married to you if you were half as funny as you think you are."

"Time's up." I twisted the key in the ignition and the Honda roared back to life.

Before I could ram the shift lever into reverse, Kenneth snaked his hand out and turned the car off. "Wait. I apologize. Now will you come inside with me?"

He didn't even say *please*. By now I was sure I knew what he was doing, but I decided to play along and get this over with.

I followed him into the "spacious" great room that "flowed" into the "eat-in" kitchen, pretending to admire the kitchen island, and acting delighted with the "fauxing" on the bedroom walls. We finished with a quick look at the two "stylish" bathrooms before exiting through the "huge" single garage.

"Now what?" I braced myself for his next move.

"Let's go back to the office and talk."

Go back to his territory where Mona and Kendra could come to his defense if I decided to kill him? Good thing I was driving.

This meeting cried out for neutral ground and I knew exactly where to find it.

Chapter 5

Kenneth stared out the window while I eased the car back onto the palm tree lined main street. "I hope you're not upset about me marrying Doreen."

I snorted. "Why should your wedding plans concern me for even one second?" The new city park was practically deserted. I yanked the Honda's wheel to aim it into the nearest parking spot.

Kenneth frowned. "I wanted to go back to my office so I can show you some other floor plans."

"Uh-uh. I'm done playing real estate."

"You've gotten awfully...I don't know. Snotty."

I rolled my eyes so far up in my head they hurt. What had I ever seen in this man?

We sat across from each other on trendy little benches the city had recently installed as part of the *Keep Del Canto People Friendly* campaign. So far the local citizens had hardly noticed such people-friendly touches as the benches and a row of spindly gardenia bushes bordering the new sidewalk. I expected they'd perk up, though, when the restrooms and water fountains were completed.

I stared at the harbor while Kenneth shifted around, trying to get comfortable. A mix of sailboats and bulkier cabin cruisers dotted the dark blue water, and the sky had pinked up behind the arch of the I-75 bridge as the sun plunged lower on the horizon. Too bad I was in the presence of my ex or I would have enjoyed the scenery a lot more.

Kenneth finally settled himself on the hard concrete seat and cleared his throat before steepling his fingers. "This matter with the horses—I've had time to give it some thought."

"Really? I thought you were too busy writing contracts for pricey estate homes to do any thinking."

He shot me a warning glance. "You once fell off a horse and broke your arm, correct?"

"You know it is. But why should that matter?"

"Use your brain. What if Whitney had been the one who broke her arm?"

"Then I'd take her to the ER and get it casted. I told you, horses aren't vicious. An accident can happen to anyone."

"When it comes to my daughter, I'm not willing to take that kind of chance. After all, you wouldn't let her ride a motorcycle."

It didn't take a psychic to see exactly where he was going with this. My blood pressure shot up a couple hundred points. "You have really got your nerve. I knew you were controlling, but this is too much."

"You've had your way with this horse hobby long enough. You'd better find buyers for your little herd, starting with the new one, the one I paid for."

"Sonny Joe? You paid half. I traded a filly for my half, remember?"

"Half, a whole, a sixteenth, who cares?" He dismissed my argument with a contemptuous wave of his right hand. "I want this done quickly and painlessly. Someone named Brenda Harper called me this afternoon and made an offer on the horse. She tried calling you directly, but couldn't get an answer."

"I know Brenda; she's part of the horse crowd. But I'm not selling to her or to anyone else. And you can't make me."

"Can't I? Correct me if I'm wrong, but I'm part owner of your house and your ten acres. I want my half in cash." He snapped his fingers. "Unless you can afford to buy me out, we're selling. And don't look at me like that. It isn't as if you and Whitney are going to end up in the street."

"Yeah, I know. That model in Hansen Haven is waiting in the wings."

"It's very affordable for the location, and convenient to my new place so Doreen and I can spend more time with Whitney. You might as well grab it while you can. But if you want to get something closer to your job, your share of the equity might be enough to buy a condo."

"What about Whitney's feelings? You know she's crazy about horses."

"She'll have to learn to deal with life's little disappointments. Doreen says she's dying to take Whitney to ballet and art classes."

"No!" I exploded. "You're crazy if you think Whitney is going to give up her horses so she can prance around in a tutu with your girlfriend."

"Fiancée." Kenneth rose to his feet, signaling he was done.

He could issue all the orders he wanted, but there wasn't any way I was going to let him control me. I gave him a minute's head start before I got up and stomped back to the car.

I had taken only a few steps when I saw Adam stroll by with a redhead, and it wasn't even a month since we'd broken up. I knew I'd have to pay close attention to my driving or I'd drive the Honda into a tree without even trying.

Back at Kenneth's office, he let himself out of the car. Slowly I pulled onto the highway as though my car were arthritic and had to be babied. I didn't realize I was home until the Honda coughed to a stop in front of my house, waiting quietly for me to crawl out.

I'd promised to see that Rita's fish and guinea pigs didn't die of neglect, and I wanted to check to make sure Doug had looked after the horses and cats out at the barn. It would be dark before long and if the chores at Rita's hadn't been done, I figured it was up to me. Half-dreading the call, I took my time going into the house and turning on a light.

I rang Rita's number, hoping someone was there. To my relief, a female voice answered after two rings.

"Hello," I said hesitantly, "is this Rita Cameron's residence?"

"Yes, Maggie Cameron speaking."

I should have recognized her voice. "This is Leigh McRae. I was calling to make sure the animals had been looked after."

"The police told me about Rita. I came out to look after the animals as soon as I closed my shop for the day. Just got here, in fact."

"I'm so sorry about Rita."

"Thank you. Wait a minute. Didn't you find her body?"

"I'm afraid so. I came by to pick up a load of hay, and the neighbor and I found her in front of the hay barn. But it was too late to do anything for her."

"That's what Doug Reilly told me. He was feeding the horses when I got here." Maggie's voice was totally without expression and I had the impression she was trying to block her feelings. Or control them.

Or maybe I was simply projecting my own emotions. How was I supposed to know how people should sound when they lost a sister they couldn't stand? It would be different with Sammi and me, of course. We were only cousins, but we were tight.

I snatched up a business card off my end table and crumpled it into a ball. Whoops. Now I wouldn't know whom to call when my air conditioning needed repair. "Umm, I hope you don't mind me asking, but are you opening your shop tomorrow?"

"Of course. Rita would do the same in my position."

I doubted that. I picked up another business card, but this one didn't meet the same fate as the first. Instead I gently ran my fingers over the raised lettering on the front while I contemplated my next move. Guilt is a mean thing. Rita would still be alive if she hadn't been in the hayloft getting bales of hay for me.

"If I can be of any help, please call. Doug's not the most reliable person in the world, and I'd be more than happy to do whatever I can to look after the horses."

"That's awfully kind of you. I'll see how it goes and let you know."

We rang off after I gave her my number and promised once more to help out. Then I drew my brows together in a frown and sat down to think.

Inheriting Rita's millions was going to make a big change in Maggie's life. She hadn't wasted any time taking over at Rita's, either. What if Maggie had hastened the inheritance process? I twisted a loose piece of thread on my blouse, then snapped it loose.

Careful, Leigh, I told myself. You're being unnecessarily bitchy. Accident, remember? Except, something wasn't right. I closed my eyes and tried to grasp the stray thought that kept flitting out of reach. No luck.

I thought about calling my parents in North Carolina. Maybe talking to them would bring me some comfort. Then I remembered they were in San Antonio visiting my brother and his wife. No point in spoiling their vacation with sad news. Besides, my father, a man even more overbearing than Kenneth, might decide Kenneth was right about selling the horses. I didn't need the extra pressure.

I sighed, blowing out enough air to inflate a weather balloon. Why was it that when you wanted to be around people they all seemed to have packed up and moved to another continent? My clock was digital, but I was sure I could hear it ticking. I shivered and hauled myself up from my chair to draw the drapes at the front of the house.

I locked the door. As an afterthought, I checked my message machine and found a message from Brenda Harper asking me to get in touch with her. Fat chance. I was not overly fond of Brenda even if she hadn't called Kenneth and given him the idea of selling my horses. And I was not stupid enough to believe that Kenneth, one week after he'd enthusiastically granted Whitney's wish for a new show horse, had suddenly become terrified of all things equine. No, there was another reason for his actions, but I didn't know yet what it was. Not any more than I knew what seemed so wrong about Rita's accident, something that pointed toward murder.

I showered and wrapped myself in a shapeless pink robe that was long past its prime and had shed so much lint over the years it was held together by a few threads in places. I frowned into the refrigerator, seeing nothing that appealed. I ended up in my recliner with the remote close at hand. After ten minutes of running through channels, I settled for a vintage black and white mystery, judging it would be suitably mind numbing.

I was wrong. The show was about a man who'd committed suicide and then turned up as a ghost to haunt his family. It seemed he hadn't killed himself after all, but had been murdered by his greedy business partner. His family was a dense bunch who took nearly the whole movie to figure out their dearly departed was attempting to communicate the truth from beyond the grave. Exactly what I needed—the idea that Rita's ghostly form might be lurking in my living room, trying to tell me she didn't fall, she was pushed. But, hey, that could have happened. All I had to do was figure out what was bothering me about the scene.

I found myself jumping every time a car went by or a dog barked in the distance. There were only two houses anywhere near mine, and the occupants always kept to themselves. I didn't think they'd notice if a criminal showed up to kill me.

It was nearly one o'clock when I crawled into bed. I lay awake listening to insects thwacking against the screen outside my window. The screen was dotted with fat tree frogs feasting on the insects, but apparently they weren't able to make a dent in such a vast population. After a long time, I dropped off to sleep, no closer to knowing what was bothering me than I was this afternoon.

Chapter 6

No one would have been surprised if I'd had nightmares about Rita, but instead I slept hard, my left arm going numb from my lying on it. It was that, as well as the ringing phone, that woke me, and I jerked awake, sitting straight up in bed. I shook my arm and picked up the receiver.

"Hello," I mumbled.

"You sound like you've swallowed a frog."

"What time is it, Sammi?" I squinted at my clock, but couldn't read the time with my puffy eyes.

"Nine, sleepyhead. I started my new job and I'm calling from the patient's house. She lives in this fabulous place on a canal."

I blinked, trying to make sense of what Sammi was saying. "Nine!" I said finally.

"Relax, it's Saturday. I called to find out how you're feeling."

"About as you'd expect." I yawned.

"It will get better, Leigh, trust me. Ray let me borrow this great book about the stages of life's tragedies, and I'm going to insist that you read it."

Wow. An ex-con who read self help books. There was hope for the world after all. "I don't have time, Sammi."

"Wait a minute." I heard background noises that suggested water running. "My patient's up and I'm fixing her breakfast, so I can't talk. Want to meet me at the park this evening? You could use a little therapeutic walk with Jeeves and me. Hey, have you asked Kenneth to tell Kendra about Ray's case yet?"

"I can't go to the park. My house is a mess and I have a ton of laundry to take care of. And as for asking Kenneth, I'm not going to. I'm sorry."

She muttered something about how she was always there for me. Of course, this remark jolted me back onto the guilt road after she hung up, but I knew I was right.

Really the house was okay, if I ignored the clutter and squinched my eyes way down so I didn't see the dust. But I didn't feel like having another discussion with Sammi about her boyfriend and besides, no walk that included Jeeves could honestly be described as therapeutic.

I pulled on faded jeans and a tee shirt, ran my fingers through my hair, and trudged out to the barn. It was going to be hot today, hotter than yesterday.

I kept the mares up and turned Sonny Joe out. He waited politely while I unsnapped his lead and slipped back out through the metal pasture gate. Then he snorted and took off, running and bucking for a good five minutes before he lowered his head to bury his nose in the thick pangola grass.

He was so beautiful I caught my breath. The sun sparked metallic copper and red from his blood bay coat, and his well-defined muscles rippled as he moved. The raven black on his legs rose high above his knees and hocks, the prettiest kind of marking for a bay. His black tail was long, almost reaching the ground, and it was thick, as was his mane.

And to think, this time last week Whitney and I were studying a show schedule deciding which classes we'd enter, and Rita was planning to give Whitney jumping lessons. When I got back to the barn, there was a lump in my throat almost big enough to choke me.

By the time I finished cleaning the stalls, I decided it was time for lunch, not breakfast, but I had Wheaties and coffee anyway. I cleaned the kitchen, ran a vacuum over the bedroom carpets, and damp mopped the tile floors in the bathrooms. Keeping busy at least gave my mind something to think about besides Rita's death.

Sure enough, as soon as I hung the mop to dry on the line out back, the persistent picture popped back into my head. I practically stopped breathing trying to remember what it was that seemed out of place.

"There you are. I've been hunting for at least ten minutes."

I spun around with my hand over my heart. "Adam Malone! For God's sake, why did you sneak up on me like that?"

"If I frightened you, I apologize." He raised one dark eyebrow and crossed his arms over his chest.

"There's no 'if' about it. Of course you frightened me, showing up like some kind of stealth fighter when my back was turned. What are you doing here anyway?"

"I'm ecstatic to see you, too."

"I didn't mean that the way it sounded."

"I stopped by to drop off the wrench I borrowed last month. It's in my truck." He headed back to the driveway.

I followed, though I supposed he didn't care one way or the other now that our relationship was finished.

He usually left his tools on his boat. One Sunday when Whitney and I were at his house for a cookout, a guest backed his car too close to the well and broke a pipe. My house was closer than the harbor where Adam kept his boat, and water was shooting up like a geyser, so I went home and got the wrench. Being that I so seldom go in for household repairs, I'd forgotten about the wrench 'til now.

He turned with his hand on the truck's tailgate and waited for me to catch up. I glanced at the cab to see if he'd brought along the redhead I'd seen him with yesterday, but the only sign of life came from George, his bulldog puppy.

George wriggled his plump little body and tried to climb out the window to greet me.

I moved closer to pat his head. "Hey, George. Who's a good

baby, hmmm?"

George went ecstatic and got even more single-minded in his plan to escape from the truck, managing to hook one hind leg on the window.

"Get back in there you wicked little hound." Adam grinned and pushed him down.

I laughed. "I didn't mean to get him started."

"He's a stubborn guy." His expression softened. "Leigh, I heard the news. I'm sorry you lost a friend."

I studied his face. When we broke up, we said some childish things to each other. I'd told him that Kenneth had paid for new cross fencing and fertilizer for the front pasture. After all, as Kenneth said, he had to maintain the place that was half his. My relationship with Adam had ended with him telling me to run home and phone Mr. Moneybags to have him buy me something pretty to go with all the other pretty things he bought me. Not that cross fences and fertilizer were anything to look at, but I got the picture.

I half expected him to get in another dig. I was unjust. His brown eyes were filled with concern, and I was ashamed of myself for going on the defensive.

I shoved my hands in my pockets. "It's hard to imagine I'll never hear Rita's voice again. She's been showing horses ever since I can remember. She was Whitney's riding instructor."

"The police know what happened?"

"They don't know the exact details, but they're pretty sure she overbalanced and slipped while she was trying to toss a bale of hay down."

"I don't expect they'd conclude she leaped out on purpose." Adam fished the wrench out of the back of the truck. "Thanks. I've bought a duplicate set of tools to keep at home, which is what I should have done to begin with instead of keeping my only set on the boat."

Adam owned his own charter boat that he used to take parties of tourists fishing and on tours. Dozens of small islands dotted the harbor, most of which were covered with mangroves and millions of fiddler crabs. A few were rumored to hide pirates' treasure, supposedly still safely buried under tons of wet sand and dank smelling seaweed. Adam took the boat out almost every day during the season.

"The worst thing is, Kenneth is insisting I sell my horses, as if he's really afraid of them now simply because they eat hay and hay causes loft accidents. I don't know if I can talk him into..." I broke off, feeling my face heat up as though I'd stuck it in a hot oven.

"Still haven't cut the cord, have you, Leigh?"

"You don't understand!" I burst out, but I was speaking to empty space. Adam was already in his truck, and a second later the truck was bouncing down the driveway in a cloud of dust, no doubt flinging George around like a brindle and white dishrag.

I marched back into the house, forgetting I had the wrench until I was inside. I shoved it out of sight under the kitchen sink. A puddle had formed under a pipe. I kicked the cabinet and bent back my big toe, which sent a jolt of pain all the way to my ankle. When I was done hopping around the kitchen on one foot, I placed a dented, seldom-used saucepan under the leak, and slammed the cabinet door closed.

The phone rang while I was still massaging the pain out of my throbbing foot. I hobbled across the room, snatched up the receiver, and snarled, "Hello."

"This is Parker Fielding. I hope I'm not bothering you."

Whoops. "No, of course not."

Parker was a friend of Rita's. I'd met him at a horse show where Rita had introduced him as her financial advisor. She probably needed one. She was the richest woman in the county as well as one of the busiest.

"I hope you don't think I'm being too forward. I'm—I was—engaged to Rita. I need help with the horses and I found your number next to the phone along with a note saying you'd offered to help."

Engaged? This was the first I'd heard and I'd never have guessed. Rita was in her late fifties and this would be her first marriage. You never knew, I supposed, when you were going to find romance. Or lose it.

"Yes, I spoke with Maggie last night." I imagined Maggie was already at her grooming shop.

"Doug Reilly seems to have quit, and I'm relatively clueless when it comes to animals."

I agreed to come over right away. When I pulled up at Rita's fifteen minutes later, a gray Toyota Camry was parked in front of the house.

As soon as I got out of the car, Parker walked out on the porch. He was limping and I wondered how he'd hurt himself.

When he got close enough, he held out his hand and said, "I'm Parker Fielding." He clearly didn't remember Rita had introduced us at a horse show. But he'd certainly started off right by not calling me darlin', even though his handshake was the limp, weak kind that make you think the owner of the hand needs immediate treatment for anemia.

"Leigh McRae."

"Before we get started, would you like to come inside for a cup of coffee?"

"I suppose that would be all right." I looked around, half expecting Rita to stride out of the barn and tell me it was all a dream.

Rita's house—a white, cinderblock square with a red tile roof—was cluttered. A stack of books and papers on the floor next to the kitchen table was tumbled randomly toward the window. I knew from having been here before that she had boxes of books and magazines in her living room, as well as in her barn office, and way more furniture than she needed.

I plunked myself down on a wooden stool at the breakfast bar while Parker fixed our coffee. I watched him, wondering if I was being mean to think he wasn't acting terribly upset over Rita.

He turned to bring our cups to the table and banged his leg on the kitchen island. It was the same leg he was favoring. "Ouch," he said, putting my cup in front of me. "I tripped on the steps carrying my bag to the house yesterday and bruised my shin. It's still pretty sore."

So he'd spent the night. Maggie must have asked him to keep her company. I didn't blame her. I knew I wouldn't have wanted to stay out here alone if my loved one had been the one who died.

"I'm sure Maggie appreciated the company."

"Maggie?" A shadow crossed his face. "I'm afraid I had to ask her to leave."

My surprise registered on my face, I knew it did, though I tried hard to have no expression at all. "Well, you…I guess she…" What could I say that wouldn't sound either nosy or stupid?

"Rita had made it quite clear that she was getting her will changed right away and was leaving everything to me. Of course, Maggie objected when I told her, but what could she do? When the will is read, she'll see I'm right and she'll stop threatening to call the police to have me thrown off the place."

I didn't respond. I never commented when people talked about fighting over wills. But I wished I hadn't gotten myself in the middle of a family dispute. And I wondered why Maggie hadn't put up more of a fight. Maybe she was saving that for the courts.

Parker sat on the empty stool on my right. "I don't usually drink coffee, but I didn't sleep last night."

I swiveled my stool to face him. "Is there anything else I can do to help? It can't be easy having to face her death alone."

"Thanks, but I can't think of anything. I don't know much about horses. Guess I'll end up selling them after all the legal formalities with the will."

I battled my eyebrows to keep them from merging with my hair. He seemed determined to convince me he was the new owner of Rita's possessions. Could Rita really have written a will making Parker her sole heir in anticipation of her marriage? "As far as the horses go, I'll be glad to do whatever I can," I said after a few seconds, keeping things neutral and pretending a disinterest I didn't feel, while my mind screamed, *motive, motive!*

"Appreciate it. Besides the fact that he doesn't work here anymore, Doug Reilly didn't strike me as someone I could count on." He nodded as if he already knew about Doug. Rita had probably told him. "Do you mind telling me about finding Rita? I'm sure it was a terrible shock."

"It was a shock, all right." I gave Parker a sanitized version.

"Ironic. As much as she loved horses, it was taking care of horses that killed her."

I frowned. Like Kenneth, he seemed to be blaming horses for Rita's death. But I'd allow him that. In his grief, he'd try to find some kind of logic, some reason for what had happened. "She'd never have given them up, even if someone could have foretold her death."

"That's true. But I'm not going to say I'm glad she died doing what she loved. Rita didn't want to die."

I stared at my cup. At least he was finally showing some emotion. Even so, our conversation dwindled after that to safe remarks about the weather, and how if we didn't hurry it would be too hot to work.

We went back to the barn and I fetched the notebook Rita kept for her horses. Parker had apparently already started clearing the office because the magazines and other papers Rita had left on her desk were now in the box with other magazines. Even her calendar was gone from the wall. At this rate, there would soon be no sign of Rita's existence.

I paged through the notebook, showing Parker which kinds of feed and the amount to give each horse. She had two old geldings that were more or less retired, as well as three two-year-old fillies in training. Parker and I each cleaned two stalls, then did the fifth one together. I took care of Tinker. She was used to me, and besides, I thought Parker might not feel comfortable doctoring her shoulder.

When we finished spreading the last of the new sawdust bedding, he leaned against the stall boards. "I'm about to melt. I can't imagine how Rita managed by herself."

We washed our hands at the spigot in front of the barn. Parker offered iced tea and I followed him back to the house. We'd no sooner walked inside when a car door slammed.

"I'd better see who that is. Hopefully not Maggie Cameron returning for round two." When he rose to go out the front door, I followed, intending to cut out and leave him to his visitor.

I hung back and watched as a woman—young, shapely, and looking somehow familiar—got out on the passenger side of a mint-colored mini van in front of the house. She had beautiful hair, long and auburn with gold highlights.

The driver's door opened and a large man—a man big enough to pass for a football lineman—hauled himself out. He was balding, but hadn't bothered with a comb-over. His tan looked like it came from a bottle and his clothes looked like they came from a tailor's shop. I disliked him on sight, but didn't know why.

The woman strode up to Parker and put her hands on her hips. "I'm looking for Rita Cameron."

Chapter 7

Parker and I exchanged glances.

He cleared his throat about ninety-five times. "I regret to have to tell you, but Ms. Cameron was killed yesterday."

"God, no, what happened?" The woman swayed and the large man moved closer and put his arm around her shoulders. "Aunt Rita's dead?"

Aunt Rita? I hadn't known Rita had other family besides Maggie. Apparently Parker hadn't either, judging by the wide-eyed look he shot me. Tthat seemed strange if they'd planned to marry and if, as he'd told me, he'd inherited the estate.

I helped direct the woman up the steps and into the living room, where she collapsed on the couch. Then I went to the kitchen to get her a cold drink. When I returned, she'd gotten over her shock enough to have gotten into an argument with Parker. I hesitated in the doorway, clutching a glass of iced tea and wondering if I could quietly escape out the back door.

"You have no right to be here." High spots of color had appeared on the woman's cheeks.

"Rita and I were engaged." Parker had drawn himself up so

straight, you could have dropped a plumb line down his back to the floor and not been off more than an eighth of an inch. "I'm sure she'd already changed her will making me her heir, as she'd promised. She didn't want her sister to inherit. She never said a word about having a niece."

"I'm not her real niece; she was my godmother. So when you heard she'd died, you waltzed onto the place and took over?"

"I wouldn't call it waltzing. Surely you can understand my position." He sounded entirely reasonable.

The man who'd arrived with her stepped closer to Parker. "I think you'd better leave." Smooth baritone, not the gravel tones I'd expected from his appearance.

"I don't think so. If Rita did favor me in her will, it's up to me to protect my interests." Parker rocked back and forth on his heels, the only sign that he was less than calm.

I stared at the floor. Why hadn't I stayed home today? Would anyone notice if I slipped out of the room? I didn't know what would have happened next if the goddaughter hadn't stepped between the two men with her hands out.

"Aunt Rita is dead, and it looks terrible that we're arguing over the will. Since I'm her goddaughter—and I can prove it—and you, Mr. Fielding, are not related to her in any way, I think I'm entitled to stay until we know exactly what Aunt Rita intended. I'm not a lawyer, but I believe if we called the police to come out here, they'd agree with me."

I wasn't so sure. The police might throw everyone out until the will was read, and then there might be trouble getting the animals taken care of. And there would definitely be some vicious gossip.

Parker drew a deep breath and said, "Of course. And if it turns out she rewrote her will to make me her heir, there will be no hard feelings, Mrs..."

"Angie Loring." The spots of color had disappeared, but she didn't seem any more kindly disposed toward Parker than she had five minutes ago.

"Pleased to meet you."

Right. I could tell. His expression was about as welcoming as that of a cat treed by a German Shepherd.

With a quick nod in my direction, Parker was out the door.

Now I was the new center of attention. "I'm Leigh McRae. Rita was a friend and I was here helping with the horses." I remembered the iced tea I was holding and thrust it in the direction of Angie. "I guess I'd better go."

Angie took the glass. "No, don't go. Please, as long as you're not here trying for a piece of my godmother's estate, stay and tell us what happened." She took a gulp of tea. "We'd come down to visit. The last thing we expected was to learn that Aunt Rita is dead." She seemed to suddenly remember her companion. "Goodness, I'm rude, aren't I? The knight in shining armor standing beside me is my husband, Stanley."

"Hardly a knight in shining armor. But savvy enough to chase away that maggot who was trying to steal your inheritance." He sent me an appraising look that lingered too long on my chest. "You can call me Stan."

I was more likely to call him jerk. He didn't even know Parker and he was talking about him as if he were on the FBI's most wanted list and it was Stanley Loring's job to capture him. Not that I was wild about Parker myself, but still.

He read my expression. "Sorry. I don't even know the man and he's probably a friend of yours."

"Not really. But Rita had high standards and if she was planning to marry him, he must be okay."

Angie plunked her glass down on the coffee table. "But she never said..."

Stanley and I both turned to look at Angie and she clamped her mouth shut.

"Never mind. Let's go in the kitchen and talk." She sent me a wobbly grin. "If Aunt Rita were here she'd tell me to quit whining and shape up."

"Yes, that sounds like her." So Rita hadn't even told her goddaughter about the impending nuptials. Stranger and stranger.

"I hadn't seen a lot of her for the past few years, though I imagine she hadn't changed." She walked ahead of me, her strides quick and business-like, the same as Rita's.

"Had you been here before, Angie?" Rita had never mentioned a goddaughter. We were back in the kitchen where I got two more glasses out of the cabinet and poured tea for myself and for

Stanley. I resisted the impulse to look over my shoulder to see if Rita's plumber or her yardman had shown up to claim the estate.

"Only once. All the other times I saw her, she traveled to Pennsylvania to visit us. Then about two weeks ago she called and insisted I come to Del Canto. She said she had something important to discuss, too important to get into on the phone. It was bad timing, but I agreed."

"Now you'll never know what she wanted," I said.

"I suppose not. It could have been that she planned to tell me she was getting married and she was changing her will." Color flooded her cheeks. "She'd told me a thousand times she was leaving me the bulk of her estate. It would be her style to tell me in person if the situation changed."

"If she and Parker were marrying, I'm sure she'd want you to attend her wedding."

"She might. But she lit into me over the phone a few months back. And when she called to ask me to come see her, I thought she was going to cut me…never mind."

I studied my glass. Amber liquid, lemon wedge, ice cubes. Yep, it was tea all right.

"So what happened with Rita?" Stanley asked, looking at me. "Car accident?"

Rescued by change of subject. Maybe he *was* a knight in shining armor. That didn't mean I had to like him.

I was glad I'd had practice telling the story. Angie snuffled back tears when I got to the part about finding Rita's body, and again when I mentioned she'd planned to buy a mare to breed in hopes of raising a champion.

"Now she'll never get the chance." Angie got up and wandered to the back door. She slid her fingers over the doorknob. "I'm changing the locks. I don't know who has a key, but I suspect Parker Fielding or Maggie might."

One of the cats had come to the back door meowing pitifully, and I realized Parker and I had forgotten to feed the barn cats. Stanley finally got up and went outside with a bag of cat food and the cat followed him across the porch, yowling as if it hadn't eaten for a month.

Angie refilled her glass, then gestured to the pitcher, but

I shook my head. My kidneys were floating. I moved my foot, hitting something under the table. Angie had put her purse under her chair and I'd knocked it over.

As I righted the purse, I couldn't help but see that loose papers had fallen out and were lying next to the table leg. One was a receipt for a room at a Day's Inn in Bradenton for Friday night and the other was a computer printout repair slip from Hal's Jiffy Car Repair, also in Bradenton. The Hal's Jiffy receipt had the time listed. Car into the shop at 7 AM Friday and out at 4 PM. So Angie and Stanley had been only a couple of hours away while Rita was dying. A wave of sadness passed over me, and I was still squatting half under the table when Angie put her glass down and bent to peer under the table at me.

Stiffly I stood, putting the receipts on the kitchen counter. "These fell out of your purse."

"Thanks." Her eyes widened. "Wow, do you know what thought I just had? If the van hadn't broken down in Bradenton Thursday evening, so we ended up staying overnight, we might have been here in time to save her."

"She wouldn't have been in the loft if she weren't getting hay for me," I said.

Her expression didn't change. "How awful. I can tell you feel bad about that, but she could have been getting her own hay. The accident wasn't your fault."

"Like you, I feel that I if I'd gotten here sooner I could have saved her." I shrugged.

"Please don't feel that way. Look, why don't you stay for lunch and tell us more about Aunt Rita. I'd really appreciate it."

"Okay, if you let me help." I volunteered to make sandwiches.

While I worked on tuna salad and another pitcher of tea, Angie sat at the table tracing lines across her place mat with her fingers. "I spoke with Aunt Rita often on the phone." She whooshed out a gentle sigh. "She was so good to me, even paid for my college tuition. Aunt Rita always had a big say in my life, and my parents encouraged her. But from the time she first told me she'd saved a college fund for me, she really pushed me to be a doctor. We compromised and I studied nursing. But then I quit the hospital to help Stan in his antique store." She blinked at me helplessly, making her look exactly like a particularly air-headed Barbie doll. But when she'd first gone into the kitchen, I'd thought she was frank and take-charge like Rita. Obviously the shock of Rita's death still had her reeling.

"And Rita wasn't pleased."

"Definitely not. But I was so burnt out at work I had to do something!" She pounded her fist against the tabletop. "Sorry."

"It's okay," I said, though I was more startled than I'd let on about her outburst. She'd seemed so amiable up to now that I'd never have suspected her of having a temper.

"You must think I have no manners, rattling on about myself. What do you do, Leigh?"

I suspected she'd be bored listening to me detail my life, unless I wanted to talk about Kenneth and his plans to force me into the Summer Breeze, Elevation A, the model I'd toured in Hansen Haven. "Nothing too exciting. I work for a banking center doing word processing and data entry. Ten thousand keystrokes a minute." I didn't add that I, too, hated my job.

When I'd taken the job, I'd told my parents it was an introvert's dream and at the time, that was what I needed to heal from my divorce. But now, the hours alone at my desk made me feel as if I were in a sensory deprivation chamber. I hadn't had the courage to actually change careers. On the other hand, I had Whitney to think about, and no idea what I might want to do instead of sitting in front of a computer monitor pounding a keyboard until my fingers ached.

Stan came in and we sat down to lunch. Right after we finished, Angie got a phone call, which she took in the living room while I started clearing up the dishes. Stan excused himself, saying he wanted to see the horses. I didn't know where to find the dishcloths and had to open four drawers before I found the right one.

Like Rita's barn office, her kitchen drawers were unbelievably cluttered, filled with papers, silverware, and assorted office supplies. The fourth drawer held dishcloths, but when I picked one up, I saw a small red notebook at the back of the drawer. The notebook was open, so I pulled it closer so could read what was on the page.

It was a list in Rita's handwriting. First she'd written, "Contact Angie about leaving her job." I grinned. Angie was right on target. Second on the list was, "Write to feed company about the quality of the last batch of rolled oats." Last she'd penned in, "Write to the ACHR about the Harper's new Dawn Lady colt."

I shook my head. I shouldn't be prying into Rita's things. I could see the list continued onto the next page, but I dropped the notebook, pushed it to the back of the drawer, and covered it with a dishcloth.

Still, I couldn't stop wondering. The Harpers, like most of us in the horse club, owned cattle horses. Cattle horses were registered with the American Cattle Horse Registry or ACHR. What could Rita want to tell the ACHR about Brenda and Scott Harper? I supposed we'd never know unless Rita had actually gotten around to sending off her letter before her death.

I was wiping the last of the dishes, when Angie returned.

"I really appreciate all your help. And your friendship. I can consider you a friend, can't I?" She looked at me like a little girl begging for a piece of candy.

"Sure." I didn't usually make friends this quickly, but what could it hurt to let her think I was her new best bud?

"Thank you. That means so much now with Aunt Rita gone, and with Stan and I being strangers here." She rubbed her eyes. "The director at the funeral home wants to know about arrangements for Aunt Rita. Apparently the medical examiner had to do an autopsy first." She shuddered. "The funeral's Tuesday. I'd thought about cremation, but then I remembered Aunt Rita said once she'd left specific instructions and she wanted to be buried next to her parents."

"I guess that's to be expected." I looked at my watch. "I have to go. I'm taking my cousin's dog to be groomed. Are you going to be all right?"

"Sure." Her expression brightened and she put a hand on my arm. "Hold up a minute. I'd like you to have some of Aunt Rita's things—a box of horse books I saw in the living room. I haven't been through the box, but it looks like there are magazines, too."

I protested, but she'd already pointed out a cardboard carton next to the door leading into the hallway. Like its counterpart in the barn office, it seemed to be filled with back issues of horse magazines and horse books, something Whitney and I would both enjoy.

"If you're sure…"

Stan had come in while we were talking and he picked up the box. "Angie told me Rita didn't throw away anything. I was out at the barn and saw there were about a million magazines in the barn office, too. You'd be doing us a favor to take them off our hands."

"Guess I can't resist, then." I held the door and we walked out together.

I opened the Honda's trunk, and Stan fitted the carton in neatly. Then he had me stop at the barn where he loaded the second box.

As I drove away, I couldn't help speculating. I wouldn't be human, after this morning's drama, if I didn't wonder about Rita's will. How would Angie react if she found out next week that Rita had cut her off without a dime, and Parker or Maggie were taking over? That would be hard to accept after a lifetime of having the expectation of being her only heir.

Chapter 8

Sammi lived in a neat, but small, wood frame house in town. She had nearly a half acre of yard, fenced for Jeeves, and she was close enough to the center of Del Canto to walk to the shops as well as the park. If I were willing to give up my horses, I'd live in a place like hers.

When I opened the back door, Jeeves greeted me by planting a pair of shaggy paws on my shoulders. Sammi wasn't kidding about him needing a grooming. I couldn't even see his eyes through the shaggy mass of hair in front of his face. I found his leash and hurried him out to the car.

There was a new grooming shop in town within walking distance of Sammi's home and when I drove by I could see the parking lot was full. But Sammi had always gone to Maggie's and she said Jeeves loved Maggie, and she wouldn't sacrifice his happiness for convenience. I couldn't blame her. I'd used the same farrier for years because my horses were so comfortable with him and if he hadn't retired last month, he'd still be making regular trips to my barn.

Maggie's shop was in an out of the way location, through

town and down a side road to a strip mall that didn't have direct access to the new highway. Most of the surrounding businesses had given up when customers wouldn't go the extra distance, but Maggie's Tabby and Rover Boutique and a consignment shop were still bravely displaying "Open" signs.

I let Jeeves drag me into the shop before I consulted my watch. Three-fifteen. Almost on time. Maggie sat on a stool behind the register looking through an appointment book. She nodded a greeting and snapped the book shut.

"Sammi asked me to bring Jeeves in for her. Sorry I'm late, but I was over at Rita's helping Parker with the horses." Wait. Shouldn't have mentioned Parker. I clamped my mouth shut.

She glanced at me sharply. "It doesn't matter, I'm not exactly busy this afternoon. But even with my sister's death, I can't afford to close on a Saturday when I've got appointments on the book. I'm not rich like some people."

Especially not since Parker took over what she'd thought was her inheritance. I wondered if she knew that Parker had since been displaced by Angie Loring.

Maggie slid off the stool. Jeeves greeted her by spinning in circles, but dropped to the floor as soon as she ordered him to lie down.

Maggie was a tall, athletic looking woman. Her hair had been gray for so many years I'd almost forgotten her natural color was a dark reddish shade. Her eyes were blue, but not the icy hue Rita had. Maggie's eye color had more than a hint of purple mixed in with the blue, her prettiest feature.

She turned her gaze on me and cocked an eyebrow as if to say, "Anything else I can do for you?"

"You certainly know how to handle Jeeves," I remarked.

"I've had a lot of experience with dogs." No change of facial expression.

I'd expected the low-key mood. Who wouldn't feel bad after losing a family member? "Uhmm…Maggie, as I said last night, I'm really sorry about Rita."

She shrugged. "We were sisters, but we were never close. We had our differences. Still." She turned her back, busying herself pulling dog combs and assorted brushes out of a drawer. The silence hung in the air. I wondered if the fact that I'd gone to help Parker had made her angry with me.

"See you," I said after a minute.

"Okay." As if Jeeves weighed only a few ounces instead of about eighty pounds, she hoisted him onto a table and started brushing him out.

I walked out of her shop into bright sunlight in time to see a silver truck pull into a spot next to my Honda. Jared Beaumont, the would-be horse buyer I'd met at Rita's yesterday, was behind the wheel, and I waved a greeting. He got out of the car and returned the wave.

"We meet again. Give me a minute—Leigh McRae, right?"

"Points for a great memory."

"I always remember beautiful ladies."

"Watch it. I don't give points for flattery." I fished in my purse for my keys.

He put his hand over his heart and said, "I swear the compliment is one hundred percent true."

He was exaggerating about my beauty, but maybe not too much, I hoped immodestly. "So what brings you to this side of town?"

"Business." Jared waved in the direction of the consignment shop. "Look, Leigh, I've been thinking. I still plan to buy horses, and I was wondering if you could help me out, maybe introduce me to some horse people in the area."

"I'd be glad to." I wrote my number on a scrap of paper and handed it to him. Then I finally found my keys, slid behind the Honda's wheel, and backed out. When I looked up again, Jared was standing in front of the consignment store. He sent me a broad grin and a final wave.

Traffic back through town was light, but that was typical of a Saturday. I passed planters filled with brightly colored spring blooms in front of every shop and office on Main Street, and smelled fresh mown grass when I took a short cut down a side street that led through a residential neighborhood. It could have been an ordinary Saturday instead of a day when I couldn't stop thinking about Rita's accident.

When I got home, though my back and legs begged me to

stretch out in my chair, I headed straight for the horses. There I measured out feed and hay before I brought Sonny Joe into his stall. Belle, her sides sticking out and making her look as if she'd swallowed Adam's charter boat edgewise, still showed no signs of foaling.

I patted her neck. "Going to hold that baby forever, old lady?"

She flicked her ears and stuck her nose in her feed tub. The three cats meowed and wove themselves around my ankles, threatening to trip me up until I fed them. They were former strays that Whitney had dragged home. I'd had all three cats spayed, and they did a good job of keeping the barn rat free. And right now they were keeping my mind off Rita. Sort of.

Brenda Harper called about ten minutes after I walked into the house. Hot, sticky, and grimy, I'd been on my way to the shower, but I knew if I didn't talk to her, she'd keep calling.

"Leigh, sorry about you finding Rita. I heard your horse Tinker got hurt, too." Brenda talked twice as fast as anyone else and she had a grating quality to her voice that never failed to set my teeth on edge.

"Ex-horse." I tried to disguise my annoyance, but failed.

"Whatever." Brenda wasn't particularly thick-skinned, but she carried on as though I'd gone into ecstasies of delight over her call. "Anyway, your husband says he wants you to give up your horses, and I thought you'd sell me Sonny Joe for my show string."

"You thought wrong." I scratched my stomach, feeling hay and feed crumbs under my shirt. I shook the mess out onto the floor.

"Think about it. We—Scott and I—talked it over yesterday. We can offer half what you paid for him."

My jaw dropped in outrage. They knew what I'd paid because Doug Reilly had overheard Rita quote me the price, and he'd blabbed to everyone in town. But I'd paid for my half with Tinker. Brenda's check would go to Kenneth, if I knew Kenneth.

"I'm not selling, especially not at that price." I pictured Brenda narrowing her tiny eyes to slits.

"You paid too much for that horse," she informed me. "Rita

knew how much you wanted him for Whitney and she took advantage. You won't get a better offer." She sounded like an overly aggressive salesman promising that this fantastic deal was good for the next three minutes only, so I'd better act now.

"Look, Brenda, I was about to step into the shower."

"Call you next week then. But I talked to your husband, and he agreed to the sale." She banged her receiver down before I could have the satisfaction of telling her Kenneth was not my husband and he did not own Sonny Joe.

After I showered, I stepped onto the bath mat with the realization I was past exhaustion. A minute later, I crawled into bed wearing a well-worn yellow nightgown. After a nap I'd hop up, fix my dinner, and maybe even sort through the mail accumulating on my desk. I reached for a book on my bedside table. Sammi had forced this volume on me months ago, and I still hadn't gotten past the second chapter. It was all about positive thinking and how one's life would improve like magic as long as one kept smiling and thinking happy thoughts. I gave up on expecting magic. I let the book drop after reading a couple of pages that could have been written by a second grader who'd just figured out why he always ended up with the gray crayon.

Rita's accident kept crowding itself into my mind. I quieted my thinking and went over the scene again as though I were running a video in super slow motion, and making liberal use of instant replays to fix certain frames in my head. This time I finally remembered. I gasped and sat straight up, flinging the unread book across the bed. It slid off the end of my flowered bedspread and thunked onto the carpet.

I stared into my reflection in the mirror on my dresser. My face was the color of buttered grits. Something about Rita's death wasn't right, and I'd known all along, but hadn't allowed myself to focus or to entertain bad thoughts about people who'd benefit from Rita's death.

The usual motive for murder was greed, but there was also revenge. Who would want Rita dead? Angie believed she was Rita's sole heir. Rita had inherited a lot of money from the grandparents who'd raised her. She'd managed well over the years and now she owned a house and barn, a new truck and horse trailer, an orange grove, three hundred acres of prime pastureland and five well-bred Cattle Horses, plus a horse training business. I'd heard rumors she had a sizable bank account as well as money in investments. If that were true, then even a conservative estimate would place her total worth at more than two million dollars. I'd even heard the figure was closer to five million, but of course, I had no way of knowing.

I frowned at my image in the mirror. Angie couldn't be a killer. She was too normal, too nice. She'd called me her friend. She'd invited me to lunch and given me a couple of boxes of books and magazines—which I'd forgotten about and left in the trunk of my car. But her husband might have done the job. Maybe while their car was in the shop he'd snuck off to Del Canto and shoved Rita out of the loft so his wife could inherit.

The next thing that popped into my mind was that I'd spent part of the day at Rita's. With people who were sort of murder suspects, if I was right about what really happened to Rita.

God, what was I doing? I'd never be able to sleep. I was likely all wrong, fantasizing a murder that wasn't because it made some kind of weird sense to me. I reached for the phone by the bed and frantically dialed Sammi's number.

"What are you doing?" I said as soon as she answered.

"Besides talking to you? I just finished taking Jeeves outside for a potty run and now I'm fixing to watch a movie I rented at Blockbuster. *Gladiator*. Can you believe I haven't seen it yet?"

"You can't talk now?"

"I really want to see this movie. What's wrong, Leigh?"

"I have a wild idea. A bizarre thought about murder that I need to run by you."

"You sound all cloak and dagger. I can see the movie another time."

"No, I probably need more time to think, and I wouldn't dream of spoiling your evening. All right if I come over tomorrow?" I desperately needed her input before I called the police.

"Of course."

"After I tell you the story, you'll probably end up advising me to seek professional help as soon as possible." If she did, it wouldn't be the first time. The only other person I could possibly tell any of this to was Adam, and I didn't consider that option for more than two seconds.

I ended up spending half the night watching old videos of Whitney's birthday parties and horse shows where she'd won high point youth. Even then I couldn't stop thinking of Rita's death.

I dragged myself out of bed in the morning, feeling like I'd worked in the pasture all night. By the time I finished the last of my chores and headed for Sammi's, it looked like a thunderstorm was on the way. Even though the sky had darkened to the color of a new bruise and was hung with lavender clouds that held the temperature down, it was so humid it felt about twenty degrees hotter than it really was.

Sammi met me at the back door. Her kitchen table was a wooden square that barely fit in a corner near the refrigerator. I took one of the two chairs. A fan on the counter whirred at top speed.

"Iced tea?"

I nodded and grabbed a *Redbook* off the table, using it to fan myself. The air conditioner switched on with a low hum. The kitchen was darker than I'd ever seen it. Normally a skylight over the sink kept it as bright as the outdoors, but now the storm clouds had become a thick curtain drawn across the face of the sun.

"Crackers? Cookies? Sandwich?" She flicked on a light and waved in the general direction of the refrigerator.

"No, thanks. Tea is exactly what I need. The air in my car is threatening to go out, and I nearly melted coming over." I couldn't really complain about my faithful little Honda. It had over two hundred thousand miles on the odometer and had never needed a major repair.

"And I nearly melted from suspense. What's going on, Leigh?"

I put down my glass. "I'm not sure. Listen and then tell me if I'm crazy."

"Haven't I always?" She leaned over and patted my arm.

"Yeah, you've been my island of sanity. I got this thought that Rita's accident might have been on purpose. I mean, what if she was murdered, instead of falling out of the loft?"

She didn't reach for the phone to dial 1-800-loony bin. She

didn't even laugh. Her eyes darkened and she gripped the table edge. "Tell me more."

"The police think it was an accident, but I'm not sure." I still had a feeling I was indulging in an overactive imagination instead of facing up to grim reality.

Sammi nodded thoughtfully. "Rita was worth a fortune. If someone wanted to kill her, it would be easy to set up a barn accident."

"Exactly. All along I've wondered how someone with Rita's experience could have been so careless. She must have been in that loft a million times."

"Maybe you're letting your imagination run away with you."

"That crossed my mind."

"Then what do you do? Go to the police?"

"That's the big question. The thought of getting laughed out of the station doesn't appeal. On the other hand, I don't want some sleazeball getting away with murder."

"Leigh, have I ever told you I think you have the most overdeveloped sense of justice of anyone I've ever known?"

"Lots of times. But I don't think it's an overdeveloped sense of justice to want a killer to get put away." When we were kids, we'd never played with dolls. Instead we played cops and robbers or even—when I could talk Sammi into cooperating—trials and prisons. I was always the cop, the judge, or the prison warden, while Sammie was the hapless perp. One time I'd locked her in an old shed for an entire afternoon, and brought her bread and water for lunch. Until I'd ended my college career prematurely to marry Kenneth, I'd been majoring in criminology with vague plans to go into law enforcement, much to my mother's horror.

"Let's think this through. If you really believe she was murdered and you make it sound plausible, the police will *have* to keep investigating."

"Right. And how do I do that?" I was all for finding out who the real killer was, if there was one, but it wasn't like I was a master detective.

"We have to figure out why anyone would want to kill Rita."

I watched while she got up and pulled a piece of notebook paper and a pen out of a kitchen drawer. If it were me looking for something to write on, I'd still be fishing around, and I'd finally have to settle for a broken crayon and the back of a business card.

"I've given this a lot of thought, Sammi, and apparently Angie, her goddaughter, has the best motive. As far as I know, she's the one who inherits everything. And Angie's husband is a big guy, certainly strong enough to kill a woman." I didn't add that I disliked him for no apparent reason. "And there's Parker Fielding. He was Rita's financial advisor, but he said he and Rita were planning to get married. As far as I know, Parker had no motive except money, and I've heard he's well off. Unless she'd already changed her will, Parker wouldn't be stupid enough to kill her before they got married."

"True." She twisted her iced tea glass in her hands. "So, unless she'd already changed her will to leave him at least part of the money, that gives Angie more of a motive. Angie would have to kill Rita before she had a chance to see her lawyer about making Parker her heir."

"But having a motive isn't reason enough to conclude murder. There's something else." I replayed Friday morning in my mind, the same way I'd been doing since Saturday. The awful picture was exactly the same, but it always stopped at the stables when I was leading Tinker to put her back in her stall. Something wasn't right. It had nagged at me since Friday and until last night, it felt like straw caught under my shirt that poked me every time I moved.

"Leigh? The whole idea of Rita being murdered is probably too way out there to even consider." Sammi's voice sounded far away.

"No." I raised my head and slowly swiveled it from side to side, surprised I was still seated at her table instead of out at Rita's barn, reliving the whole horrible event. "Someone killed Rita. I'm positive."

Chapter 9

"You saw something? A clue?" Sammi put her hands over mine.

"I'm not sure how much of a clue it is, but I'm convinced." I was still probing my subconscious where I'd stored the scene that was now so clear. "The police came, along with an ambulance and a bunch of medics. Detectives questioned me and Millie Destin, and then Jared Beaumont showed up. He's a man who was supposed to be seeing Rita about buying a horse, and they questioned him, too. All this time, I was still out of it. But after they took Rita away, I realized I couldn't leave the horse standing in the washrack all day, so I told one of the detectives I'd put her away."

Sammi nodded. She'd clipped her hair on top of her head, but now most of the wayward tresses had come loose from the barrette and fallen over the right side of her face. She didn't seem to notice.

"When I first got to Rita's, a filly was running loose and Millie Destin was chasing her with a branch. That filly—Tinker—had opened her stall latch and gotten loose before, so I thought she'd done it again. I led her to her stall to put her away…and the stall door was closed and latched."

"Wow, I see what you're getting at. The filly could have let herself out, but she couldn't have closed and latched her door behind her. But maybe Rita took her out."

"That makes no sense. If Rita had opened the stall, it's unlikely Tinker would have broken loose from an experienced horsewoman like she was. And if she had, Rita wouldn't have simply said, 'That pesky filly is running loose. Guess I'll shut the stall and climb into the loft to get the hay, and I'll worry about her later.' No, she'd have caught Tinker and put her up."

"If that's your only clue, something tells me the police are going to brush you off with a warning to stop watching so many *Law and Order* reruns."

I drummed my fingers on the table. "It isn't my only clue. There's the saddle and bridle in the barn aisleway. You know what a show bridle looks like."

"You mean one of those with polished silver trim all over it."

"Right. I wondered why Rita was using it at home. Especially since it was next to an old beat up work saddle that didn't match the bridle. I looked in the tack room and saw her work bridle was taken apart on the table. At the time, I figured that was a simple enough explanation, but now that I've thought about it, it wasn't like Rita to leave a chore half done. She'd have put the bridle back together rather than substitute a show bridle."

"That could be a clue, but hardly proof of murder. You need real proof you can take to the police."

I sighed. "You may not think it's real proof. But I *know* it is."

"So the killer, if there is one, might or might not be clueless about which saddle and bridle to use on a horse."

I let out my breath in a whoosh. Yep, exactly the way I expected, Sammi brought me back to earth. Except, I was positive Rita wouldn't have used a show bridle with her work saddle just to put a few miles on a filly in training. Someone else had to have taken the tack out of the tackroom and left it in the aisle.

"Here's what I think. Someone killed Rita. Then they decided to set up an accident, make it look like one of the horses threw her. They took the saddle and bridle out of the tackroom and left them in the barn aisle. Next they went for the nearest horse, which would be Tinker in stall one. After they took her out of the stall and closed it, Tinker broke loose. She's a young filly with a lot of spirit. Someone who isn't used to horses wouldn't know how to handle her. Once she was loose, they changed their mind and hauled Rita up to the loft, then pushed her out. Or else, they'd already pushed her out of the loft and decided to stage a riding accident."

Sammi eyed me thoughtfully. "Okay, I'm convinced there's at least room to question the obvious. But I still don't believe the police are going to leap to check into things."

"I know. And Angie probably has the best motive, so I suppose she'll be the chief suspect. That's sad because except for Maggie, she's Rita's closest relative, if a goddaughter can be called a relative."

"Yeah, relatives should give each other lots of love." She got up and planted a big wet kiss on my cheek.

"Cut it out," I said, pushing her away. "This isn't funny."

"Angie doesn't have to be the killer; Parker Fielding might have done it. And what about those Harper people? You told me once they couldn't stand Rita."

"They couldn't, but I can't think of a motive, except maybe jealousy."

"What if something happened? Something we don't know about, and the Harpers realized there was only one solution."

"Such as Rita had something on them and maybe she'd resorted to blackmail?" I tried to picture Rita calling up the Harpers from a pay phone, instructing them to leave cash in unmarked bills at a convenient location or she'd reveal that Brenda and Scott Harper were total idiots.

"You're the one who thinks someone killed the woman. Work with me, Leigh."

"I'm trying. I have to have facts for the police."

"Didn't you say Rita and Doug Reilly didn't get along too well?"

"True," I said. "Everybody in the horse club saw them argue. I suppose we'd have to list him."

"What about that guy, the one the detectives questioned?" She tapped her pen against the paper and wiggled her eyebrows up and down.

"Jared? What about him?"

"What's his connection with Rita?"

"I told you, he was there to buy horses. That's not a motive unless he planned to steal them instead."

"Okay, we'll leave him out. For now." She'd started writing suspects' names in a column on her notebook paper. She had another column for clues. She turned the paper over and started a third column labeled *what to tell the police*. That one was blank. "Didn't the medical examiner do an autopsy?" she said, looking up at me.

"He did, but I suppose he'd write fractured skull or something in Latin that means the same thing. Fracturus skullus."

"Behave yourself. On TV they'd figure out all kinds of evidence from an autopsy."

"This isn't TV. As far as the coroner and the police are concerned, the fall killed her and—" I stopped in mid-sentence. An unsettling mental picture had interrupted my train of thought. Rita was a fighter. Rita wouldn't have simply stood quietly and waited for the killing blow. Unless the killer had snuck up behind her. "Sammi, do you suppose the autopsy showed defensive wounds and the coroner missed it because he assumed she died from an accident?"

"If they weren't looking for something like that, they could easily miss the clues."

"Damn. I really hoped I could have solid evidence for the police instead of a lame theory. We're doing nothing but going in circles."

"Yeah, and I have to get ready for a date." She shook a forefinger at me. "Don't you dare say anything about Ray."

I made a lip-zipping motion. "Call you tomorrow."

My talk with Sammi had helped sort my thoughts from a jumble of mixed scenes and impressions, but left me with jumbled emotions instead. I was sure Rita had been murdered, and now I wouldn't be able to rest until Detective Frazier and his partner had the killer in handcuffs.

It had been over a week since I'd shopped for food and I knew I'd have to get groceries before Whitney came home. Tiny as she is, she still has the appetite of a swarm of locusts. I headed to Publix to stock up, but I would rather have stayed home to wait out the impending storm, and maybe ponder my next move.

I was in aisle four, fruit juice and cereal, when Parker turned the corner pushing a grocery cart. We stopped and stared at each other, mutually surprised to cross paths at Publix instead of at Rita's or a show.

"Hello," I said finally, switching gears from grape juice to social encounter.

"Good afternoon." He was wearing gray slacks, a gray sports coat, and a white shirt and gray tie. "I'm sorry about the scene with the Lorings at Rita's place yesterday. I was out of line."

"No problem. I understand."

His jaw tightened and he looked away from me for a long moment.

A thought popped into my head—where was Parker on Friday morning? I didn't dare ask and he didn't seem inclined to further conversation. I watched as he carefully maneuvered his cart around mine, then continued down the aisle, stopping only to select a bottle of cranberry juice, holding it up to the light as though he were choosing the finest wine.

"I'll see you at the funeral," I called. He didn't answer. You'd never have guessed we'd spent Saturday morning working companionably together cleaning stalls.

Seeing Parker started my mind spinning again. I was so deep in thought at the checkout that the bagboy had to say "paper or plastic, Ma'am?" three times, each time sounding increasingly annoyed. I finally snapped to attention, narrowing my eyes and staring him down.

"Plastic is fine," I spat out, knowing I sounded like a shrew. I instantly developed a guilt complex—one of my specialties—so I stared out the front window of the store, watching Parker carry his bag of groceries across the parking lot. I felt as though my eyes were popping out of my head when I saw him get behind the wheel of a shiny white Lexus. I actually swiveled my head from side to side, searching for the trusty Toyota I'd seen on Saturday, as if waiting for it to pull up and say, "Parker, stop! *I'm* your car!" Maybe if I were a financial advisor like Parker, I could afford a new car. But if I ever get up the nerve to actually change jobs, high finance wouldn't be my first choice.

I consulted my watch. If I didn't get home within the next fifteen minutes, Kenneth would have to wait out front with Whitney, which would make him work himself into a mood worthy of Attila the Hun. I did not feel like coping with an angry Hun. I tossed my grocery bags into the Honda's back seat and zipped out of the parking lot.

About the time I finished putting the groceries away, Whitney trudged up to the house, her overnight bag slung over her shoulder. Kenneth escorted her to the door, half raised a hand in greeting when he saw me, then started to disappear back into the shadows without taking the opportunity to remind me he expected me to sell Sonny to Brenda Harper.

"Kenneth, wait," I called.

He turned in slow motion and one eyebrow shot up. "Well?"

I'd been about to ask him to fix the leak under the kitchen sink, but then something in the way he stared down his nose brought up thoughts of Adam. Not that Adam ever stares down his nose. I opened my mouth, but no words came out.

"Well?" he said again. "I don't plan to wait here all night watching you jitter around looking confused, especially since it's going to storm any second." Even as he spoke, rain began to fall, a few gentle drops at a time.

"It's nothing," I snapped, stepping aside to let Whitney pass. I deliberately turned my back on Kenneth and shut the door, harder than I needed to. "Hi, sweets," I said, smiling at Whitney. "How was your visit?"

"The usual. Daddy took me to out to play video games at the arcade. Doreen showed me how to make an over-dazzled tee shirt for myself. You know she's all arts and crafts and ballet and pageants. I didn't want to hurt her feelings, so I didn't tell her nobody in my school would wear one of these." She bent down and dragged a pink tee shirt out of her bag.

I winced when I saw the bright green and blue stones forming a random pattern between the silver and gold lines of glitter that snaked back and forth across the shirt. Some people do beautiful work with similar materials. Doreen, despite her interest in arts and crafts, seems to lack their talent. "I'm glad you weren't rude about it. Don't you like Doreen?" I was fishing. I prided myself on not quizzing her when she returned from visiting Daddy and his dearest, but being all too human, I occasionally gave in to a little curiosity.

"Sometimes I do and sometimes I don't. But I always act polite to her. Doreen gets her feelings hurt really easily. Even Daddy knows that. Doreen said she wants new dining room furniture and Daddy said they just got furniture. I thought she was going to cry, so then Daddy said she could buy whatever she wanted. I went with her to the furniture store and she used Daddy's credit card and bought a whole truckload of stuff. After that, she bought a gold tennis bracelet and makeup at the mall. When we got home, she showed me how to put on nail polish without smearing, and we talked about Heath."

"Heath?"

She set a course for the refrigerator. "Doreen says she plans to have a baby right away when they're married, and she wants a boy. She's naming him Heath something. One of those J names that are so popular—Jordan, Jacob, Justin. That's it. Justin. He'll be Heath Justin.

"Daddy said they couldn't afford a baby because they spent too much on their house and they'd go broke. Doreen said babies were little and didn't cost that much. I thought they were going to fight, but Daddy made that kind of face that looks like he ate something rotten, and he said he'd sell some more real estate and Doreen could have whatever she wanted."

My eyebrows rocketed toward my hairline. You go, Doreen. Kenneth had never made me that kind of offer. But I was starting to believe the real estate he was going to sell was my own ten acres.

Whitney opened a bag of chips, and I poured her a glass of calcium fortified orange juice. I knew Doreen's knowledge of nutrition was about on a par with that of one of my horses, and Kenneth seemed oblivious to the fact that Whitney drank nothing but soft drinks while she was at their house.

"I really hope the baby's a boy," she went on. "Because Doreen wants to name it Beatrice Angelica if it's a girl, and call it Bea-Angel. I really hate that name. It sounds like the name of a poodle or something. Daddy doesn't like it either and he said he hopes Doreen changes her mind."

"Can't say I blame him." I pawed around in the refrigerator and found a lemon yogurt.

"But you know what, Daddy shouldn't be so mean."

I heard the catch in her voice and turned. "Mean? What's wrong, sweets?"

"He says I can't keep Sonny Joe. He says you're going to sell him and the other horses. He *told* you to." Her bottom lip quivered like Jell-O.

I took a deep breath, dipped my spoon into my cup, and did not scream that "Daddy" could not force me to sell so much as a toothpick.

"Horses are my life," she said dramatically. She flung both arms out to the sides, nearly clipping me on the side of the head.

"Don't worry, sweetheart, I'm not selling the horses."

"I heard Daddy tell Doreen that he can force you to sell. She thinks I'm going to get hurt in a barn accident like Rita did. She says he's doing the right thing and she'll back him up, no matter what you say."

Doreen? Sweet Thing? Doormat woman?

Right then the storm finally cut loose, rain pouring down as though a dam in the sky had burst. Lightning flashed, thunder boomed, and I stood in one spot for a good five minutes before I remembered to unplug all the appliances and turn off the air conditioning.

Whitney ran to her room, and I let her have her space. I knew she was grieving over Rita and sure I'd give in and let Kenneth dictate how we were to live. I shook my head. Except for the divorce, which he'd wanted as much as I had, when had I ever given her reason to think I'd stand up to him?

I went back to the kitchen and found the wrench Adam had returned, where I'd left it under the sink. The smell of mildew wafted out from where I'd placed old rags under the pan I was using to collect the water drips.

I'd never before tackled a chore like this, but I grabbed the wrench and went to work, lying on my back under the sink with my legs poking out of the cabinet. A drop of scummy water landed on my forehead, making me curse out loud. It took only a minute of tinkering and speculation to find the problem. A loose connection on the pipe from the garbage disposal to the drain was the source of the leak. I gave it a few turns with the wrench and miraculously the dripping stopped.

Adam was wrong, I didn't have to depend on Kenneth for everything. And I didn't have to depend on Adam either. I'd just fixed a leak all by myself. And tomorrow I would contact the police to set them straight about Rita, and no one was going to stop me.

Chapter 10

I whined all the way to Whitney's school about the unfairness of it being Monday. Then, my audience gone, I switched on the car radio and continued up palm-tree lined Rucker Avenue into downtown Del Canto. The older section of town was located on the waterfront, where renovated wooden fish houses served as trendy shops with a view of hundreds of well-tended yachts and charter boats moored at the city docks. The bank where I worked was past the shops. Thanks to the strict zoning laws, all the new buildings had to fit in with the surroundings—skyscrapers definitely forbidden. My company's building was a flamingo-colored, stucco rectangle set discreetly back from the road. It was nearly hidden behind a jungle of tropical vegetation that included palms and banana trees, as well as magenta colored bougainvillea cascading over a low concrete wall near the door.

I parked in my usual spot under a light post, guessing from the full parking lot I was running late. I gulped in a deep breath of salt-scented air blowing in off the harbor, and took the stairs as fast as I dared, pausing only to grab a coffee out of the break room on my way to my cubicle.

Fiona, my supervisor, stopped by as I was powering up my computer. She graced me with a concerned smile. "Are you okay, Leigh? You've got some sick days coming if you need more time to recover from that horrible experience." She fluttered her fingers when she said horrible as if to ward off evil.

Frowning, I swiveled my chair to face her. I'd almost forgotten about being on the local news. "I really appreciate your offer, but I'm fine, and I think it will do me good to keep busy. I need part of Tuesday off to go to the funeral, though."

"Of course you do. Remind me later and I'll mark you off the schedule."

Seconds after Fiona disappeared down the hall, Camilla Reed peeped furtively around the corner, giving the impression she'd been waiting for Fiona to leave. Camilla was a part-timer who filled in with word processing, but she was also recently admitted to the Florida Bar and practiced law, as well as did accounting, from her home.

One thing you had to say about Camilla, she was ambitious. When she hadn't been able to get a job at a local firm, she set up an office in her home. She told me once she really needed the money from the word processing and the accounting—home based lawyers not being all that popular—and anyway she'd get bored doing the same job all the time, so the hectic schedule suited her. She was saving to rent an office in town.

We sometimes ate lunch together, but I'd never felt I knew her well. She talked a lot, but she was one of those people who kept everything on a casual, surface level, so their words were only the top layer, never the real substance.

She slipped up to my desk and shot me a look I couldn't read. "Leigh, I'm sorry about Rita Cameron. I mean, what a total shock finding her."

I'd no sooner thanked her for her kind words, then she shook her head and marched briskly away, the heels of her shoes clicking on the tile floor. As usual, I was left wondering what she was *really* thinking.

At lunchtime I called Detective Frazier and arranged for him to come to the house after I got off work. I told him I wanted to add something to my statement about Rita Cameron's death, and he didn't ask any questions, for which I was grateful. What I had to say would come across better face to face.

"Mom, guess what?" Whitney burst in the door after school all smiles, last night's mood a thing of the past. The Jekyll and Hyde bit was starting to get to me. But with embarrassment, I remembered myself at that age when my mood swings and my attitude of utter superiority toward my poor mother had her wondering daily if it was too late to leave me in a basket on someone's doorstep.

I'd known Whitney would head straight for the kitchen, so I'd strategically placed myself next to the refrigerator as soon as I heard the squeal of the school bus brakes. "You don't have homework?"

"Yes, but that's not it. Brad Dakman beat up Donnie Holt at the bus stop. It was neat!" Two spots of color stood out on her cheekbones.

"Since when did you get to be such a fight fan?" I handed her a glass of milk and an apple.

"I'm not, but you have to admit it's kind of exciting. You know Brad, right? He was in the school play with me…he played the banker who wouldn't loan money to the poor farmer. Brad's a really nice boy, but he's kind of chubby. Anyway, Donnie's a jerk and he likes to make fun of Brad's weight. Usually Brad doesn't do anything, he just says he'll get even. Of course, he's said that a million times, so no one believes him. But Donnie finally crossed the line when he played this mean joke on Brad last Friday. He bought a whole bunch of Twinkies and dropped them all along the sidewalk from the bus stop right up to Brad's front door. He made a sign that said, 'follow the trail to the fat boy.'"

"How did Brad know who did it?"

"Mom, get a *clue*, it was so obvious." She rolled her eyes. "Donnie's the one who always picks on him, so who else would it be? So Brad jumped Donnie at the bus stop this afternoon and gave him a bloody nose. Now Brad is suspended from the school bus for ten days, even though nobody is punishing Donnie for being so mean. Would it be okay if Brad rode to school with us in the mornings?"

"How will he get home?"

"His older brother can pick him up."

"That's fine, then." I paused with my hand on the door. "I'm going out to feed the horses. Are you sure you don't want to come with me?"

Whitney clunked her glass down on the table. Her eyes took on an extra brightness. "Mom, there's no point in me hanging around the horses if you're going to sell them like a bunch of used cars."

"I am *not* selling them. You'll see, and then I'll expect an apology."

"Whatever."

Yeah, whatever. I was not proud of myself for powering down into permanent zombie mode ever since I'd met Kenneth McRae—and that was when I was twenty. I was thirty-five now. At least I'd finally realized I'd done a pretty good job of demonstrating to my daughter that Daddy called the shots and Mommy obeyed. I lifted my chin. Those days were over, but Whitney wasn't going to believe me until I showed her I was serious.

Detective Frazier drove up alone as I was finishing the last of the feeding. We shook hands and I motioned him into my stable office. It's not much, only a ten by ten room with plywood walls painted white, a phone, a desk with wobbly legs, and a couple of folding chairs against the back wall. But I didn't want to talk in the house where Whitney might overhear.

Frazier settled himself in the nearest chair, and I took the one closest to the desk. He opened his pocket notebook, the one I'd seen him with at Rita's, and said, "You've thought of something I should know concerning Ms. Cameron's accident?"

I took a shaky breath and reminded myself that my tax dollars were paying his salary, no matter what he thought of my theory. "I have. It's eating me alive."

He closed the notebook. "Darlin', it's normal to feel emotional about an accident involving the death of a friend."

I shook my head. "No, that isn't it. I've done a lot of thinking about what I saw that morning, and I'm convinced Rita's death wasn't an accident."

"You think she went out of the loft on purpose?" He crossed his arms over his chest. "Even if she wanted to commit—"

"Not a suicide," I broke in. "Someone murdered Rita."

"Why do you think it was murder?"

I explained about the show bridle, the latched stall door, and how Rita had a lot of money, and might have been about to cause trouble for some people, or disinherit others. When I finished, I half-expected Frazier to steeple his fingers ala Kenneth, tell me I was "imagining things, darlin'," and head smirking for the door.

Instead he nodded soberly. "Ms. Cameron's death looks like an accident. There was nothing unusual in the autopsy report. She had injuries from falling of course, and a few bruises on her hands and arms. Nothing severe."

"But?" My heart bumped into a higher gear and I gripped the edges of the chair seat so tightly, my knuckles turned white.

"It looks like an accident."

"Won't you even consider my theory?" I wanted to sound indignant, but even to me my voice sounded shaky. I inwardly cursed myself for being such a wimp. "The bruises could have been from her trying to defend herself."

"If she *was* murdered, they could be. On the other hand, she may have hurt her hands some other way. Like this." He held out his left hand with fingers spread to demonstrate. "I've got a half-grown lab puppy at home, and he plays pretty rough. There were also bruises on the upper part of Ms. Cameron's right arm. Someone gripping her arm tightly during an argument or to keep her from escaping could have caused that. *Or* she could have sustained an injury while working in the barn. In fact, that's the most likely explanation."

"If the killer confronted her, Rita wouldn't go quietly. You know, she was mugged last Thanksgiving in the parking lot at the mall, and she kicked the guy in the leg so hard, he was still limping at his trial."

"It could be you're feeling guilty because you couldn't save her." His voice sounded kind.

"No." I shook my head. "I really believe someone killed her. The horse could have flipped the latch up and turned herself loose, but there's no way she could have shut the door and re-latched it."

"It's possible you're not remembering the scene exactly as

it was. I deal with witnesses every day, and you'd be surprised how many different colors the same getaway car can be. Every witness swears they're right. That door could have been hanging wide open. In fact, as I remember the scene, it was."

It hadn't been, but I had no way to prove it. "Will you at least think about the possibility?"

"I'll speak with Stephanie Groves, my partner, and tell her what you said. I promise we'll take a closer look. But I'm pretty sure it will go down as an accident when we close the investigation, probably in a few days."

"I see." My voice was barely above a whisper. I had to think of a way to convince him. "There are other people who didn't get along with Rita. And Angie Loring, Rita's goddaughter, is probably her only heir. She had reason to believe Rita was planning to disinherit her since Rita was getting married." I felt like a traitor, but if Angie had killed Rita I wanted her caught.

Detective Frazier flipped back a few pages in his notebook. "Angie Loring wasn't even close to Del Canto when Ms. Cameron died."

"Oh." Obviously if the police were doing their job, Angie would be one of the first people they'd talk to. I already knew she had an alibi for the time of Rita's death. She'd been in Bradenton getting her car repaired. And now I knew the police had checked her story.

He stood and tucked his pen into his shirt pocket. "Thanks for the information, darlin'."

His casual stroll on the way back to his car told me all I needed to know. Ready to snap someone's head off, I stormed back to the house. I'd gone into my office with Frazier absolutely convinced the police would agree with me, and subsequently had gotten nowhere. I shook my finger at a hibiscus bush in frustration.

Chapter 11

Tuesday, funeral day, dawned ungodly hot. I raced around trying to piece together my outfit, eat breakfast, and keep Whitney moving so she wouldn't be late for school. I wouldn't have time to come back to the house to get ready, so I had to wear my dress to work. But I wasn't about to torture my feet by jamming them into my pointy-toed, spike-heeled shoes all day. I left the shoes in a bag on the front seat of the car to wear later, and put on my running shoes for work.

Today *would* have to be the first day to pick up Brad Dakman, as if I weren't stressed out enough. On time at least, Brad slid into the back seat and dropped his bookbag beside him. He didn't look like a kid who'd get into trouble for violence, but then I suppose all of us have a breaking point. Brad was, as Whitney had said, chubby. He also had neatly combed sandy hair and gray eyes that crinkled up at the corners when he smiled. And I suspected, from the shy smile she sent his way, Whitney had a crush on him.

"Hey, Mrs. McRae. Thanks for the ride."

"Hi, Brad," I said absently. Brad lived in an overcrowded subdivision of cloned floor plan houses painted in Florida pastels.

I was glad to get back onto the main road so I didn't have to keep dodging cats, dogs, and cars parked in the narrow streets.

"Were your parents really mad about you beating up Donnie?" Whitney asked.

"Not at first. They thought Donnie should have got in trouble, too, for picking on me. Then Mr. Griffith called from the school and said I beat up the wrong kid."

I glanced at Brad in the rear view mirror. He rolled his eyes and drew a finger across his neck at noose level. "Oh, man," he squawked. "It turned out that new kid, Richie, did it. He admitted the whole thing, and man, I felt stupid when I found out."

"How could you have known?" I said. "Donnie was the one who always picked on you and what he did was awfully mean."

"This kid Richie? His dad owns one of those outdated bakery stuff places, and that's where he got all the Twinkies. So my dad thinks I should be like a detective or something and add up the clues before I hit people. He said I'm just like everybody else. I jump to conclusions."

"You're not a cop or anything," Whitney said.

"True, but I should have known Donnie could never afford that many Twinkies, and even if he could, he wouldn't waste them on me. And my dad said things aren't always the way they seem."

I caught my breath. That's exactly what I'd been telling myself whenever I thought about Rita's death and how it seemed like an accident, but it could have been murder. Why couldn't the police figure that out?

When I was in school, if I was looking forward to going out or maybe anticipating the weekend on Friday afternoons, the day would crawl by as though all time had stopped. Today was like that, even though I definitely wasn't looking forward to the funeral, I was simply looking forward to getting it over with. I found myself clock watching and having to hit my backspace key every few seconds. I'd entered a time warp where my cubicle seemed to dissolve away and I could almost smell chalk dust and hear old man Gardner droning on about equilateral triangles.

I eventually finished my last report and punched out, thinking I'd be late, but cars and trucks were still arriving at the church when I pulled up. I recognized most of them as belonging to people in the horse show crowd. I slid the Honda in next to Parker's new Lexus, then squeezed my feet into my torture shoes.

A black Buick rolled to a stop in the spot on the other side of me. Sammi waved and got out. She waited while I took a few tottering steps like a colt trying out its legs for the first time.

"I didn't know you were coming." I concentrated on keeping my balance after I stepped on a crumbly spot in the asphalt.

"I *did* know Rita from seeing her around town. Have you talked to the police yet?"

"Shhh. I'll tell you later." I caught a glimpse of a black hearse parked at the side door. My stomach lurched and my mood shifted like beach sand. I frowned at Sammi. "Why are you wearing that dress?"

Her glance slid down the front of her cobalt blue top. "It's not a dress, it's a skirt and blouse. What's wrong with it?"

"You know very well. It's the same color as mine, so now we'll walk in together looking like the Olsen twins." I tripped on the first step into the building and she grabbed my elbow, pulling me upright.

"My hair hangs past my shoulders and yours is shorter and curly instead of straight. I outweigh you by—never mind, I outweigh you. We don't look like twins. We don't even look like cousins."

"And your hair is like Whitney's, honey-blond like a Golden Retriever's coat, while mine is grocery bag brown. That's not the point, is it?"

"You're in a horrible mood, Leigh."

"Okay, I admit it. My nerves are stretched way out like soft taffy." I twisted the strap of my purse. Unlike my stretchy nerves, the strap was not soft and it dug into my hands.

"Sorry about the matching dress."

I mumbled that it wasn't really a match, and I promised to stop being so bitchy.

Angie and Stan, smiling and looking relieved to see someone they knew in a crowd of strangers, hurried forward to greet us.

"Thank you for coming," Angie said, reaching out to me.

I took her hand in mine. It was icy and dry, and I pulled her into a hug. I'd thought her so strong on Saturday when I'd met her, but now she seemed as vulnerable as a child.

A dark-suited man, obviously the funeral director, approached from my right and said, "Mrs. Loring?"

With an apologetic look, Angie went off to consult with him, Stan marching behind her with his chin thrust out. Sammi and I exchanged glances. I wondered if she was thinking the same thing I was—Stan Loring looked every inch a suspect.

Together we pushed past a crowd at the doorway. We didn't get far. Someone stepped forward and locked eyes with me.

Jared Beaumont. It was nice of him to come to the funeral, since he hadn't really known Rita.

My face lit in a smile. "Hello, Jared. Meet my cousin Sammi Hollister," I said, remembering the manners my mother had spent years drilling into me.

"Hi, Sammi. Jared Beaumont."

"I'm pleased to meet you." Little vibes were dancing around Sammi and shooting in my direction. I could tell she'd gone into full matchmaking mode when she saw that Jared was an attractive man about my age.

"Same here."

"We have to get going." I excused us, pulling Sammi with me down the church aisle.

As soon as we were out of earshot, she leaned toward me and whispered, "Where did you find him and why didn't you tell me? Is he the guy you were telling me about who was going to buy horses from Rita?"

"Bingo. I met him at Rita's, the day I found her body. He's new in town." I shook my head. "I'm not interested. Why don't you take him for yourself?"

"I'm in love with Ray. Anyway, I know you're dying for a man to call your own so you can show Adam and Kenneth that you don't need them any more than a cat needs a pet alligator." She said the last sentence at a volume I'd have expected her to use if she wanted to call me from town without the benefit of a telephone.

Mr. Cadbury, owner of the feed store, snapped around and peered myopically from side to side.

I pinched Sammi's arm. "I can't take you anywhere. And, no, I am not. Looking for a man. Pining for a man. Needing a man."

Sammi pulled away, stalking down the aisle, and I followed, forced by my shoes to maintain a tentative wobble. Naturally Sammi didn't have any trouble walking in *her* shoes—she'd worn an unfashionable pair of flats that could have doubled for beach shoes.

Parker Fielding was sitting alone up front, his head bowed. Stan and Angie eventually took places across the aisle from him. Then Maggie walked in and sat beside Parker—not close, but on the same bench. I could almost see lines of tension crackling back and forth among the four of them like an impending lightning strike.

Jared walked to the front and Maggie glanced up at him. Her lips were pulled into a thin line, though that might have been because she'd tortured her hair into a bun that looked tight enough to rip her scalp loose. Jared hesitated, then backpedaled to sit a few pews behind her.

Sammi elbowed me. We had elbowing down to a private code. The nudge was her way of signaling that I should have invited Jared to sit with us. He was a stranger in town and had no way of knowing Maggie was not only family of the deceased, but apparently she didn't want his company. I nudged Sammi back, my way of telling her it wasn't my fault Maggie was in a foul mood. But I wished I'd made the offer. I'd probably been rude to rush off and leave him at the back of the church, and if I hadn't been so intent on telling Sammi to cut out the matchmaking I would have been more thoughtful.

From my angle I couldn't see anything of Angie except the back of her head, but half of Parker's face was visible and his complexion had gone from a glowing tan to plum colored. He took out a handkerchief and held it to his eyes. I wondered if Parker had really loved Rita or if he had he been more interested in her money. But I'd heard Parker was well off on his own. It was the same with Maggie.

She'd owned her pet grooming business for years and apparently the shop was successful, even if business was in a slump right now. She'd done well enough to buy herself some acreage to add to the little plot she'd inherited from her grandparents, and she was putting in a boarding kennel.

As for Angie, she and Stan owned an antique store and had a solid alibi.

A white-robed woman at the front of the church lit candles and I snapped back to the present. I forced myself to glance away from those I'd marked as suspects to concentrate on Rita.

The sun poured light through a stained glass window at the front of the building. Green and red and blue tinted rays slanted across the coffin. The lid was closed, and I was positive that would have been Rita's choice. I didn't imagine she'd selected the music, though. I would have put her down for ordinary church hymns instead of the solemn dark tones of a classical piece I didn't recognize. The organist was doing her best to play something funereal I was sure, but to me it came across like what I'd expect to hear as mood music for a horror flick about ghosts.

Even though the horse club secretary had called around for donations for a bouquet, I'd sent flowers on my own. Besides mine and the horse club's carnations, the only other arrangements were red roses—probably from Parker—as well as a simple spray of white and yellow roses on the coffin itself. Despite the relative paucity of flowers, a heavy perfume—the roses predominating—scented the air. I found myself wishing for a one of those cardboard church fans I remembered from my childhood, when my father would drive me and my mother to church, then go fishing with my brother.

Brenda and Scott Harper were sitting in front of us, but I noticed after it was too late to move.

Brenda turned around once, moments before the service started, her pale green eyes widening. "Leigh! Talk to you about the horse later."

I stared straight ahead, concentrating on getting through the service without boring holes into the back of Brenda's red-haired skull with my eyes.

Then, slowly I let my gaze wander over the mourners, trying to determine if everyone seemed suitably bereaved or if they looked more like homicidal maniacs. My crowd study stopped for a long moment when I spotted Camilla Reed sitting in the next to last row on my right. I hadn't known she was acquainted with Rita.

If there were any clues to Rita's killer in the crowd, I missed them. But then, unless someone had typed out a full confession and pinned it to their chest, I would have no way of knowing if the murderer was at the funeral.

Eventually we filed out and headed for the cemetery. Parker didn't go to the graveside. I saw him turn in the opposite direction when the rest of us left the church in a convoy.

Oddly, though I knew almost everyone in attendance at the graveside from horse shows, they all seemed like strangers today. I'd never seen them dressed up and so subdued that even their personalities seemed to have changed. Lily Hagen, normally wearing an impish smile, was known around the show circuit as a prankster. Now she actually wiped away a tear or two. Or maybe it was sweat.

Maggie stood to one side with a group of horse people who were also into showing dogs. They were conversing in voices too low for me to make out what they were saying, though I did catch a couple of references to Pomapoos and Border Jacks. Rita was dead, but life—and the breeding of designer dogs—went on.

Florida had gifted us with yet another cloudless day of bright sunshine; ecstasy to pale-skinned, snow-weary northerners, but all too familiar to us locals. Sweat rolled down my back and pooled above my waist. The backs of my knees as well as my armpits were sticky, and I could feel my hair hanging limp, my bangs falling in front of my eyes like a wet curtain. To add to my misery, my feet were on fire in my narrow-toed shoes. I was ready to politely say, "excuse me," and rip my footwear off entirely, when the service abruptly came to a close.

I decided I could keep the shoes on for five more minutes. Most of the horse people came up and spoke, offering their sympathies to the unfortunate woman who'd found Rita.

Doug Reilly was dressed in a white shirt, a tired blue coat, and shiny brown trousers. Probably the best clothes he had, but then he likely didn't have many occasions to dress up. Doug was handsome in a rough kind of way. Sammi had once told me Doug's face reminded her of Richard Gere playing the role of a debauched cowboy.

"Tough luck finding Rita dead," he drawled, pulling at the frayed cuffs on his shirtsleeves. A frown appeared on his lean face. "Course everybody knows you have to be careful doing farm work by yourself. I told Rita a week or so ago that she ought to give me a few more hours instead of doing so much on her own."

"Guess you were right about that, Doug." Brenda, a purse attached to one arm and Scott to the other, marched up. "Too bad Rita didn't take your advice. But then everyone knows Rita was entirely too overconfident about herself. She strutted around like she was immortal and we all know where she ended up."

I clenched my fists so tight, my fingernails dug into my palms. Sammi saved me from committing murder by looping her arm through mine and hanging on.

Brenda was wearing a rose-colored blazer and skirt that clashed with her carroty hair, and the thick material had to be making her feel like she was enveloped in a sweat soaked horse blanket. She wiped a line of moisture off her face and made a point of looking at her watch. "Leigh, someone's coming to see my Cocoa Bars filly, so I'm really pressed for time. What about that deal?"

Sammi inserted herself between the Harpers and me. "Hello, Brenda."

"Hello." Brenda flashed her teeth long enough for me to conclude she might be attempting a smile.

"I think you've picked the wrong place and time to conduct business. This is a *cemetery* for heaven's sake." Sammi frowned, managing to look suitably shocked.

Brenda licked her lips and turned to Scott, as if for once needing his guidance. He grinned sheepishly and dug the toe of one of his black shoes into the dirt.

"Leigh, I'll call you," Brenda said when Scott remained silent.

"My, ain't it hot?" Barbara Snyder fanned herself with a damp handkerchief. Barbara was about Rita's age and she was raised in Del Canto, so she'd known Rita longer than any of us. "Shocking for me to hear the news. I was unloading feed Friday morning, all the while thinking it was another fine day and I didn't have a sad thought in my head. You always remember what you were doing at the time when someone you know dies."

This led to a lot of head nodding. Everyone had to say where they were at the time Rita was dying. Brenda, of course, had to proclaim that she was going about routine chores at her farm with Scott, as they were always *so* busy with an operation that size, though the rest of us, being amateurs, couldn't *imagine* how much work they did. The Harpers were getting their horses' hooves trimmed or something. I didn't pay much attention because my feet were screaming at me in stereo to get them unpointed *now*.

People gradually drifted away until everyone had left except Angie and Stan, and the Harpers. And, of course, Sammi and me. Now Brenda and Scott were picking their way between tombstones back to the road, Brenda yapping orders in Scott's ear while he nodded like a robot.

Sammi put her arm around my shoulders. "She has her nerve. Rita's not cold in the ground, and she's trying to deal you out of a horse?"

"Kenneth says I have to sell the gelding I bought from Rita. All of a sudden he's got this wild hair about horses being dangerous. Brenda's wanted that horse since the moment she saw him, but Rita would never sell to her. Rita wouldn't have sold her a roach."

Sammi snorted. "It's nothing but a control thing with Kenneth and you know it. And Rita was right about Brenda. I wouldn't sell the horse to that witch, either."

"I'm not going to sell him."

"Yeah, right. If you ever crawl out from under Kenneth's thumb, I'm going to throw you a party."

I scowled at her. "And I'll throw you a bigger party if you dump Ray."

"Watch it, babe."

"Would you think I was terrible if I took off these heels and shredded the bottoms of my pantyhose walking back to the car?"

"I don't know how you stood it this long, and I hope you never wear those shoes again. I would suggest you donate them to a good cause, but it would actually be more charitable to throw them away."

I used her for support while I pulled off the shoes. I made delighted sounds of oohing and aahing and stood between two tombstones wiggling my burning toes in the grass to bring the circulation back. "My feet seem to have swollen past the point of shoe return."

Sammi and I had ridden together in my car from the funeral home, so I had to take her back to the church to get her Buick. I was still barefoot except for my hose, picking my way along the edge of the path between headstones and back to the road while trying to avoid stray patches of sandspurs.

"Sammi, we need to talk," I said as soon as we got into the car. I turned the key and tromped on the gas pedal with my shoeless foot.

"Careful, Leigh, there are potholes the size of Lake Okeechobee in this road."

"I don't care." The Honda's right front tire slipped in and out of a pothole, and I winced at the jolt. "Why were you being so friendly to everyone? They could be murderers."

"What's wrong with you all of a sudden? Get a grip. Ever since you got the idea that Rita was murdered, you've acted like a twit."

"A twit? Is that what you call it when someone finds a murder victim?" A station wagon pulled out of a side street in front of me and I slowed. Three charcoal colored clouds had appeared on the horizon, and I hoped they didn't mean rain, especially after last night's downpour.

"You need to stop seeing evil behind every bush. And how can you say I was being overly friendly? I came down pretty hard on Brenda."

"True. But she deserved it. I am not seeing evil, I'm simply seeing the truth. Someone killed Rita and that someone might have been at the funeral pretending to care."

Chapter 12

On the way back to the church, I filled Sammi in on my talk with Detective Frazier. "He doesn't believe Rita was murdered," I said. "But I've been thinking. Since we don't know who the killer is and it's probably someone we know, it might be better if we don't tell anyone we believe Rita's death was a murder."

"Give me some credit. I haven't told a soul, not even Ray. Only Jeeves knows and he can't talk." Sammi fiddled with her seat belt, adjusting it tighter across her shoulder. "So if Stan or Angie didn't do it, who did? Parker? Maggie? A stranger, maybe Jared Beaumont? Someone we've never met?"

I shrugged. "It's possible we'll never know unless I can convince the police to see things my way. It's scary thinking there's a killer out there who's probably someone we know. The worst thing is, sometimes I imagine Rita's following me around and imploring me to bring her killer to justice."

Sammi arched an eyebrow. "I won't tell a soul you said that. Not good for your reputation."

"I'm not all that worried about my reputation these days." I stopped in the church parking lot and let the Honda idle in the baking heat, waiting for Sammi to pull out ahead of me. Thank God I didn't have to go back to work. Now that the ordeal of Rita's funeral was over, I wanted nothing more than some down time. I headed home at warp speed.

A sour, time-to-empty-the-trash odor hit me when I pushed my front door open. It's Whitney's chore to take out the garbage, but most times she needs reminding. I changed out of my funeral dress into a pair of shorts and a blue tee shirt with a feed stain on the front. I was writing Whitney a do not disturb note when the school bus rumbled up out front. I rested my head on my hands. It seemed like years since I'd had restful sleep and I couldn't see any prospects for improvement.

Whitney took forever getting to the house. She finally strolled into the kitchen with a black and white, curly-haired dog tucked under her arm. It looked like a cross between a toy poodle, a mop, and a Shih Tzu. Maybe it was a designer dog like the ones the dog people had talked about at the funeral—a Tzu Noodle or a Shih Bop a Loodle, or something equally exotic. I'd have to ask Sammi.

"Great," I said. "Don't tell me someone dumped off a dog."

"Isn't she cute, Mom?" Whitney stroked the little dog's head and it licked her face. She'd wanted a puppy for a long time, but I'd told her that as long as I had to work, we'd have to forget about getting a dog. Dogs, unlike cats and horses, need a lot of human companionship. This didn't stop her from re-asking every month or so to see if I'd gone mushy in the head.

"We are not keeping a stray dog, Whitney."

Whitney held the dog out in front of her. "Actually, I don't think she's a stray. See, she has a collar."

I trudged over to take a look. "Collar, but no tag. So maybe she's lost instead of abandoned."

"Yeah, she's too nice for someone to dump off and speed away into the night." Whitney thrust the dog into my arms and headed for the refrigerator.

Matter of opinion. Some people got animals on impulse and got rid of them as easily as they tossed out yesterday's newspaper.

I gave the dog a bowl of water. She wagged her tail in

appreciation before she started slurping, pushing the bowl ahead of her with her nose until it banged up against the wall with a loud clatter. At the same time the phone rang. I grabbed the receiver in one hand and a roll of paper towels in the other.

"Leigh, I've just had a call from Brenda Harper." Kenneth spoke before I could identify myself. His voice sounded like he'd been possessed by the spirit of Alexander The Great and he could do nothing except issue orders and plan his next world conquest.

My entire body went tight at as an over-wound guitar string, a familiar feeling that gripped me whenever Kenneth called. "Let me guess. She hasn't been able to make a deal with me, so she told you again that she wants to buy the horse. She's going to do us a real favor now that you're in a panic over imagined danger from a horse that wouldn't bite your hand if you stuck it in his mouth. Per your plan, Whitney is going to forget she ever loved horses and go ecstatic over toe shoes and dance recitals."

Whitney put down her sandwich and raised an eyebrow. She knew her dad wanted her to give up horses, but this was probably the first she'd heard about the ballet lessons.

"Brenda informs me you've been putting her off since Sunday. We've already discussed the sale." Obviously Kenneth was annoyed that I was causing him to waste a few minutes of his precious time. I pictured him at his desk with a line of customers snaking out the door.

"I am not selling Sonny Joe or any of my other horses. Rita's funeral was held today and that greedy, profit-worshiping horse trader was trying to finalize a sale right out among the tombstones." The little dog finished drinking and trotted over to lie next to Whitney's chair. I frowned at all the water she'd sloshed across the floor. "Why didn't she just bring her trailer to the cemetery so she could run by here after the service and get the horse?"

"I don't care how bad this Harper woman's timing is. Call her now and arrange for her to get that animal. I've already agreed to her price."

"You what?" I exploded.

"Don't shout at me. I gave you plenty of time to take care of this problem and you're still twiddling your thumbs. I'm selling the horse to the Harpers. All you have to do is arrange to be there when the woman shows up."

"*You're* selling the horse? Just who do you think you are? You may have paid for half that horse, but for your information, Kenneth, *my* name is on the bill of sale and *my* name is on the registration papers. You can call Brenda Harper yourself and tell her there's no deal. There will never be a deal!" I slammed the receiver down.

The phone rang again immediately. I took my time wiping up the dog's water, then plopped down in a kitchen chair to study my ragged, bitten-off nails. Hard to do because my hands were shaking so badly. After twenty rings or so, there was silence.

"Wow, Mom," Whitney said softly. "I've never seen you stand up to Dad."

"I should have done that a long time ago."

"Dad's going to come over here to force you to do what he wants. You know he is."

Kenneth was, no doubt, strapped behind the wheel of his Chevy Tahoe at this very moment, speeding in my direction at about half the speed of light.

"Mom? When Daddy makes you sell Sonny Joe, please don't let the Harpers get him." Whitney slipped out of her chair and picked up the little dog. She padded down the hall to her room, shutting the door shut with a thud.

I sat for a long time staring at the floor. I'd always prided myself on being a good mother. For years I'd given in to Kenneth and his tirades, thinking I was sparing my child the ordeal of watching her parents fight. Now I knew better. All I'd done was teach her it was okay to let a man boss her around and run—or ruin—her life for her. I pictured her in a few years getting into an abusive relationship with some Neanderthal of a boyfriend and I shuddered.

No, that was not going to happen. I'd made a mistake marrying Kenneth and then, even after the divorce, I'd refused to oppose him in front of Whitney. It was the only way I knew. My own parents had never fought, and I'd grown up thinking they had the perfect marriage and that it was fine that Dad bossed Mom around. Then when Whitney was eight and I told my mother Kenneth and I were splitting up, she revealed that she'd deliberately refused to argue with my father or go against his wishes "for the sake of you children."

She expected me to do the same. She pointed out that the one time Kenneth and I had shouted at each other in front of Whitney, our daughter had thrown up. I'd had enough sense to go through with the divorce anyway, but afterward I'd stayed true to my upbringing. Great move. Now my daughter believed I leaped to obey every time her father issued another order.

Time for me to shape up. Past time.

I was doing the afternoon chores when Kenneth roared up the driveway in a cloud of dust. I was surprised there weren't flames shooting out of his nostrils and scorching his dashboard.

I deliberately turned my back and opened Belle's stall door to check for signs of imminent foaling. Not yet. Her udder was full, but not leaking milk. I knew from past experience she'd be streaming milk off and on for about twelve hours before giving birth.

"What in the hell do you think you're playing at?"

I'd heard Kenneth yank open the gate across the barn aisle right after I heard his car door slam. I straightened up slowly from where I squatted at Belle's side. "Hello, Kenneth. I'm fine, other than a few sore spots on my toes from wearing a bad pair of shoes to the funeral today. How are you?"

He stood with his head lowered, his feet planted wide apart and his hands on his hips. I should have a poster made of Kenneth in that pose, a warning poster for any women who think it's sweet when their boyfriends make their decisions for them. A little muscle at the right side of his face went into visible spasm and was soon followed by a matching muscle on the left side, which created a fascinating effect. "Well, Leigh?"

"Could you move, please? I have to get into that stall." I was proud of the way I was keeping my cool, though my heart was thumping along at about six hundred beats a minute.

"What are you doing? I've decided I don't want Whitney riding anymore, we have a buyer for her horse, and now *you're opposing me.*" He shot the words out, obviously expecting me to cringe and grovel before him while I promised to mend my ways.

He watched in disbelief while I ignored him and opened Lena's stall door to pour sweet feed into her tub. His eyebrows furrowed into a long angry line. "Is that Whitney's new horse?"

"You've seen her ride. Don't you recognize Belle's Red Lena Dot, former youth show horse and now broodmare to be?" I shut the stall door and latched it.

"I can't tell one horse from another and you know it. I'm dependent on you when it comes to getting horses sold."

"You? Dependent on me?" I snorted. "If you're trying to get me to work up some sympathy for you, you'll still be waiting when you're in a nursing home."

"You're going to have to sell sooner or later. I don't know what's gotten into you in the past few days, but your stubborn behavior has got to stop. You might as well fall in line with the deal I've arranged. Then start packing your bags."

"What?" My voice came out in a crow-like squawk.

"You heard me. I want my share of the equity in this place. You can buy the house I found for you in Hansen Haven or get a condo. But you can't keep horses in town so it's time you faced up to that fact and started looking for buyers for all of them."

He planned to force a sale? I almost dropped the feed bucket I was holding. I couldn't have been any angrier if he'd popped me in the face. "You're not being fair."

"This discussion is about doing what's best for our daughter."

"Selling her horse? Making her move out of her home?" I sputtered. "How is that best?

"I don't like the direction her life is taking. Doreen and I are going to have more of a say in her activities from now on."

"You're being unreasonable." But he *could* force me to sell my house—which also meant selling my horses—unless I could get him to hold off long enough for me to come up with a workable alternative. "There's something you don't know." I hated to tell Kenneth, but I had to buy time. Kenneth didn't make threats he didn't intend to act on. "Rita didn't fall out of that hayloft. She was murdered." I quickly outlined my theory and told Kenneth I'd had a talk with Detective Frazier.

Kenneth didn't give any signs that he was awed by my powers

of deduction. "That's the most..." He worked his mouth for a few seconds. "What did the detective say?"

"He said the case is still open." I didn't add that Frazier didn't believe I was right. "So there's no way I can sell the horses and move while I've got Rita's murder on my mind. That's too much to ask of anyone."

"You're being ridiculous."

"Me? You're the one who acts like horses came straight up from hell to directly or indirectly cause death and destruction to any human they encounter."

His eyes glinted as he stared at me. "Whether Rita Cameron was murdered or not," he ground out finally, "I've made my decision. I'll give you one week to find another buyer. After that, the horse is sold to the Harper woman, even if I have to rent a trailer and come over here to get it myself. And you might as well decide whether you want the condo or the Hansen Haven model, or I'll make the decision for you." He spun and barreled toward his SUV like he planned to tackle it.

"Control freak," I shouted at his back. Sure, he'd be over to get Sonny Joe. I could just see him loading a horse and hauling it, even assuming he could figure out which animal to put in the trailer.

With trembling hands, I went back to measuring portions of sweet smelling hay into various nets. This was a chore my daughter and I had shared since the time she could walk. We spent hours together feeding, grooming, training, and cleaning. Show dates were carefully plotted on our barn calendar, as were breeding dates for Belle. We'd sat side by side in the barn office planning Belle's foals, poring through stacks of advertisements for the services of well-bred stallions.

Now Kenneth wanted to take all of this away from us. And because of my foolishness, he had the legal right.

I'd been wrong, thinking he was simply in a bad mood the day he'd first told me he wanted me to sell Sonny Joe to Brenda. And I'd been wrong thinking that if I could show him horses weren't dangerous, that Rita had been murdered, he'd change his mind. Kenneth's decision had nothing to do with danger and everything to do with—what? Control? No, he'd never gone this far. It had been five years since our divorce and he'd been content with only minor rampages. Something else was motivating him. I didn't know what and I wasn't sure it mattered.

Whitney waited for me on the couch, the little dog resting contentedly on her lap. "Are you and Daddy still fighting?" She twisted strands of the dog's hair into a braid.

"Not exactly. By the way, I meant to ask you earlier if you wanted to go to the horse club meeting in Fort Myers with me on Saturday. If not, I can ask your dad if you can stay with him."

"Definitely no to the meeting." She pursed her lips and stared at the opposite wall.

"You could wish me luck. After all, it's been a long time since I helped plan a show that size."

"Good luck, Mother." The dog, now sporting a braid in the middle of its back, jumped down and Whitney stood. "I don't want to think about horses right now since Daddy's making us sell them. I hope you're not too lonely without me."

"I'll mange fine. And I already said, I am not selling our horses."

Right. If I didn't come up with a plan, and soon, they were going to look cute in the garage of my new home in downtown Del Canto.

Chapter 13

The little dog trotted back and forth through a morning sunbeam slanting across the kitchen floor. The braid was gone, but the hair on top of her head had been pulled into a topknot, held together with a pink barrette. I stopped short in the kitchen doorway.

"Whoops. I forgot about that animal."

"I know," Whitney said. "You seemed halfway to Jupiter last night, so I didn't bother you. I fed her slices of bologna and cheese for dinner."

"The poor thing. I'll call the pound while I'm on lunch break to see if anyone's reported her missing. And, Whitney? I might be stopping by Sammi's after work today, so you'll probably be alone longer than usual after school."

"Big conference with Sammi? Going to tell her all about your horse club meeting and how you won't need to be in the horse club 'cause we won't have any horses?" She bit her lower lip and turned away from me.

"Have some faith in me, kid." I grabbed the jar of coffee out of the cabinet and slammed it down on the counter.

One cup of coffee wasn't nearly enough this morning, so I had two. Even so, I drove so slowly going over to Brad's that Whitney made a big show of holding her watch up in front of her face and clearing her throat.

I turned sedately down a side road and headed into Brad's neighborhood. There were cars parked in the street, kids on bikes, kids standing in packs at bus stops. I pulled up in front of Brad's home, a neat cinderblock ranch house painted sea foam green. While I waited, I idly took in the scenery, watching in amusement as two little girls chased down a loose dachshund dragging a rope from its collar.

A car pulled into a driveway at the end of the block. I felt my eyes widen. I knew that house; it was Camilla Reed's. I'd given her a ride home from work once when her car went dead in the middle of a summer downpour. But what caught my eye was the white Lexus, exactly like Parker Fielding's, that had just pulled into the driveway. I stared at the driver until I was *sure* he was Parker Fielding.

A door slammed, and I jerked my attention back to my own business. Brad settled himself onto the back seat. He stuffed a toaster pastry into his mouth and chewed noisily, crumbs littering the front of his shirt like oversized dandruff.

"Brad," I said, "what was it you told me yesterday about fighting the wrong boy? Something your father said."

"My dad said people jump to conclusions. Things aren't always the way they seem." Brad's puzzled eyes met mine in the rearview mirror.

I smiled. "I think your father is a very wise man."

As soon as I got into the building, I headed straight to my cubicle and got down to work without stopping in the break room for another cup of coffee. Even I have limits.

Camilla came by in the middle of the morning, bringing a stack of forms for me to process. "I won't need these back until next week, so take your time if you want. By the way, would you like to join me for lunch?"

"Sure." My mood brightened. Camilla was good company and I hated to eat alone. I glanced at the forms she'd given me. I'd have them ready before noon, even if I followed her advice to take my time. I picked up the first copy and opened a file. It was exactly 11:55 when I finished—just in time for lunch.

Usually I ate in the break room or outside on the patio behind the building. But we'd steam ourselves if we sat outside today, so we stayed in. I put my machine issued tea on the table next to my bagged lunch—a tuna sandwich and a hard-boiled egg.

Camilla had brought salad and a container of blueberry yogurt. "Kind of cloudy out," she said, waving toward the window. "It might rain."

"We need it. Before the storm Sunday night my pasture was getting almost too dry to let the horses out."

This conversation was not typical Camilla chatter. Any minute now she'd get so perky I'd half expect her to break into a song and dance routine. Then she'd tell me a funny story about one of her neighbors and have me rolling on the floor.

Instead there was dead silence except for Camilla clinking her fork against her salad bowl. I cleared my throat twice, drank half my tea, and bit into my sandwich. She put her fork down and raked her fingers through her black hair, thoroughly messing it up, so I could see the light brown roots above her freckled forehead.

We'd already covered the weather, so I said, "I saw you at Rita's funeral yesterday. I didn't know you knew her."

After a long hesitation she said softly, "I'm her attorney and I've done accounting for her, too. Last month she introduced me to her hired hand, Doug Reilly, and we went out. Strictly a favor for Rita, though God knows why I felt the need to do anything for her after she criticized practically everything in my house. What did she expect? If she wanted to do business in a luxurious office, she should have gone to Kendra McRae. But she was too cheap to pay Kendra's prices. Anyway, she talked me into going out with Doug. She said she wanted to get him out of the way while she talked over a business deal with Parker and didn't want him hanging around and eavesdropping."

"That was nice of you," I said.

"Oh, yes, I'm a real Samaritan." She grinned ruefully. "I admit I was attracted to Rita's money. I thought I might get steady work from her and maybe a bonus like I get from some of my other clients. After all, if she had money to leave to her sister and she didn't even like Maggie, I figured she might have plenty of work to pass on to a struggling attorney."

"Maggie gets Rita's estate?" The question hung in the air. I knew I was out of line, but I had to find out if Maggie had a motive.

"Whoops." She put her hand over her mouth. "Shouldn't have revealed privileged information. You won't tell anyone, will you?"

"Of course not. You went out with Doug as a favor to Rita?"

"Twice." She pretended to gag. "Enough said. I dumped him and found someone else."

I shrugged. I hated it when people dropped hints but then wouldn't tell you anything. Sammi and I both agreed that if a person didn't want to tell you details, they shouldn't drop comments indicating they had juicy gossip and then leave you wondering.

"How nice for you," I said idly.

"It was. Until I figured out he was exaggerating his financial status. I don't mean to sound mercenary, but money in a relationship is really important to me. I was brought up poor. This new guy came across like he had money, but it turned out to be a lie." Her eyes bored into me as if she were daring me to criticize her desire to be rich.

I stared down at the table. Now that she'd mentioned it, I'd never known her to bother with a man who didn't have money.

"That was really something about Rita, wasn't it? When was the last time you saw or talked to her?" I asked, more to change the subject than from any desire to ferret out more information.

"Not for a couple of weeks, I suppose. I was working at home the day she died, and didn't even find out until hours later. I remember at the time thinking I hadn't seen her for a while, though we'd spoken on the phone two days before her accident. She said she had something important to discuss and she'd call for an appointment in a few days."

I went to full alert. "That's right. I forgot you work at home when you're not filling in here," I said after a few seconds of pretending I was only mildly interested in Rita's personal dealings with her attorney.

"Until I can afford a real office." She dug a compact out of her purse, flipped it open, and studied a spot on her chin.

"You know Parker Fielding, too. Rita's fiancé. I saw him at your house this morning when I went to pick up a friend of Whitney's." As I wrapped up the remains of my lunch and stuffed them into a trash bag, I watched her out of the corner of my eye.

She snapped the compact shut. "He brings work to the house two or three times a month. In fact he was there Friday morning, the day Rita died."

"How...sad." An alibi for Parker. I could cross him off my list. Unless she was lying. Darn it, why was detecting so convoluted?

"Of course, we didn't know about Rita at the time." She glanced at the wall clock near the door. "Wow, I can't believe it's almost time to get back to my desk, and I've got a ton of work waiting for me when I get home. Business is finally picking up. We'll have to do lunch again next week."

We parted company at the water cooler. I wandered back to my cubicle, so deep in thought I nearly collided with a trash bucket someone had left in the hall. Did Parker have an alibi or not?

During afternoon break, I went to the pay phone near the water fountain. There was no report at the pound of a lost black and white dog. I was so sure someone was looking for her, I was struck silent for a few seconds.

"You're positive? She's probably part Shih Tzu—shaggy and cute."

"You might try calling the vets' offices." The male voice on the other end of the line sounded annoyed. "Or you could bring her here. If no one claims her, we'll try to find her a home."

"And if you don't?" I didn't really need to ask.

"We try for up to a week and then we have to euthanize."

"Thanks. I'll probably put an ad in the paper." Whitney was already attached to the dog and there was no way I could take her to the pound where she might not survive. If I couldn't locate the owner, I'd find her a home myself.

Quitting time at last, I rushed around tidying my workstation. After that I planned to go home and get in some quality time thinking over what I'd learned from Camilla. My mind in turmoil, I dashed for the door, nearly running Fiona down when she walked around a corner.

"Sorry." I grabbed her shoulder to steady her, hoping I hadn't hurt more than her dignity when I'd caused her to flatten herself against the wall and nearly drop the stack of manila folders tucked under one arm.

"It's quite all right, Leigh. By the way, are you sure about that time off? The work volume is way down and you have the hours accumulated. You could stay out until a week from Monday to recover from all the stress."

I started to turn her down, but then I had a thought. The police were unlikely to find the killer if they didn't even believe Rita was murdered. If I had more time, I could quietly ask around and jumpstart the investigation. Detective Frazier would probably welcome my information if it led to him solving an important case.

"Okay, Fiona, you've convinced me," I said, not even pretending reluctance.

She let out her breath, patting my arm soothingly. "It's for the best. Sometimes we're overstressed and we don't even know it."

I nodded vigorously. "Yes, sometimes we push ourselves right over the edge."

Fiona might not know it, but I was well acquainted with stress. Let her spend the next week thinking I was relaxing in a dark room listening to *The Sounds of Nature* CD collection with a wet cloth over my eyes. My time off would bring her a lot of comfort and bring me time to work out the puzzle surrounding Rita's death.

I sent a silent thought heavenward. *Don't worry, Rita. I won't rest until I bring you justice.*

The storm broke before I got to my car, lasting long enough to drench me while I fumbled for my keys. By the time I pulled up in front of the house, the rain had eased to a steady drizzle while the lightning had moved off over the Gulf of Mexico to strike far offshore from a deep purple sky. All this spring rain, unusual for so early in the year, was doing a lot toward easing the recent drought, but it wasn't making my life any easier.

Strands of wet hair clinging to my face, I dodged puddles all the way to the house. Hey, my bad. If I'd gone for that Hansen Haven model, I'd have an attached garage and a garage door opener so rain would not be the slightest inconvenience.

Whitney met me at the door. "Brenda Harper called. She says she'll try again this evening."

"The witch. I hope you weren't rude." I pulled off my shoes. "I wish you'd put the mares in before the rain started."

"I was asleep. Besides, I told you I'm staying away from Sonny Joe so I don't get attached."

I lowered my chin and studied a spot of mud on the tile floor. She didn't have any faith in me and I didn't blame her. It wasn't like I could say, "Hey, girl, your father and I fought plenty when you weren't around. I won a few."

The dog trotted out from behind the kitchen island to sniff my shoes. The she sat up and begged. I was willing to bet Whitney had taught her that trick.

"I called the pound but no one's reported the dog missing."

"Good. I want to keep her. By the way, a friend of yours called. Jared, he claimed his name is. He'd like you to call him back." Her voice had gone icy.

"He's not a friend, he's merely someone who needs help with his horses." Horses to be; he hadn't actually bought them yet. I'd bent down to pat the dog's head and now I straightened up.

Her eyes narrowed and she put her hands on her hips. "His name is Jared? One of the super popular J names, of course. He must be quite a hunk, probably a salesman, huh?"

"Stop it, young lady. You haven't even met Jared, who happens to be very nice. And he's not a salesman, he does something with computers."

"Computers? Forget the trendy name, he's a nerd with a pot gut who wears white socks with his business suit. Maybe I should be like Richie with the Twinkies, only I'll leave a trail of mouse pads and pocket protectors from his car to his front door and make a sign that says this way to the geek boy."

"I've told you before it's wrong to stereotype people. Since you're determined to react like a wolf defending its food over any man I meet, there's no point in arguing. Besides, this isn't even a date." I raised my chin.

"I like Adam, but you broke up with *him*."

I stiffened as if she'd poked me in the back with a sharp stick.

"I told you never to mention Adam's name to me again."

Her expression went to stone. "Okay, Mom, but by the time you figure out what a huge mistake you made dumping the one whose name I can't mention, it will be way too late."

I gritted my teeth. If this was how she acted at the prospect of me spending a few hours in the company of a man she hadn't even met, how would she react if I ever decided to get married again? A voice in my head, a voice that was getting all too pushy lately, broke in to inform me that my daughter would be ecstatic if the groom-to-be were Adam and she'd boycott the ceremony if it were anyone else. I stilled the voice and regrouped before I went into my room to dial the number Whitney had jotted down.

Jared answered on the first ring. "Leigh, I heard something about a horse club meeting Saturday and I thought it might be a good idea for me to go. I've got a couple of younger sisters in Connecticut begging me to stock my place with riding horses before they visit. Anyway, I figured you might be going and wondered if I could tag along. We could go out to dinner afterward."

"Gosh, uh..." Wheels spun in my brain. I definitely did not want to get involved with anyone right now, despite Sammi's hopes for my lasting love and happiness with the one right man. On the other hand, a horse club meeting and dinner were not involvement, they weren't even exactly a date. "Sure, that would be fine. But the meeting's in the afternoon, in Fort Myers. We'd have to get together later for dinner."

"That sounds good."

After I agreed and ended the conversation, I changed into barn clothes. But despite having a club meeting and dinner to look forward to, I was in a grumpy mood. The horses were in a grumpy mood. Sometimes barn chores are not fun and this was one of those times. Kenneth's insistence on selling my home hung over me like a storm cloud, and I wondered how many more times I'd feed my horses before the barn stood empty and a moving truck waited in the driveway. Not too many, unless an idea presented itself.

Belle pinned her ears while I filled her bucket. I shook a finger at her in warning. She was usually pretty cranky at this stage of pregnancy, like a woman who'd gone overdue and was sick to death of carrying around all that extra weight.

Brenda Harper called after I'd taken a hot shower. It seemed she planned to wear me down a few millimeters at a time.

"Leigh, how are you?" Chirp, chirp. Don't really care.

"Fine," I said. "How about you?"

"Great, absolutely terrific. Your husband called and agreed to sell me the horse. When can I pick him up?"

"*Ex-husband.*" I ground my teeth. "And he was mistaken. I'm not selling Sonny Joe. So there won't be any picking up. Unless you meant the ex. Him you can have."

"Ha ha. But he seemed so sure about selling, said the two of you had decided Whitney is going to do something besides horses. Dance, gymnastics, whatever. Still, if you want to wait, that's fine with us, though you won't get a better price. While I've got you on the line, I wondered if you'd like to come over and see our new stud."

Brenda was a businesswoman to the core. I supposed Kenneth hadn't told her he wanted me to sell my place and my other horses, too, or she'd be offering half price for them as well.

"Oakdale Prime? I saw him at the Tampa show last month, Brenda."

"Isn't he gorgeous? I can't *believe* the Tremaines sold him to us."

I could. The Tremaines, horse trainers on a budget, had ignored his conformation faults and bought him cheap on the strength of his breeding. They'd given him two years to produce, but his foals hadn't made the grade. Did Brenda think I was stupid?

"He's a horse all right," I said. It wouldn't be good form to tell her what I really thought.

"I expect Belle will be foaling any day now and, of course, you'll want to breed Lena. Prime would make a wonderful cross on your mares."

"I have the mares booked, but thanks for asking."

"Don't be too quick to decide. Any time you want to stop by, I'll be glad to trot him out for your inspection."

Whitney had come in while I was talking. As soon as she realized who was on the phone, she'd started clutching her throat and pretending to faint.

I finally had to turn around and face the wall to keep from laughing. "I'll let you know," I sang into the phone.

Brenda was turning out to be even more persistent than Kenneth. But if she was expecting me to waste my investigating time to go look at her horse, she had a long wait.

Chapter 14

Fiona would have been shocked to see how I started my first day of recovery. As soon as I'd taken Whitney and Brad to school, I stopped at Target and got myself a red notebook exactly like Rita's. Then I sat on a bench in front of the store to jot down notes. Passersby, mostly women herding small children and a few elderly retirees out walking, eyed me curiously. I smiled and casually waved.

Sammi loomed into view before I finished writing about Parker. She reminded me of a giant pulltoy at the end of a leash. Jeeves flung his shaggy gray and white body forward in a series of jerks that propelled her along the sidewalk until she finally dug in her heels and grabbed the side of my bench, anchoring herself so he had to stop. The overwound sheepdog plopped down on his stomach, panting like a steam engine. A puddle of slobber formed in front of him.

"What are you doing home in the middle of the day?"

"Fiona decided I needed time to recuperate, so I'm on vacation."

"Good for you. Hey, thanks for taking Jeeves for a haircut

Saturday. You'd think he'd hate going to Maggie's. He always comes out wearing a little bow and smelling like he swam around in cheap perfume all afternoon. But as soon as she clips him, he gets so excited, he drags me around at double speed for a week like all he wants to do is go outside to show off."

"Maybe he gets excited because he can see better with the hair clipped out of his face."

"Probably so. He loves Maggie, too, so I hope she doesn't go out of business."

"Why would she? Maggie's had her shop for years."

"True, but her end of town's practically deserted since the new highway came in. She wants to move her shop out to her boarding kennel where there's plenty of traffic and she can keep an eye on the boarders, but first she has to get the money to finish the building. She's been worried sick she'll lose everything."

"I'm sorry to hear that, but she really couldn't expect to be the only shop in town forever, not with the way the town is growing. Speaking of dogs, Whitney found a stray in front of the house. Have you heard of a missing dog—small female, black and white, maybe part Shih Tzu?"

Sammi shook her head. "You might try asking Maggie."

"That's a good idea." I scooted over to make room for her to sit beside me. "By the way, how did things go with Ray and his problems with the police?"

Her cheeks pinked up. "I called Kenneth myself."

"You what?" I said in flat tones.

"I told you Ray and I are in love and I'd do anything to help him," she said, flipping her hair out of her face.

"Great. I imagine Kenneth thought I put you up to it. Sammi, I don't need more trouble from him right now, not when he's trying his best to ruin my life." I was surprised he hadn't added "problem relatives" to my list of sins when he last lectured me.

"Who cares what he thought? Anyway, he called Kendra and she recommended some other lawyer. I forget his name, he's in that fancy brick office near the courthouse. Only of course when I called, he wanted thousands up front, as if I'm really rich and I all I have to do is write a check."

"There's a surprise. A lawyer who wants thousands before he

even lets you talk to him."

"Kendra can keep her stupid recommendation. The police have backed off Ray for lack of evidence."

"Lucky Ray."

"You've never gotten to know him. Anyway, I told you he was innocent. He hasn't even been to that side of town since last Friday, and there was another burglary on Monday when he was definitely with me, so obviously he isn't responsible."

Something clanged in my brain. "Wait, what did you say about last Friday?"

I was speaking to empty space. Jeeves had decided it was time to continue his speed walk to wherever he was going. Still holding tight to his leash, Sammi leaped off the bench and trotted down the sidewalk away from me.

The area Sammi was talking about, the small neighborhood where all the burglaries had taken place, was within couple of miles of Rita's house. According to Sammi, Ray was out that way the day Rita was killed. Suppose Rita had caught him trying to break in. But then, why would her body be found out at the hay barn if he were at the house burglarizing it? Besides, Ray wouldn't go near horses.

He'd once done some fence work for the horse show club, he and his son. The son, Junior Ray, was an unpromising youth with an out of control shock of sandy hair and more crooked teeth than I'd ever seen on one human being.

At one point Ray came into the meeting room and said that anyone who had their horses tied near the fence had better move them because if there was one thing he didn't get along with it was horses. I'd watched in amusement as Brenda led two gentle old geldings back to her trailer while Ray ran and leaped in his truck as they plodded by.

I thought of Ray as likable, not bad looking, but a little lazy. I didn't consider him or his son suspects for more than about five seconds, especially since Ray would have been too afraid of Tinker to open her stall and try to saddle her. Yet maybe he'd seen something if he was near Rita's place on the fateful day. It could be worthwhile to ask, so I made a note on the second page of what I was now calling my clue notebook. While I was thinking about it, I also wrote myself a note to speak with Millie again.

Then I turned back to the first page where I'd written, "Discreetly find out where Doug was on Friday morning."

Doug lived with his mother in a forty-year-old trailer home in the woods east of town. I didn't know if he'd gone back to work at Rita's, so I decided to drive out and check his home first.

I parked in front of the trailer on the bare dirt that passed for a driveway. Doug had lived here all his life. His parents were nice people, hard workers who'd always seemed to be in one crisis situation or another. Doug's father had died a few years ago of a heart attack while he was building a storage shed at the back of the lot. The shed was still unfinished. Doug's mother, Ellen, worked part time at a convenience store, and I knew her well enough to say hello if I ran across her.

She wasn't at work today. She was hanging clothes on the line beside the trailer. Her green shorts and red striped blouse hung loose on her skinny frame. Her hair was iron gray, and though her eyes were the same shade of green-blue as Doug's, the expression was entirely different—sad and defeated—in vivid contrast to Doug's cockiness.

I joined her at the line, helping pin up the last few shirts. "Nice breeze for drying today."

"Sure is." She looked at me curiously. "You're a friend of Rita Cameron's. Saw you at Rita's one day when I stopped by to bring Doug a few dollars."

"I'm Leigh McRae. Would you mind talking with me for a few minutes? About Rita?"

"Reckon I could do that." She turned toward the trailer, waving for me to follow.

I'd never been inside Doug's place. An overstuffed chair in the corner of the living room sagged, its seat permanently indented with the shape of someone's bottom. One corner of the faded couch rested on a stack of books instead of on a couch leg. A Bible with a ragged cover lay in the middle of the coffee table next to an envelope addressed to Doug. I didn't have to strain to see that it was a past due notice from a finance company. I looked toward the kitchen and wrinkled my nose without meaning to. A faint smell of used cat litter scented the air, no doubt helped to circulate by the wobbly box fan spinning away in a corner.

"Did you come to see Doug? He's working today."

"Actually, I thought you could help me." I hesitated, looking for the right way to phrase my question without making it obvious that I wanted to know if Doug had an alibi. "I'm the one who found Rita Cameron dead last week. I've felt guilty about her death. You know how it is...if I'd gotten there earlier maybe she wouldn't have been killed. I wondered if Doug could say something that might reassure me. Has he said anything to you?" Lame, but all I could think of.

Ellen cleared a gray and white cat off the couch, then motioned for me to sit. "Doug didn't seem real surprised about Rita, said she did pretty much what she wanted and took chances when she didn't have to. I asked about that hayloft, thinking maybe she tripped over something, but Doug said wasn't anything up there but hay, and the floor was smooth. Goes to show you can't ever tell can you? I don't mind saying I'm awful glad Doug wasn't over there that day. He might've been hurt trying to help Rita or he might've gotten blamed. She didn't really deserve his help after she fired him, though Doug would have done the Christian thing."

"Rita fired Doug?" My mouth dropped open.

She nodded. "After all he done for her, too. She claimed she was missing some money she left out at the barn in her desk drawer and she knew Doug was the one took it, though he swears he never went near her desk."

Doug hadn't said a word about being fired. He'd carried on working as though he and Rita were on the greatest of terms. Could he have been angry enough with Rita to kill her in revenge?

"So Doug was *home* that morning," I said. The gray and white cat returned to claim his seat, and when I didn't move after he'd insistently butted his head against my legs and swiped at me with both paws, he jumped onto the back of the couch.

"I worked at the store last Thursday night. Doug wasn't here when I left about seven. He...he spent the night away and I didn't see him again until sometime Friday." Her lips pressed into a thin line.

Doug had mentioned Buddy's Motel and being with his girlfriend Tina when I called him Friday. Ellen Reilly would never let Doug bring a woman to the trailer to spend the night, and Tina lived with her sister and her brother-in-law, who was a Methodist preacher. I didn't imagine they'd take kindly to Doug and Tina having a romantic tryst in their home, either. So Doug's story about the motel was probably true.

"Doug said he was going to apply for a job in Sarasota at Palmetto Horse Farm," she went on. "So I expect that's where he was that day."

I fought down a yelp of surprise. Palmetto Horse Farm was quite a few cuts above where I would expect Doug to find work. For one thing, they'd insist on an honest day's labor. For another, they'd never tolerate his drinking. It was one of the finest Cattle Horse farms in the state. In fact, Sonny Joe had been foaled there. Maybe the story was a lie and he'd left the motel in Sarasota early and gotten back to Del Canto in time to kill Rita.

I stood. "I'm sure I'll be seeing Doug around, and I'll ask him myself if I have any more questions."

"I know he'll help you out any way he can. He's a good person, never stole a thing from anyone. Rita Cameron had no right to fire him without even checking the facts." Belatedly she offered me a drink of lemonade, which I turned down.

I could ask Doug's neighbors if they'd happened to notice what time he got home last Friday, but somehow I got the impression they wouldn't be terribly helpful. When I'd driven past, I'd noticed that their front yard was peppered with hand-painted signs: Keep Out—We Shoot to Kill; Real Mean Dogs; and Big Bad Ex-Marine.

I didn't have a clue whether Doug had stolen Rita's money. Didn't sound like him. He wouldn't have wanted to risk his job and he certainly didn't have a reputation as a thief. But had someone else been prowling around Rita's and taken the money?

I'd have to try to track down Doug and see if I could get the straight story out of him without arousing his suspicions. Right now, though, I had a better idea for checking his alibi.

Chapter 15

I drove back across town, made a quick stop at Publix for dog food, and got home by noon. After I verified that the horses were alive and well, I called Sammi.

"I'm going to Sarasota Friday morning. Want to come with?"

"I thought you were supposed to be recuperating."

I could hear the radio in the background playing what sounded like a string orchestra's version of "Yellow Submarine."

"Remember what we talked about yesterday? I've come up with some alibis I need to check out. For example, Doug bragged that he was with Tina at a motel in Sarasota on Thursday night, and never went near Rita's 'til after she was killed. And he supposedly applied for a job at Palmetto Horse Farm in Sarasota. But I was able to reach him at home right after I got back from her place and that was mid-morning. Pretty fast if he'd gone to a job interview and then gotten home so soon."

"I get it. You want to check out his story. I'm not working until tomorrow evening, so I'll go as long as this trip doesn't turn into some kind of wild adventure. I know how you are when you get started on something, Leigh, when you can't rest until you bring justice down on some hapless perp. Like that time you thought you saw a guy who was featured on *American's Most Wanted* and you called 911 and it turned out he was the new preacher at the Baptist church and the newspaper printed—"

"Of course not," I interrupted, before she brought up more embarrassing memories. "This trip is strictly two little old ladies out for a Sunday drive."

"*Old* ladies? Speak for yourself, Miss Daisy."

"And one more thing. If Kenneth and Doreen can't keep Whitney until evening for me on Saturday, could she stay with you? I'm going to a horse club meeting in the afternoon and then out to dinner with Jared Beaumont."

"Dinner with Jared Beaumont?" she replied after a pause. "That nice looking guy I met at Rita's funeral? Now that's interesting."

"For heaven's sake, Sammi. He only wants to thank me for taking him to the meeting."

"I'll be glad to keep Whitney on Saturday, in fact she can spend the night. But be careful, Leigh. I'm not ready to eliminate *anyone* from the 'who killed Rita' list; I don't care what the police say. So don't let your guard down. The killer could be someone from the club."

And she'd accused *me* of seeing evil behind every bush. As soon as she hung up, I called Millie Destin.

"I already talked to the police. They did me the same as they did you that day. Asked questions. Then I had to go home to feed my animals, and they came by before they headed back to town and looked at the damage that horse did racing loose in my yard. Ain't no one paid me for it, though." I heard muffled chomping on the other end of the line; I'd interrupted her lunch.

"All I want to know is whether you saw or heard anything unusual before I got there to pick up my hay." Which I still hadn't picked up. Wouldn't need it, though, if I had to sell my horses.

"Same thing the police asked." She noisily slurped up something liquid. "I don't waste time spying on my neighbors. I know Rita said I did, but it wasn't true. Rita made a lot of false accusations about my hogs—even called animal control once."

"So you don't have a clue about who might have been there

that day?" I heard the disappointment creep into my voice.

"If I did, I'd have told the police. But I didn't see a thing. Got all them pepper trees blocking her fence line, anyway. Before the horse came into my yard I heard something, though."

I leaped to my feet, nearly knocking my chair over. "You did?"

"That fool dog of my neighbor's, the ones that have the milk cows? He like to barked his head off that morning."

"Was that before nine o'clock?"

"Now tell me, do you ever notice what time it is when you hear a dog bark? Especially one that makes a habit of it. Usually he'll bark for a while, then shut up, but that morning he went on and on until I thought my head would split plumb open. I'm thinking it might have been about eight-thirty when he started because I was watching a garden show on TV. Starts at eight-thirty. Between that dog and Rita's horse, I didn't have a moment's peace. Dog finally shut up. I wish I'd thought to call animal control and tell them who was the *real* neighborhood nuisance."

"Sorry I bothered you." I lowered my chin and sighed. "Thanks, anyway, Millie."

For a few seconds, I'd had real hopes she'd give me some important information about last Friday. Now I was back to the beginning. So a dog had barked. He'd probably heard the killer out at the barn with Rita, and then Tinker running around. But that wasn't evidence I could use.

I'd fed the little stray before I left and refilled her water when I got home. Now she curled up next to my chair and emitted a big sigh.

"What's the matter, sweetie?" I said, bending forward to rub her ears. "Miss your family, don't you?"

This was as good a time as any. I could call Maggie and the people at the new grooming shop and ask if they knew the dog, but seeing her in the flesh was more likely to jog their memories. I gathered up the dog and carried her out to the car.

I took her to the new shop first. As soon as I stepped inside, I could see why people might be tempted to drop Maggie and come here. Not everyone was as loyal as Sammi and Jeeves. This shop was not only air-conditioned, it featured a magazine filled waiting room for clients to enjoy themselves reading celebrity gossip while they waited for their pampered darlings to emerge from the grooming salon after their visits to the "pet makeover specialists." The tile floor sparkled, the walls were freshly painted, and the shop was well-lit. It even smelled like a day in the mountains instead of Maggie's shop that smelled of musky doggie cologne mixed with coconut scented dog shampoo.

A perky girl in a dog hair encrusted blue smock greeted me, then busied herself fussing over the dog I held in my arms. "What a sweet baby! Do you want a groom or just a bath?"

I blinked. I'd been busy going into shock at the prices posted on the sign behind the register. "Actually, neither one. My daughter found this dog on the road near our house. I wondered if anyone recognized her."

"Oh, gee, I've never seen her. Let me ask the other girls."

She whisked the dog away. In a few minutes she returned from the back room, shaking her head. "No luck. You might try the vet's or even that other grooming shop, but it's way out of town. You probably don't want to drive that far."

Unfortunately, I already knew how far it was. I stopped at two vet's offices on the way, but no one recognized the dog. I hoped I had better luck at Maggie's because I was starting to get attached to the dog myself.

Maggie had one customer when I arrived, a cocker spaniel. But even if her face hadn't lit up in recognition when she saw the dog, I would have known from the animal's reaction that she'd been here before. She wiggled and squirmed and whined until Maggie took her from me.

"What are you doing with Heidi?" Maggie planted a kiss on top of the dog's head.

"Heidi? So that's her name. My daughter found her in front of our house and I've been trying to track down her owner. Sammi thought you might know."

"Sure. The Allbrights brought her in all the time. But they moved out of the country last month."

"You mean they abandoned her?" My voice went up half an octave.

"The Allbrights wouldn't do something like that. They

couldn't take her along, so they gave her to the people next door. It about broke their hearts." Maggie flipped through a nearly empty Rolodex and showed me a card. "I tried calling to see if they wanted to keep bringing her in, but never got an answer. Then I stopped by, and their landlord said they'd skipped out on the rent. I never imagined they'd dumped Heidi."

The phone rang, and Maggie walked over to the desk to pick it up. While I waited for her to finish talking, I picked up a ceramic dachshund next to the cash register. My mother collected ceramic dogs so I tended to notice them. When I put the dachshund back in its place, I saw that Maggie's appointment book was open.

Her back was turned, so I took advantage of the opportunity to flip over a few pages, back to last Friday morning. Maggie had two appointments listed. Sammi and Jeeves at nine-thirty and someone named Vivian Reinhardt picking up Baby at eight-thirty. Sammi had postponed her appointment—I'd ended up bringing Jeeves to the shop on Saturday—but Maggie had to be here for Vivian Reinhardt's Baby at eight-thirty. So there was no way she could have gotten to Rita's at eight-thirty when Millie had heard the neighbor's dog barking. I'd found the body at nine. It was impossible for Maggie to have killed Rita.

Maggie hung up and turned around. I jumped and flipped the book closed, hoping she hadn't seen me snooping.

"Guess you got yourself a dog." She grinned. Her mood had improved considerably since I'd seen her Saturday. Maybe she'd gotten the good news about her inheritance. "Heidi's about two years old, mixed-breed, mostly Shih Tzu. Really sweet and well-behaved."

"I hadn't planned to keep her," I said doubtfully.

"Wish I could help you, but I've got too much going on right now with keeping this place going, building my new shop and kennel, and taking care of my own dogs." Her face had become animated, almost pretty when she mentioned the new place. She smiled when she handed the dog back to me.

"My daughter has really fallen in love with Heidi. But are you sure you don't want another dog?"

"Positive. You know Heidi needs regular grooming to keep her looking neat. I'm leaving the shop early today to meet the man who's doing the work on my new kennel, and I'm busy all day tomorrow, but you could bring her by on Saturday."

"Saturday I'm going to a horse club meeting. After that I have to stop by Rita's place to see Angie. I can call you next week."

A momentary flicker of displeasure crossed her face. Maybe I shouldn't have mentioned Angie. Was there bad blood between the two women?

"Next week then. I'm always happy to get new clients." She opened a cage and took out a black and tan Chihuahua. "This is Leo—one of *my* babies. Say hello, Leo."

I made suitable comments about what a precious dog he was, then watched while she opened a foil packet and took out what I knew was a gelcap containing deworming medicine. Leo struggled in her arms while she worked on prying his little jaws apart.

"Peanut butter helps," I said. "Whenever I deworm my cats I put the pills in a glob of peanut butter. They gulp it down, never realizing they're getting duped."

"I've heard of that, but I'm allergic. Last time I got near a peanut, I passed out and almost died."

"Goodness. As common as peanut products are, that must make things awkward." A girl in Whitney's class was so allergic that no one in the school was allowed to bring peanut butter in their lunch.

"Tell me about it."

Leo finally gave in and let Maggie poke the gelcap down his throat. The phone rang again and she waved a hand at me in dismissal.

Friday morning began with the promise of cool breezes and sunshine. A flock of birds had congregated around the bird feeder in the back yard, and I wished I could sit near the window all day sipping coffee and enjoying them. Instead, I got dressed in record time and drove directly to Sammi's after dropping Whitney and Brad at school.

Sammi insisted on driving to Sarasota, saying it was her turn to give me a ride. When I climbed into her Buick, I let my purse fall to the floor between my feet but kept my notebook on my lap.

She eyed the red notebook. "Directions?"

"No, it's my, uh, clue notebook. I have a section for each suspect, a section for clues, and a section for new evidence to get the police up off their tails and busy solving the murder."

I'd spent almost an hour last night writing up my sections. Whitney complained bitterly that there were no signs of supper and likely all she'd get would be some old warmed up casserole, which she was sick of.

I finally gave in and took her out for pizza. I couldn't tell her I was involved in some very important detective work to bring justice for Rita and to convince her father horses weren't dangerous, even though I knew by now that convincing him would not get him to change his mind. Something else was motivating him and I would find out what it was. In my spare time.

"I hope you've got a big fat list of clues pointing to the Harpers. There's something about Brenda that irritates me."

"You and half the people in town. The horse people, anyway. I don't believe the Harpers killed Rita, but there *is* something to think about. After I decided to write things down, I thought about how Rita kept notebooks. The day I was there talking to Angie I saw one of them in her kitchen drawer. She'd written a list of chores that included reporting the Harpers to the ACHR."

Sammi merged smoothly onto the interstate and urged the Buick to pick up speed. "ACHR? Isn't that the registry for American Cattle Horses?"

"I've taught you well. The question is, what would she have on the Harpers?"

"Whatever it is, it would have to be pretty serious for them to kill her."

I flipped pages until I reached the entry for Brenda and Scott. "The thing is, the ACHR can ban you from showing or registering horses, stuff like that. It's not like they'd throw you in prison or impose the death penalty for an infraction."

"If Brenda couldn't register horses, that would put her out of a job, wouldn't it?"

"Pretty much," I said, squinting my eyes against the sun coming into the car from my right. "They've got a real money making horse business there." Last night I'd written, *Rita reporting the Harpers to ACHR?* Now I added an arrow pointing to the word *Greed.*

"I wonder what Rita knew that she was going to report?"

I thought about the Harpers. Brenda was short and, despite hours spent riding, she was built round and her body was going plump. Even her face was round and full, and she had a sprinkling of freckles across her nose. Somehow this made her look fresh-faced and younger than her age. She looked impish rather than sinister, the last suspect anyone would pick out of a lineup. Scott didn't appear any more menacing than Brenda did. He was tall and lanky with thick, wiry, sand-colored hair. His eyebrows angled low over his hazel eyes and arched at the outer corners, giving him an eternally perplexed look. He was sharper than he looked, but he depended on Brenda to do his thinking for him more often than not. They looked about as murderous as a pair of first graders.

"It could have been nothing. Maybe she just wanted to cause trouble, Leigh."

"Could be. She never went over to their place; too much bad blood. Whatever she knew, she would have to have seen it at a show." I stared out the window at endless palmettos. They gave way to a clearing and then to a pasture where a herd of black Angus grazed in contentment. Occasionally we passed fields full of horses, some with spring foals. For me, they made more enjoyable viewing than the calves.

A flicker of a thought ignited in my mind. "Sammi, I know this sounds weird, but Rita had to pass the Harper's farm every time she went to Fort Myers. She could have seen something from the road."

"That almost takes us back to square one."

"I know. There's Doug who fought with Rita. Angie who stands to inherit a lot of money, but has a solid alibi. Her husband Stan, who'd benefit if Angie gets money, but was with Angie in Bradenton. Parker—who thought he was inheriting—also has an alibi. Camilla does his accounting and she said he was at her house working on Friday morning. And Maggie inherits, but I don't know how much. Besides, I was at her shop yesterday and her appointment book shows someone picking up a dog at eight-thirty, so she has an alibi. Then there are any number of people who didn't know her that well, people like Jared Beaumont coming to her place looking to buy horses, and others coming over for lessons."

"Babe, something tells me Doug didn't do it. He's rough, but he's not totally stupid. Killing Rita would be like killing the golden goose who paid his salary. After all, who else would put up with Doug?"

"You have a point there. But I talked to his mother this morning and she claims Rita fired Doug for stealing."

Sammi took her eyes off the road long enough to flash me a look of surprise. "So he may have gone ballistic and killed her if he thought he was out of a job."

"I had the same thought. Still, it may sound silly, but I don't want Doug to be the killer. It's true that Doug isn't exactly a son to be proud of, but he's good to his mother. She doesn't deserve any more pain in her life." I clenched my hands. Rita's murder might never be solved. And even if it was, I'd still have to sell my home unless I could come up with a miracle.

Chapter 16

Traffic went from heavy to troublesome as we neared Sarasota. There were too many cars using too little highway and, with the Gulf of Mexico forming the western boundary, not much room for the city to spread out. I directed Sammi to the exit for Bee Ridge, and from there to where quiet neighborhoods eventually gave way to pastureland. I had her turn north onto a connecting highway and then after a few more miles, Palmetto Horse Farm loomed into view.

White board fences enclosed what looked like dozens of pastures where the horses were loosely divided into groups by ages. Sammi squealed with delight when she spotted mares with fuzzy foals.

"Pull up near this first barn," I said. A white cottage next to the barn was enclosed by a picket fence. There was a sign on the fence and I paused to read it. "Office. V. Reinhardt, Manager." V. Reinhardt. Why did that sound so familiar?

The flat roofed house had a wall of windows across the enclosed front porch. The walkway was lined with marigolds in shades of orange and pale yellow, and someone had put an assortment of brightly painted concrete gnomes on either side of the door. I figured V. Reinhardt must live here; one of the perks of what was already a dream job for anyone who loved horses.

Sammi accompanied me to the front door, but I didn't get a chance to knock. A pleasant faced woman wearing jeans and a blue tee shirt pulled open the door. I spared a second for envy. I might have had a job like this if I'd known sooner what I wanted to do with my life.

The woman stuck out her hand. "Viv Reinhardt. Can I help you?"

I shook her hand. "Leigh McRae. This is my cousin, Sammi Hollister. I bought a horse that originally came from this farm and I wanted to learn something about his background." I smiled to show I was nothing more than a talented horsewoman from Del Canto out to learn about her horse.

"Sure, come on in." She held the door.

The front room was used as an office and was furnished with a desk, computer, and file cabinets, but was also equipped with a couch and two chairs. I sank onto the couch. A chocolate and white Chihuahua puppy in a blanket lined box stirred in its sleep.

Viv sat in an armchair. Her hair was short and wavy, and her tan showed how much time she spent outdoors. She looked young for the position of farm manager, but the confidence in her manner made me think she'd have no trouble handling the job. "Which horse are wanting to know about? I've been here five years and I remember all the babies. We don't sell many older horses."

"He's a blood bay gelding. Palmetto Sonny Joe."

Her face lit. "I sold that colt to Rita Cameron last year. He was one of the nicest in his year's foal crop—really a fine animal."

"Yes, he is," I said. "I bought him for my daughter, but now that Rita Cameron has died, we've lost our trainer and I suppose we'll have to manage on our own."

"I was sorry to hear about Rita. I know it's a long way for you to come, but I give youth lessons if you're interested."

"I'll keep that in mind." If I found a way to keep my horses, I'd need a trainer.

"Like I said, Sonny was a great colt, and so beautiful. Are you familiar with his sire? Palmetto Bold Son? Every one of his babies has a great mind."

"I've heard that." This was my opening. "In fact, Rita's hired hand, Doug Reilly, said Sonny was a nice horse to work with."

Viv wrinkled her nose at the mention of Doug. "That's right, he worked for Rita Cameron."

"You know Doug?" I said brightly.

"Not well. He was here a few times with Rita, and he came out to look for a job last week."

I leaned forward. "Really? When was that?"

"Thursday, I think. No, it was Friday morning. I couldn't tell you what time, maybe eight, but I remember it was Friday because one of the mares foaled breech, and we had to have the vet out and I had to cancel another appointment. Doug Reilly came parading up to the stall with a cheap looking blonde draped all over him." Viv shook her head. "I don't like people wandering into the barn without permission. I didn't have time for Doug and I sure didn't have time for his girlfriend to pull a fainting spell when she saw the blood."

"So you didn't hire him?"

"No," she said quietly. The puppy in the box woke and started whimpering. Viv reached over and picked the baby up to cuddle him against her chest. "Little sweetie isn't used to me yet; I just got him a few days ago. In fact that was the appointment I had to cancel Friday. I was supposed to go to a shop in Del Canto to pick him up, but had to postpone because of the breech foal."

Something clicked. Now I knew why her name seemed so familiar. "You bought the puppy from Maggie Cameron."

"Yes, do you know her?"

"Sammi gets her dog groomed at Maggie's shop."

Viv chuckled. "It seems that everyone in Del Canto knows everyone else. Listen, I hate to rush you, but I have a full schedule."

"Thanks for your help. I'm sure we'll manage fine with Sonny, and I'll let you know about the training."

"Thanks. And keep me posted about how he's doing, though I suppose I'll see you at the spring shows." She got to her feet and Sammi and I took our cue to leave.

Sammi had the Buick moving out of the driveway before I

was completely in.

"What are you trying to do?" I gasped, leaning sideways to grab the door handle. "I didn't wear my running shoes."

"I'm anxious to get this cleared up. I'm really into it, now. When we get to that motel, I'm sure we're going to find that Doug checked out too late to have gone out to this farm and then gotten to Del Canto in time to kill Rita."

"Slow down, if you don't mind. I said this was little old ladies, not a couple of CIA agents."

"Little old ladies never went after evidence in a murder except in books." Sammi swung around a corner and back onto the highway ahead of a line of approaching cars.

"There's no reason now to go to the motel. Doug couldn't have had time to take Tina home and then go kill Rita. And if Viv is right about him being here Friday morning, he was here or on the road while Rita was being murdered."

"Then what we need to do next is find out for sure where the Harpers were last Friday morning." She flicked on her radio and heavy metal boomed out of the speakers. Suddenly I longed for the string orchestra that had mutilated "Yellow Submarine" when I called her yesterday.

"That should be easy enough." I waved my hand around like a magic wand. "I'll ask them. Presto—like magic we'll have the answer."

"You sound so bitter. Why don't you work it into the conversation next time you talk to Brenda? You know, the way you did with Viv when you asked about Doug." Sammi started humming along with the noise coming from her radio, though there was no discernable melody for her to follow.

"I'll consider it. By the way, I don't suppose you have a little spare cash lying around, say about fifty or sixty grand, do you?"

"Ha! I knew something was troubling you, other than Rita's death. This is about Kenneth, isn't it?" She didn't take her eyes off the road. "And don't make any sarcastic remarks about me being Einstein or a psychic, just tell me what's going on."

"Actually, I was going to say Sherlock Holmes. Didn't I tell you Kenneth wants me to sell Sonny Joe and give him back what he paid?"

"Ah, Mr. Control Freak has figured out another way to pull your strings. But you're not telling me you paid fifty grand for a horse." She nearly ran off the road and had to yank the wheel to keep the car pointed west.

"Don't be an idiot. Kenneth says if I don't give him what he paid for Sonny Joe, as well as his share of the equity in my place, he'll force a sale. He's picked out a place for me in town and that means no more horses."

"Leigh, why did you...wait, you know my thoughts about your present, past, and future relationship with Kenneth McRae. And his shrewd lawyer sister, who left you in this mess with your property. Or maybe I should say shrew lawyer."

"Might as well."

"So why don't you just sell your place? Give him his money and tell him where he can stuff his plans for selling your horses."

"Are you crazy? I have no place to keep my horses if I sell, unless the Del Canto zoning board allows me to stable them in the garage of my new cottage. Forget I ever mentioned Kenneth. Let me buy you lunch and then I'm going home. I intend to spend the rest of the day not thinking about Rita or Kenneth."

"You got it, babe." Sammi swung the wheel and accelerated up the I-75 southbound ramp like she was trying for the pole position at the Daytona 500.

On the way home, I settled to flipping aimlessly back and forth through my mostly empty notebook, and wondering how I could get Kenneth to change his mind. Even if I dredged up a rich client to buy all his listings, he'd still have half an interest in my home and could pull the same stunt whenever he wanted. I couldn't ask my parents for money. They were retired and, given the fact that they'd tried to talk me out of marrying Kenneth to begin with, they wouldn't help. My dad is big into tough love and my mother does whatever he wants her to do.

I slathered on my best makeup, the kind with the built in sunscreen and the heavy-duty blemish concealer.

Whitney whistled when she saw me. "Are you going to a horse club meeting or lunch at the country club?"

"Hush, Whitney. This is a big meeting, so I don't see any

need to wear my lucky shirt with the mismatched buttons." I was wearing a brand new pair of jeans and a pink blouse. I'd put on lipstick and even a pair of earrings, which I seldom wore.

The day was gorgeous, perfect for a spring show, and if Rita hadn't died, that's where we'd have spent the afternoon after attending the meeting. It was sunny out, but with enough of a cool breeze blowing from the north to keep the humidity and the temperature down.

I dropped Whitney at Kenneth's and headed back across town to pick up Jared. On the way I stopped for gas, where Parker Fielding ambled into the station and filled up just ahead of me. We exchanged smiles and waves. He was okay, really a nice person from what I'd heard. I already thought he was too in love with Rita to have killed her— he had an alibi provided by Camilla—and I hadn't been able to come up with a motive anyway. I'd cross him off my list.

The Harpers, though, were clever enough to have made Rita's death look like an accident, and they might have had a motive if her comments in her notebook were true. I'd have to watch them for suspicious behavior at the meeting. I didn't know what that would be, though. Shooting murderous glances at their fellow equine enthusiasts perhaps?

Chapter 17

Jared had bought a "ranchette" east of town off of Highway 17. The five acres were fenced with barbed wire, so I'd have to warn him about the danger of horses ripping themselves to shreds unless he put in horse fencing. There was a rundown two-stall barn in one corner of the property and the cinderblock house looked like it needed a lot of work, including a paint job and a new roof.

He was out front fixing the porch railings when I drove up, but must have just started the job because he'd only finished one of about two dozen broken rails. He banged in a nail, then gave it one more shot before he looked up and sent me a friendly grin.

"I'd ask you in, but I haven't finished unpacking and there's no place to sit." He rubbed at a spot on the back of his hand. It was a fresh scratch next to an old bruise, and reminded me of the dings and scrapes I got when I worked around my barn.

"That's okay. We need to leave now if we want to get there in time to talk to the horse people before the meeting starts." I glanced around the yard while he went inside and washed up. The grass was overgrown and broken cinderblocks were strewn next to the house. He couldn't have had the place long. As Kenneth would have said, the property had potential, but needed a lot of sweat equity.

Jared came back wearing a clean shirt. He'd combed his hair and put a Band-Aid on the back of his hand.

I shook my head. Men had it easy when they went out. It had taken me almost an hour to get ready and this was nothing more than a casual outing. After he got in the car, a hint of cologne wafted my way. I wrinkled my nose, but didn't tell him his cologne smelled a lot like the spray Maggie used on her dogs.

We took a back road that would get us to I-75 and then south to Fort Myers. Even though I was driving, I managed to sneak a glance at the pastures of the Harper's Summer Song Farm as we zipped by. The grounds were as neatly kept as a golf course, the front pastures enclosed with stout wooden fences painted a blinding white. The well-kept farm presented quite a contrast to the run-down place next door, the one sporting a for sale sign in the front yard next to a house that needed a lot of work. Across the road was an orange grove and a small home that belonged to my great aunt. But I didn't see anything that would have aroused Rita's suspicions about the Harpers. I made a mental note to call Great-Aunt Dorothy to see if she'd noticed anything odd.

"You're quiet today." Jared shifted sideways in the passenger seat.

"Sorry, I have a lot on my mind. But I promise to be better company for the rest of the day."

"I'll hold you to that promise. Tell me about yourself. What kind of work do you do?"

"Word processing." I grimaced. "I'd rather talk about the weather than my job. Why don't you tell me about yourself?"

"I'm from New York. I had quite a few jobs before I settled down as a manager at a computer store." He shrugged. "Got tired of the store, so I took computer classes and found a job at a technology business here in Del Canto. I think I told you about that."

Only that he did something with computers. But he must be doing okay if he'd been able to buy a place in Del Canto and if he were planning to buy horses from Rita.

I wondered where he was the morning Rita was killed. He'd shown up while the police were there, but what if he'd killed her and come back for something, like the murder weapon? Stupid thought. It was unlikely he'd have returned before the police left, and besides I didn't like the idea of thinking he was a suspect, especially not while I was alone with him. And, as a stranger, he couldn't possibly have a motive.

"What made you decide on Del Canto?"

"I broke up with my witch of a girlfriend last month and decided to make a new start. Looked around, and ended up buying this place. I've got a couple of spoiled sisters in Connecticut, and now they're begging me to stock the pasture with riding horses before they visit."

Witch girlfriend? I bit my lip, gripping the wheel so hard my fingers ached. And just when we were getting along so well.

"Sorry." Jared twisted up his mouth. "That sounded wrong even to me."

"In my experience, guys who complain about the witch they used to go out with, don't make good company."

"Ouch. I deserved that. But in my own defense, can I plead recent heartbreak?" He grinned boyishly, placing one hand over his heart.

"I'll allow it," I said, suppressing a smile. "The change of scenery could be exactly what you need." I hadn't considered leaving my home for even a minute when I divorced Kenneth. After all, I'd grown up in Del Canto and my family and friends were there. Jared obviously had a family—he was buying horses for his sisters to ride—but time on his own might be important to him.

"I hope so, Leigh. Or should I call you talented horsewoman? Unless you prefer equine enthusiast."

"Leigh is fine, thanks very much. I'm trying to forget that story in the *Del Canto Star*."

"Don't blame you. I remember how stunned you looked that day when I saw you in Rita's barn."

"I'm sure I was not at all like your ordinary talented horsewoman." He'd looked pretty stunned himself, but I didn't point that out. "I don't often find one of my friends dead."

"I know you wish you could have helped her or offered some kind of comfort."

"Of course I do, but she was dead when I found her and nothing is ever going to change that." The only thing I could ever do for Rita was to bring her killer to justice, and I was determined to keep my promise.

"It must have been tough waiting for the police and the paramedics." He reached across the console to squeeze my shoulder in sympathy.

Goosebumps rose on my arm. I could get to like this man, despite the witch in his past. "I wasn't alone, thank God. Millie Destin from across the street was with me."

"Were you close? You and Rita, I mean, not you and Millie Destin."

"Sure, we'd been friends for years and we spent a lot of time together at shows." For some reason I was unwilling to admit that spending a lot of time with Rita didn't mean I knew a lot about her private life.

I braked hard and signaled for a turn. "I nearly went right past the driveway. Jared, is it okay if I change the subject? How about if I compliment you on your new career and wish you well."

He pretended to pout. "Telling me you wish me well isn't a compliment."

"Sorry."

The Fort Myers Club, unlike the tiny Del Canto Club, had a huge show facility. Their arena was three times bigger than ours and they had a second, smaller arena for warm-ups. There were stalls for the exhibitors, and three food and drink concession wagons. At the Del Canto show grounds we had only the ancient and sagging "Snack Shack" manned by reluctant volunteers.

On the left side of the road, opposite the Fort Myers Horse Lovers' show arena, there was a building the club used for meetings. I steered the Honda down the drive and pulled into the parking lot where I found a shady spot.

I led Jared toward the end of the row where Pat Ansley was leaning against a white Blazer. Pat was a good friend of mine, a fellow Cattle Horse enthusiast. Unfortunately Brenda Harper came at her from the other side and before I got there, she'd already latched onto Pat's arm like a crab grabbing bait out of a trap.

Then Brenda spotted me and Jared. Her eyes lit and she turned Pat loose to scuttle in my direction. Pat could barely keep up, though she was about a foot taller than Brenda and built like a whippet.

"Leigh, I had no idea you'd be at today's meeting," Brenda purred.

"Couldn't stay away," I said. "I'm in charge of the trophy committee. And since I'm planning to ride Nancy Green's Teddy Boy in the jumping next month, I have to make sure to get really special trophies."

"Teddy Boy only jumps well for Nancy. You'll be lucky to get a sixth place ribbon."

"Thanks." I gritted my teeth, then remembered to introduce Jared.

"We met at Rita's funeral," Brenda said. "Did Leigh tell you she and her husband are selling me a horse she bought from Rita Cameron?"

Jared shook Brenda's fat little hand. "Actually, I'd heard Leigh was divorced."

I raised an eyebrow. Not from me, he hadn't. But leave it to Brenda to try to create drama to make me look bad.

"Yes, that's right. Somehow I keep forgetting."

"So how's your new stud, Brenda?" I glanced around as though I expected her to have brought the stud to the meeting in the crew cab of her truck. "Going to haul him to the next show?"

"We're waiting until breeding season's over and then we'll start showing him in pleasure. Come out to the farm anytime, though."

I'd set my thoughts on idle, but now sudden inspiration revved me back up to speed. Brenda and Scott were suspects because of what Rita knew about them and what she planned to report. "Would it be okay if I stopped by in the morning?"

Brenda blinked. I was sure she hadn't really expected me to agree to look at her stud. "Fine. We'll give you a discount if you breed both your mares."

I could almost hear the cash register ringing in her brain. I was saved from giving the kind of answer that Rita would have been proud of when Pat put her hand on my shoulder, gently restraining me.

"I'll probably come see your stud, too, maybe next week. We're breeding Daisy Sox this year." Pat didn't let go of my shoulder.

Brenda actually rubbed her hands together. "Prime would sire you a great foal; he's got what it takes to cancel out Daisy's ugly head."

Pat winced. Daisy was an old favorite of hers, well loved despite her coarse, slightly roman nosed head. I glared at Brenda. I couldn't wait to talk to Pat privately and tell her all about "Prime." Unlike some of the new horse people who were overwhelmed by Brenda's non-stop sales pitches and her bragging, Pat would see the stud's flaws.

"I could see your foals while I'm there. What did Dawn Lady have this year?" Pat asked.

Something odd happened to Brenda's face. Her jaw sank, so the roundness turned to a long oval. Dark pink color flowed into her cheeks and down her neck to her chest, most of which was exposed by her too-small tank top.

"Dawn Lady hasn't foaled yet." Brenda spoke through tight lips.

"Wasn't she due last month?"

"No." She laughed, but it sounded silvery and brittle like a bell tinkling. "You must be thinking of Red Dawn. Whoops, Scott's calling me. Got to run, people." Brenda bolted.

I stared after her. I was absolutely positive that Dawn Lady was due last month, in February, because Brenda had joked about naming the foal Dawn Valentine if it arrived on the fourteenth. Now that I thought about it, Brenda usually bragged about Lady's foals as though they were her own babies. Lady was one of the finest mares in the state and she'd produced a long list of champions.

I was glad I'd thought to tell Brenda I'd come see her stud. I intended to see Dawn Lady for myself. An idea had formed somewhere in the depths of my mind. What if Dawn Lady had lost her foal? Could Brenda be waiting for another of her mares to give birth, so she could pass the baby off as Dawn's? A Dawn Lady foal would be worth at least twice as much as, say, a Sweet

Susie foal, merely on the strength of its breeding. But how had Rita found out?

Lost in thought, I stumbled going up the steps to the building and Jared had to help me. I checked my knees and elbows for damages. Minor scrapes only, no blood.

"You know," I said, as we sat in folding chairs toward the front of the room. "You must think I'm a Grade A klutz."

"I'm sure you're simply coordination challenged," Jared said. He patted my shoulder and smiled into my eyes.

I turned my head and concentrated hard on the club officers. *Careful*, I told myself. *You are not interested.*

"Your friend Pat seems nice," Jared said. "But do I detect a bit of hostility between you and Ms. Harper?"

"Gosh, I didn't know you were so perceptive."

"I mentally prepared myself to witness bloodshed."

"She can be difficult."

"Doesn't she sell horses, too? I might want to go see her."

"You wouldn't want what she's selling." I turned my attention to the front. Someone had brought samples of the trophies we were voting on and arranged them on a shelf. All I had to do was point out the trophies, sound suitably impressed, then return to my seat for the voting.

The meeting, thanks to Nancy's strong leadership, was short and to the point. Except for the part concerning the trophy committee where I stood to give my report, I mostly zoned out and thought about last year's joint show when Rita had won the western pleasure futurity with a sweet little filly she'd since sold.

As soon as the meeting was over I turned to Jared. "I need to ask Nancy if she wants me to work her horse before the show. Want to come along and meet her? She doesn't have anything for sale, but she knows everyone in Lee County who does."

"That's okay. I'm going to talk to some folks on my own." He inclined his head toward a family moving toward the door. "Good way to get acquainted."

"Sure. I'll meet you outside." I didn't tell him the people he was following were also new to the club and their only horse was a twenty-year-old Welsh Pony—and it was not for sale.

Nancy was nowhere to be found when I got to the front of the room. Someone told me she might be in the restroom, so I decided I'd call her later in the week.

I pushed my way back through the crowd and went looking for Jared, but when I saw him, he was with Brenda and Scott near their truck. Brenda was talking, waving her arms around expansively. Jared nodded and laughed at something she said.

A twinge of annoyance went through me. I walked up and said, "How's it going?"

"Mission accomplished?" Jared shot me one of his charming smiles.

"Not really, but what about you?"

"Nice talking to you again." This to Brenda. Then to me, "I'm getting there. Ready?"

"Way past ready." I was already marching stiff-backed toward the Honda. It was not my business if he ended up buying from Brenda. I would manage to keep from saying "I told you so" if he ended up with a rough-gaited, stubborn-minded horse that wouldn't switch leads...unless you popped it on the shoulder with a riding crop and yelled, "Change, darn it."

He caught up to me and said, "Tell me about this horse you're going to ride in the show."

"Nancy's recovering from a serious illness. Since she's hoping to win a high point trophy she asked me to ride her horse in the jumping class."

"Jumps? You must be a pretty good rider."

We fetched up at my car and climbed in to fasten our respective seatbelts. "I do okay. The first time I rode Nancy's horse he tried to run out at the last fence and it was all I could do to get him over." I'd squeezed him with my thighs so hard, my leg muscles were in knots the next day.

"Weren't you worried he'd run into the fence?"

"Horses won't deliberately run into something if they can help it." The vivid memory of Tinker skidding to a stop in front of my truck and practically turning herself inside out to reverse direction inserted itself into my mind. Would I ever get over relating every new thought to that terrible day?

"Thanks for bringing me along. I met a lot of people. All of them knew Rita Cameron, it seems."

"Everyone in the state who has horses knew Rita." If he was checking Rita's credentials as far as being a reliable person to buy horses from, he was a little late.

"Did I tell you I've got a week off from work?" I said, starting the Honda. "My boss thinks I need to recuperate from finding Rita's body. But there's not much rest and relaxation going on in my life because my ex-husband is pressuring me to sell my horses. He's decided horses could be dangerous and our daughter belongs in dance class. Ballet lessons with her new stepmother." I wondered if Doreen would feel compelled to bedazzle Whitney's toe shoes.

"Odd how people are about things. But then, I don't have a daughter; I don't know how a father should feel."

I glanced at him, dividing my attention between his face and a too-slow Cadillac I was passing. "With Kenneth I think it's an excuse to keep controlling me more than it is any real problem with horses. But he's pushing me and right now I have enough to think about with convincing—" I bit my tongue. Hard. I'd been on the verge of telling Jared I suspected Rita had been murdered and I was determined to prove it so the police would bring the killer in. He might repeat what I'd said to the wrong person, might even let things slip to Brenda when he went to see her horses. Brenda was a suspect. And I hadn't checked Jared's alibi, but this was as good a time as any.

"When you talked to people about Rita," I said, "did they tell you where they were that day? At the funeral, everyone had to say where they were while she was dying."

"I noticed that. You and I were both on our way to see her. Coming from different directions, though."

"True." No way to check that, but then Jared did not come across as a homicidal maniac and I couldn't imagine a motive. Once again I felt frustrated over my lack of credentials as a detective.

Jared tried to bring up the subject of Rita again a minute later. I blinked and came back to the present. I knew he was only trying to help by letting me talk about my feelings, but I couldn't. Not right now when I'd been hit with a sudden wave of sadness after seeing her empty chair at the club officers' table.

"Uhmm, Jared, do you know anything about taking care of horses? Might be a good idea to learn what you're getting into."

"I'm not even up to rookie status." He made come on motions with both hands and widened his eyes at me in mock innocence. "Tell me what you know."

"Yes, okay. And by the way, I think you're a terrific brother for getting horses for your sisters."

"I hope they think so, too."

"Older or younger? Wait, they must be younger." He appeared to be about my age, thirty-five or so. Older sisters would not be looking to their brother to entice them south with horses.

"Yeah, the little prima donnas are much younger. I come from a weird family. My parents adopted me, and about the time I went to college they rocked my world like you wouldn't believe. They surprised me and everyone else in town by adopting a set of twin girls—infants."

"Wow. That is weird."

"Weird enough to make me wonder if somehow I hadn't measured up, and they had to try again to see if new kids could make up for their profound disappointment."

I opened my mouth to say I was sure his parents loved him dearly, then realized from his sudden dimpled smile he had to be kidding. Sometimes I got a little too Mom-ish, a trait that both Whitney and Sammi assured me I got from my own mother.

I launched into a recitation of the merits of hay versus grain and segued into the best pasture grasses for our area of the country. We were almost home before I realized I'd barely given him a chance to talk. I'd switched from the topic of feeding horses to a long-winded discussion on the perils of intestinal parasites and the prevalence of roundworms in subtropical climates such as south Florida. This was not a good topic of conversation for a lady, especially since tonight we were going to an Italian restaurant called "Mama's Spaghetti."

"I'm sorry," I said, stopping myself in mid-sentence. "I didn't mean to bore you with worm stories."

He smiled. "I'm not bored."

I stopped the car and he got out and came around to lean in the driver's side window. "Thanks for everything. Pick you up about seven, okay?"

"Seven's good. And, Jared? Thank's for letting me ramble on. It takes my mind off things."

"Anytime." He planted a light kiss on my cheek and stepped away from the car.

I put my fingers over the kiss, trying to decide if it meant anything and if I liked it. I finally decided Jared was simply being friendly.

Chapter 18

After dropping Jared off, I headed for Rita's, intending to keep my promise to stop by...and to look for Rita's notebook.

Stan met me in the driveway near the barn. He mopped sweat off his face with an old towel, then shot me a wounded look as if I were to blame for the heat.

"Everything okay? I went to a meeting and on my way home thought I'd stop by Rita's to see how you're doing." My face flushed. "I guess I should say Angie's, not Rita's."

"Appreciate the concern." He draped the towel over a fence rail. "And, yes, you can call it Angie's. The lawyer has let her know Rita left nearly everything to her, though there might be a delay settling. We'll get things worked out eventually."

"A delay?" I hoped he didn't think I was nosy.

"Apparently some of her money isn't where it was supposed to be. It might take time to sort out, and of course we have to make sure there's enough cash for Maggie's share or Angie might have to sell some of the property." Clearly annoyed at this turn of events, he set his lips into a thin line.

Angie strode out of the barn. "Stan, stop bothering Leigh with our problems."

I could tell from the sparks flying in Stan's direction the concern was not with bothering me, but that he'd divulged private information. Such as, the fact that Maggie was inheriting something, though I already knew that thanks to Camilla's slip.

"We're glad you're here, Leigh." She turned to me with a smile. "Perfect timing. We've been out running errands since early this morning and got back about five minutes ago. We stopped at the barn first to make sure the horses had been fed."

I didn't get to answer. A battered gray pickup roared up the driveway before screeching to a stop. The truck door banged open and Doug Reilly leaped out flapping his arms, reminding me of an oversized chicken trying to get airborne.

Stan stepped forward and positioned his lumpish body in front of Doug. "What's wrong?"

"I got here real early to feed the horses like you wanted and somebody was trying to break into the house."

"Who tried to break in?" I asked. Dumb question. "I mean, did you manage to get a look at them?" I hoped it wasn't Ray; Sammi would be devastated.

"Naw. See, I thought I'd check and see if you folks were around, and I went up to to the house. They must of heard me 'cause when I got there, all I saw was a glimpse of someone ducking into those palmettos that run into the gully behind the house."

"Did they get inside?" Angie asked.

"Don't think so. Door's still locked, but there's pry marks around the frame. I didn't chase whoever it was. You know palmettos will tear you to pieces."

I stifled a laugh. Palmettos have sawtoothed branches. They can scratch, but only if you're pushing close enough to get past the fans on the ends of the branches and reach the sharp parts on the stems. To hear Doug talk, you'd get the idea that a person would have to be hauled into intensive care if they braved a palmetto patch. The truth was, he didn't want to chase a would-be burglar. I didn't blame him, though. The thief could have been armed.

"Lord." Stan ran his hands through his hair. "What do you suppose they were after?"

"VCR and TV most likely." Doug nodded wisely. "Been a

bunch of other houses broke into out this way in the past month and that's what they took from them places. They must have figured no one was home. That's when they strike. When nobody's home."

"Burglars," I said. "I remember reading a story in the paper about some recent break-ins." I didn't bring up the part about Ray having been a suspect.

"I called the police. They came over and filled out papers, then said you all can stop by and talk to them." Doug hiked his jeans up higher on his hips and leaned against a fence post.

"You didn't see a strange car around or anything, did you?" I asked. "I mean, where could a thief go way out here without a car?"

"If he kept going, cut all the way down through the gully and up the other side through those tall palmettos, I reckon he'd come out on Slater Road."

"I didn't think of that."

A thief could have easily hidden a car along Slater Road, where there were at least six turnoffs on dirt roads into the palmettos. Slater Road cut back to Highway 17 and from a major highway, a person could go anywhere. It would be impossible from this distance to see a car. Besides, the trees and the palmettos formed a pretty good obstacle to clear vision, even if Slater Road were closer. My heart constricted for a few seconds. Rita's killer could have done the same thing. That would account for the fact that Millie Destin hadn't seen anyone coming or going before we found Rita.

"I hope he's gone for good," Stan said. "It's unsettling to think someone could break in, and Angie has enough on her mind without having to worry about thieves."

Doug's face lit. "A burglar can be pretty stubborn when there's something he wants, and he could show up while nobody's home and clean the place out. Everybody knows Rita was loaded. Why don't I stay here for a while to help guard the house? There's a nice apartment up over the garage and I wouldn't charge any extra for being the caretaker."

My mouth dropped open. Doug had tried to get Rita to rent him the garage apartment ever since he started working for her. She always refused, telling him she hardly got any work out of him now, and she'd get even less if he had an air conditioned apartment to run off to every time her back was turned.

Stan and Angie hadn't completely caught on to Doug yet. His face thoughtful, Stan glanced over at the detached garage, off to the left of the house, then turned his attention to Angie.

"That might be a good idea, Stan." She looked at me. "Thanks for stopping by. I'd offer you coffee, but I think Stan and I should see the police as soon as possible. Another time?"

"Of course." I left while Stan and Doug were finalizing the arrangement about the garage apartment. I'd definitely be back to get a look at that notebook.

Finally home, I turned Lena and Sonny Joe out together. Belle was cranky, nearing her time. She hadn't finished the last hay flake I'd given her, and her eyes held a far away expression. When I'd checked her early in the morning, I saw she'd started waxing—forming milk plugs on the ends of her teats—and now she was dripping.

"Finally, old girl." I patted her neck. I gave her water, but not feed. She wouldn't want to eat tonight, and her feed tub would be in the way. Doreen had wanted Whitney to spend the night, but I'd have to call and say I'd pick her up later. Whitney would never forgive me if I let her miss the birth.

I called Jared and asked for a rain check on dinner. "My mare probably won't foal for hours, but I can't take a chance on leaving her alone in case there are complications." Horses weren't like cows; cows could birth healthy calves even after days of labor. Horses had to get it right the first time, with little room for error and little time to summon veterinary help during an emergency.

"I understand. You sound pretty excited. I guess I would be, too, especially since I've never seen a horse foal."

"Belle is pretty predictable, so we've been there for most of her foalings." I had an inspiration, and when I couldn't come up with an objection, said, "You could watch with us if you want to."

"If you're sure you don't mind."

"Positive." Whitney would not be pleased, but Jared didn't have to know that. "I can't wait for this foal. Whitney and I even gave up our vacation trip last summer to afford the fee for a champion sire."

"You'll get a champion then?"

"There's no guarantee."

Being an optimist by nature, I had more than hope that Belle's baby would be the one that would go to the state championships, and maybe even to the nationals. Belle was no Dawn Lady, but she almost always had outstanding foals, even by the cheaper sires we'd resorted to in the past.

We arranged for Jared to come by to pick me up, then we'd go get Whitney and return to the house for the big event. I decided to get ever so slightly dressed up and made up, even though I'd have to change back into barn clothes.

Jared complimented me on my black slacks and jade colored silk blouse. I mumbled my thanks and said something predictable about my clothes being nothing special. But I was pleased he'd noticed.

I directed him past a row of "quaint souvenir shoppes" lining a narrow side street off the main drag in downtown Del Canto. A building that had been a bank in its first incarnation along with an adjoining hardware store had been sliced into more mini-shops for the sake of progress. I liked the effect, though. It was better than tearing down what was left of the beautifully designed building and putting up a block and glass monstrosity with a classless name such as *Bargain Discount Souvenirs*. Closer to the harbor, opposite the street where we turned to go to Kenneth's pricey Victorian, there had once been an upscale hotel. Now there were only a few failing stores and a crumbling parking lot, and no sign of the former luxury vacation paradise that had enticed visitors from all over the world.

Kenneth's house dated to the early nineteen hundreds and had recently been renovated to Doreen's specifications. The renovations must have cost a fortune. I hadn't known Kenneth's real estate office was doing so well. But I wouldn't have traded my own place for any house in town. As Kenneth had delighted in pointing out, town zoning doesn't allow horses.

Kenneth led us to the front parlor. Doreen appeared silently from the hallway. She caught my eye and smiled. Kenneth nodded curtly at me and then at Jared. He asked us to sit, then swaggered over to his newly installed wet bar to offer us drinks.

"None for me, thanks," Jared said.

"You know I have too much on my mind tonight to want to dull my thoughts with liquor," I said primly.

"I hope you're not still hung up on that nonsense of thinking Rita was murdered." He slipped his right arm around Doreen's shoulders and drew her closer. "Sweet Thing, let's go upstairs and tell Whitney her mother's here."

"I *meant* Belle having her foal." I shot him a dagger of a look. I'd told him I didn't want him discussing my theory with anyone. It was bad enough he'd opened his mouth in front of Jared, but I especially didn't want Doreen knowing. Doreen wouldn't see the need to spare my feelings. After all, she was the woman who'd told Winona at the Cut 'n Curl that the only reason Kenneth cheated on me before our divorce was that I spent too much time in the barn and not enough time in the bedroom. Not true, of course. He cheated on me because he's Kenneth.

Kenneth and Doreen, still wrapped together, left the room, and I was sputtering my indignation to empty space, wishing I'd thought sooner to make a remark about him acting like a dog trying to mark its territory. I turned to Jared and, trying to sound as though I were making polite conversation, said, "Don't Kenneth and Doreen have a beautiful house?"

"Yes, they do. Leigh, I don't mean to be nosy, but what was that about Rita being murdered?" One eyebrow had moved perilously close to his hairline. "I thought she fell out of her loft."

"Nothing." My heart was thumping along at twice its usual rate, and I mentally lectured myself for letting Kenneth get to me again. If stress could kill, I got another shove toward my grave every time I got near my ex.

"You don't really believe she was murdered, do you?"

I wondered if Jared might be regretting his decision to spend the day with a nutcase like Leigh McRae.

"No," I lied, opting for damage control over honesty. "She fell out of the loft. I was only trying to stall Kenneth so he'd stop thinking horse activities are dangerous, and he wouldn't sell Whitney's horse to Brenda Harper."

"Ah, Ms. Harper, your nemesis."

A blush warmed my cheeks. "If you don't mind, I'd rather not spoil what's left of the evening talking about my ex-husband and his demands. Or Brenda Harper. So tell me about your computer job," I said. "That should be a safe topic."

"Of course."

By the time Whitney came downstairs, I knew more about disk drives and RAM than your average word processing clerk. But I hadn't had to answer any more probing questions about Rita's death.

After I took Jared on a grand tour of my barn—including the feed room and the tack room—Whitney, Jared, and I sat quietly in chairs in the stall across from Belle's. When Whitney realized that Jared was staying for the birth, she'd clamped her mouth shut and pasted on a scowl that threatened be permanent. He hadn't taken the hint. I sent her one of my, "I'll speak to you later, young lady," expressions and she rolled her eyes. I knew she was remembering I'd promised Adam he could watch the foal's birth.

I concentrated on being quiet so as not to disturb Belle. When a car door slammed, I nearly toppled off my chair. "Goodness—who could that be?"

Heidi was in the house, but she barked. She'd also barked when we'd first gotten home and she saw Jared.

I didn't mind. She was just being a watchdog, barking only at strangers, not at everything that moved the way Jeeves sometimes did.

Whitney jumped up. "I'll check, Mom. You wait right here." She smiled sweetly and zipped out the door.

A minute later I knew what she was up to because Adam was following her back into the office.

He leaned his long frame against the wall and looked from me to Jared and back again. He beamed me an insolent grin. "I didn't know you had company, Leigh."

"What are you doing here?"

"You seem to be saying that to me a lot lately. Whitney called to say Belle was foaling. You did promise me last summer that I could be here for the big event, but of course I'll leave if it bothers you."

"Don't be silly," I snapped. "Nothing you do bothers me."

"Glad to hear it."

I bit back the impulse to ask if he'd left what's her name, the redhead, in the truck. I introduced him to Jared. Then Belle stamped her foot, and Whitney put a finger to her lips, signaling us to be quiet. There were no more chairs, so Adam leaned against the back of the stall, behind Whitney. I couldn't give her "the look" without him seeing, so I gritted my teeth and turned around to face the door.

I'd left the barn aisle dimly lighted, but otherwise we were in semi-darkness, not talking, so as not to disturb the laboring mare. When I checked, damp patches covered Belle's neck and flanks, and she was alternately pacing her stall and laying down.

Now, with a groan, she went down again. When she was still down after five minutes, I rose and tiptoed to her stall. She was straining and with each push, the water bag appeared briefly.

I silently motioned the others to move closer. After five more minutes, I could see two forefeet inside the water bag. I slipped into the stall and knelt behind Belle. Her water broke suddenly, drenching my legs. The foal's front hooves were properly positioned, one just behind the other, I noted with relief. Both forefeet were showing white socks, and I waited to be sure the foal's nose showed next. Another push and more of the forelegs appeared, along with a white face.

Whitney gasped and I turned to exchange horrified glances with her. *Not a lethal white*, I thought. *Please, God, don't let it be a lethal white.*

Chapter 19

I knelt and grasped both forelegs, tugging gently with Belle's next push. All at once, the rest of the foal slid out, practically on top of me. It was not a lethal white, but it wasn't a Cattle Horse either.

Whitney eased into the stall and handed me the old towels we'd brought from the house earlier. I rubbed the foal's face and cleared out its nostrils. I couldn't tell yet whether the damp coat would be chestnut or sorrel. The new baby's face was almost entirely white and now I could see that all four legs were white, with the white reaching high above the knees and hocks, nearly to the body. Quickly I checked the foal's flanks and stomach. Sure enough, the foal, a filly, had white patches with jagged edges splashed across both her sides and streaking the length of her stomach.

"Mom," Whitney said, sounding awed. "A crop-out." She dropped down beside me and took the towels out of my hands to finish the drying job.

I worked myself away from the filly and stood up. I was a mess, covered in a mixture of alkaline smelling amniotic fluid and wet straw. "It sure is," I said, rubbing my hands on the dry parts of my jeans. Good thing I'd gone to the house and changed when we got home earlier or my new outfit would have been ruined.

"What a beautiful little horse," Adam said.

I shook my head. "It's no good."

"What do you mean?" He swiveled his gaze down to look at the filly and then back to me. Then he stepped past me and into the stall. He hunched beside Whitney and put his arm around her shoulders. A lump formed in my throat. Adam was the only one I'd dated who'd completely won Whitney over.

"Leigh?" Jared said.

"The foal's got the wrong markings. We can't register it as a Cattle Horse because of all the white patches."

Whitney looked at me with pleading in her eyes. "Will the SCHR register her, Mom?"

The SCHR was the Spotted Cattle Horse Registry. Spotted Cattle Horses were stock horses like Cattle horses and they came from the same background. The SCHR would sometimes register Cattle Horses with spotted markings, but the ACHR wouldn't register spotted horses.

"I think so," I said. "It depends on the amount and the location of the markings. I guess I can call the SCHR and ask."

I was still numb with disappointment. As soon as Belle was up and the foal was nursing, I went to the house with Jared, leaving Whitney and Adam at the barn. Crop-out or not, I could see the little filly already had Whitney's unconditional love. And it least it was healthy. A lethal white foal would have inherited a genetic defect that would kill it in a few days.

Jared looked around curiously. "Nice home."

"Thanks." I didn't add that the house was part of my divorce settlement...with steel cables attached.

I took a quick shower and put on clean clothes, while Jared waited in the kitchen with Heidi feeding her snacks from a box of dog treats. The dog had barked again when we came in, but now, thanks to the attention and the treats, she was well on the way to recognizing him as a friend.

"I still don't understand what happened with the foal," Jared said when I returned. "How does a solid colored horse like your mare give birth to a spotted baby?"

"It's a crop-out." I turned to reach for the coffeepot—I used real coffee instead of instant when I had company—and noticed my clue notebook lying on top of a pile of newspapers on the table. Hopefully Jared hadn't looked inside and seen I was lying when I said I didn't believe Rita had been murdered. I didn't think he had. I hadn't been out of the room for more than ten minutes and he seemed to have spent those minutes paying attention to Heidi.

"Crop-out?" he asked, giving Heidi a final pat and putting aside the dog treats. He'd made a friend. Heidi curled up on top of his feet.

"I know it sounds like some skin disease you get from wandering around in a swamp. I assure you it isn't. Belle and the foal's sire are both solid colored Cattle Horses, not counting socks and blazes. But back in their ancestry somewhere there were horses with genes for white body markings. Now those genes have shown themselves, or cropped out. The filly's a kind of throwback." I sighed deeply and filled the pot with water. And we'd had such high hopes for a Cattle Horse Champion.

"I can see you're disappointed, but I'm not sure why," Jared said.

"Whitney and I show in open shows, which means any breed can enter. But we also show in Cattle Horse shows."

"Now you can only show the filly in open." It was a statement, not a question.

I nodded. "We could show the filly in the Spotted Horse shows if it has enough white to get it registered. But with the sire it has, it would most likely be worth more as a Cattle Horse. Anyway, I don't know the Spotted Horse people that well and it would be like starting over."

The back door slammed and Whitney tromped into the kitchen with Adam.

"Coffee?" I frowned in Adam's direction, holding the scoop, ready to add another serving or two if he didn't get the hint.

"No, thanks. Whitney's offered me cookies and milk." Wearing a goofy grin, he joined my daughter at the kitchen table where she was opening a package of mint chocolate cookies.

Jared stood. "Never mind about the coffee, Leigh. Let's call it a night."

My cheeks flamed. This was all wrong. At this point Adam was supposed to politely excuse himself and leave, and Whitney was supposed to take herself off to bed. Then Jared and I were supposed to spend a few hours talking together in my semi-dark living room.

"You don't have to go." I shot Whitney and Adam the kind of look they'd earned.

"It's late and you're busy. I'll call you." Jared nodded in the direction of the table. "Nice meeting you."

I turned off the Mr. Coffee and walked him out. I expected another kiss on the cheek, but didn't get one. "I'd like to apologize for Whitney's behavior."

"No problem. She doesn't hold a candle to my bratty sisters."

I watched him drive away, then detoured to the barn. The filly was still a crop-out.

I trudged back to the house and made a point of avoiding the kitchen. I settled myself in front of the TV and stared at the screen, watching a chef in a yellow apron prepare blackened grouper.

After twenty minutes or so, I heard the back door open and close. I got up to join Whitney at the refrigerator where she was putting away the milk.

"Whitney—"

"The filly's great. I love her, Mom. She's everything we'd hoped for, except for her color." Whitney's eyes shone and she squeezed my arm. If I'd entertained stray thoughts about selling the mis-marked filly, they were gone now.

"Your diversionary tactics show real promise. But let's talk about your behavior tonight. Jared was my guest."

"Sorry I was rude to Jared." She didn't look any more sorry than she sounded, but I figured that was about as much of an apology as I could hope for.

"I think it's about time you went to bed."

"Goodnight, Mom." She angled her head in the general direction of Heidi who was snoozing under the table. "Come on, pup."

At least she hadn't called Jared J Man or Geek Boy. Quick footsteps marched down the hall and then her door slammed.

Then I was alone in the kitchen trying, but failing, to sort out my thoughts.

I trotted out to the barn first thing in the morning. The more I saw of the crop-out filly, the less I worried over her markings. As Whitney had said last night, she was everything we'd wished for; the best Belle had ever produced.

Her mane and tail were flaxen, the color of corn silk. It was hard to tell with a foal, but the filly's mature coat would almost surely be a bright cherry color—very flashy when set off with the white markings. Still, it was her conformation that really counted. As Rita would have said, you can't ride the color or the pedigree.

With this filly, we wouldn't need to rely on flash to catch a judge's eye. Our foal had an exquisite baby doll head with doe eyes. Her neck was long and slim, promising a soft ride and good balance, and she was blessed with well-defined muscles already showing in her broad shoulders and hindquarters. Straight legs and perfectly shaped feet completed the picture.

"I guess I can become a Spotted Horse person with a filly like this," I said out loud. I finished at the barn and went back to the house to do a little work. By the time Whitney hauled herself out of bed, I was on my way out the door. "Whitney, I know you'll want to spend time with the new baby. I'll be back later."

Whitney rubbed her eyes. "Where are you going now? To see your new boyfriend?"

"Jared is *not* my boyfriend. I don't owe you any explanations, but I happen to be going over to the Harper's farm." I whisked past her and out the door before she could open her smart mouth again. Then I tromped on the gas pedal, almost flooding the Honda when I tried to start it.

Brenda escorted me from my car to the barn as if I were a visiting princess. Two of her Australian Shepherds, a tri color and a blue merle, danced beside us wearing wide grins. One of her boys roared past, and I had to flatten myself against an oak tree to keep from being run down.

The Harpers had three boys who ran nonstop. Brenda was heartbroken that none of them cared for horses, but that was probably a blessing. As energetic as her sons were, they'd most likely have Brenda ripping her hair out in frustration as they burned out one mount after another without ever coming near a high point trophy.

"Todd!" Brenda screeched as another boy, this one with red hair like hers, careened around the corner of the barn. "How many times have I told you not to run near the horses? Get your butt up to the house and get your room clean, and I mean *now*!"

I couldn't help grinning. "Bet you're glad spring break is over."

"Tell me about it. How did you manage to have a horse loving daughter?"

"I've been blessed."

"I'll say. I gave up after three tries."

I dodged another boy and followed Brenda down a long aisle with stalls on each side. The barn was immaculate, and smelled of alfalfa and sweet feed. The center section had a computer-equipped office on the left and a wash rack on the right. There were more stalls past the center hub.

Even though Brenda mostly rubbed me the wrong way, I had to admit she had a nice operation and she knew how to turn a profit with her horses.

Oakdale Prime was housed in the last stall on the left. His stall was twice the size of the others, with an extra door at the back so Prime could have his own exercise paddock. Brenda snapped a lead onto his halter and led him out for my inspection.

I hooked my thumbs in the waistband of my jeans, narrowing my eyes to study the horse's conformation. The dun stallion had a lovely head, but overall he lacked substance. He didn't look any better close up than he had at the show where I'd first seen him losing a halter class. I was sure Brenda was as aware of his faults as I was. Still, she'd gotten him at a bargain price and she'd get enough breedings to earn back her money.

When people saw he wasn't producing and quit booking their mares to him, she'd truck the stud to an out of state auction where there would be a buyer to take a chance on his pedigree. I couldn't do it, but then I didn't make a profit on my horses.

"He's tall," I said, not commenting on his too narrow frame and his long back.

"His oldest foals are two-year-olds. The Tremaines say they've been a little late to mature, but they're coming along."

Code that meant they weren't big and they probably hadn't filled out much. None of them had won at halter. And they wouldn't unless Brenda found a way to bribe a judge.

"How do they ride?"

"Too soon to tell, but you'll probably see at least one of them at the futurity."

Code for they didn't ride either or she'd be telling me exactly how many of his get were entered in the November futurity.

"He's certainly a well-bred animal. Are you using him on all your mares this season?" If a stud owner wouldn't breed her own mares to her stud, how good could he be?

Brenda turned the stallion around, hiding her expression behind his neck. She put him back in his stall. "Just Apple Trudy and Lou's Sudden Dark. My other ladies wouldn't cross well with his line. Anyway, I've already booked Dawn Lady to the Shellenberger's new champion stud."

I nodded in understanding. Apple Trudy and Sudden Dark were big, coarse mares. Sudden Dark had a rear end about as broad as my Honda. There was an outside chance mares of that type would balance the stud's weediness with their bulk, leading to a well-conformed animal, better than either parent. Dawn Lady, on the other hand, was far too fine a mare for Prime.

Mention of Dawn Lady gave me the conversational opening I'd been hoping for. "Speaking of Dawn Lady, where is she?"

We'd passed every stall in the barn. Some were empty. Some held show horses. A few housed mares with new foals, including the previously mentioned Sudden Dark—a near black mare—with her newest baby. The foal was liver chestnut and looked about as wide as it was tall. Its tanklike build insured a few quick wins at halter in foal futurities and a speedy sale to newcomers with fat wallets. The newbies wouldn't realize that foals of this type coarsened up fast and rarely won at halter after the age of ten months or so. The baby would mature into an even bigger tank, probably with a lumbering, rhinoceros-type gait. Rhinos don't win riding classes, either.

Brenda opened a stall door and led out a bright gold palomino yearling with a blazed face. "Have you seen our new colt?"

"Yeah, at last month's show, remember? Gorgeous color." I made a point of turning in a complete circle and peering from side to side in an exaggerated search. "Has something happened to Dawn Lady?"

"Of course not. What would happen?" Brenda snapped. "She's in the back pasture with the rest of the mares that haven't foaled yet."

"That reminds me," I said, deciding not to press her. "Belle foaled last night."

"What did you get?" Brenda put the palomino back in his stall, yanking her arm out of the way when he attempted a playful nip.

"A stunning sorrel filly with a flaxen mane and tail."

"Congratulations. Going to challenge us at the futurity, then?"

"I wish. She's got excessive white markings. A crop-out."

Brenda stared at me guppy-eyed. Her mouth dropped open and she made a strangling sound. "Tough luck," she said finally.

I stretched, then consulted my watch. "Not really. I'll show her as a Spotted Horse."

"Can you get her papered in the SCHR?" Brenda sounded doubtful.

"I think so. She's got white patches on her stomach and along both flanks, and has Spotted characteristics to spare. Lots of chrome. Brenda, I'll let you know about Prime."

"Let me know when I can have Sonny Joe, too. I need to start getting him ready for western pleasure at the June show."

I spun around and headed for my car. Just when we were almost getting along, Brenda had to spoil things. My trip had been wasted. I didn't know a thing more about Dawn Lady and as far as seeing the stud...

Wait a minute, I thought. *When I told Brenda about Belle's crop-out, she missed a golden opportunity to tell me her stud doesn't throw crop-outs. It's not like Brenda to pass up a sales pitch.*

Something was bothering her. I pondered this development all the way home. There was only one thing for me to do and by the time I pulled into my driveway, I had my plan worked out.

CHAPTER 20

I eased the Honda past a line of cars; my driveway looked like the Publix parking lot on a Friday evening.

While I was at the Harpers, Whitney must have called everyone we knew. After about a thousand people had gone crazy over Belle's new baby, I thought we were finished, but I was not that lucky. Kenneth and Doreen arrived just as Whitney's homeroom teacher left.

They'd brought Kendra's two boys with them. Doreen must have wanted an opportunity to show Kenneth how well she could deal with small boys so he'd agree she could have a baby right away. But I'd spent time with the boys myself and I knew they could be a handful.

"I hope you don't mind us bringing Taylor and Ford to see the foal," Doreen said. Her brow furrowed into a line of concern as she smoothed down the front of her long skirt. She was wearing a diamond bracelet and matching earrings that I'd never seen on her before. If they were real—and I suspected they were—they'd have cost what I earned in half a year.

"Not at all. Whitney loves showing off her horses to her

cousins." Whitney had offered in the past to have them come over and ride, but her Aunt Kendra was allergic to the thought of horses and wouldn't allow it. "Aren't you afraid they'll get trampled or eaten, though?"

"Huh?" Her pretty brow furrowed ever so slightly.

"Never mind."

Doreen, looking confused, took the boys to the barn, herding them ahead of her to keep them from bolting. I waited for Kenneth. He'd want to remind me about selling Sonny Joe, so I decided to get the lecture over with.

"I see *that horse* is still here." He jerked his chin in the direction of the pasture where Lena and Sonny Joe stood contentedly under an oak, head to tail so they could help each other with fly swatting. "I'm tired of waiting for my money."

"Don't waste any words greeting me or anything like that, Kenneth. I said I wasn't selling, remember?" My hands curled into fists that I hid behind my back.

"There's no point putting off the inevitable. Besides, Doreen's already signed Whitney up for ballet and tap, so she won't have time to ride."

"Why don't you leave me alone?" I'd been angry with Adam, had broken up with him, after our fight over me taking money from Kenneth. But the truth was, Kenneth's half ownership of my home gave him a lot of leverage. And Adam had been right all along about me buying a horse with Kenneth's money. It had been a huge mistake.

"Listen, Leigh—" Kenneth broke off as Sammi and Jeeves exited Sammi's Buick.

Sammi dug in her heels to stop Jeeves from dragging her toward the road, and waved a hand in greeting. She'd known at once that Kenneth and I were fighting.

"Hi, Leigh. Kenneth."

He grunted something that could have been a greeting.

"Have you seen the foal yet? Whitney says it's a beauty."

As though Kenneth were merely an old friend instead of her cousin's ex-husband who ranked just below parasites in her estimation, Sammi took his arm and led him to the barn. His face, I noted with satisfaction, was the color of a smashed beet. His mouth was set in a firm line and I doubted he was listening to Sammi's congratulations to him and Doreen on their impending marriage.

Kenneth hugged Whitney and grunted something that could have been, "Hi, princess," then gave the filly the briefest of glances. His obligations to his daughter taken care of, he signaled Doreen to round up the boys.

Taylor was occupied with poking a stick at a fly-coated manure pile, but Ford had gone into the feed room where he'd spilled feed in a long trail from the wall to the door. He'd also gotten into the jar of peanut butter I kept on the shelf, leaving the lid off and ending up with a line of peanut butter around his mouth. Good thing I was out of cat dewormer or he'd have the cleanest colon in town.

We had a padlock for the door, but I didn't bother to lock it. I usually left the padlock open and the key hanging on a nail by the door, since I never worried about feed thieves. However, I'd have to change my ways if overly curious kids like my ex-nephew were going to visit.

I had to go after Ford when he didn't respond to my polite requests to come out of the room and wash up at the spigot. While I was running him down, I nearly stepped on a giant roach that scooted across the floor and dove under an empty feed sack. I shuddered, barely managing to hold back a cowardly scream.

Roaches terrified me. Ever since a roach crawled into bed with me and tangled itself in my hair when I was a small child, I'd gone hysterical at the sight of them. I watched until I was sure the buffed-up roach was not coming back to attack me, then I ran Ford down and tucked him under my arm. He smelled like a mix of molasses and peanut butter, and his tee shirt was as sticky as his hands. I skipped the trip to the spigot and hauled him out to Kenneth, who made a face when he took him from me.

"Kenneth certainly seemed angry about something," Sammi said after the SUV had crunched back down the driveway. Jeeves tried to take off after the car and she wrapped the end of his leash around her hand. "Did you find out anything about the Harpers?"

I glanced into the barn to make sure Whitney was out of earshot. The biggest calico cat must have realized the coast was clear now that Ford was gone and she jumped out of the loft, pushed off on the top a stall door, then landed nimbly at my feet. I busied myself picking her up and stroking her fur. "Only that Brenda is being awfully evasive about her best mare." I explained about Dawn Lady.

"I think you're right, it could be a big clue." Sammi raised an eyebrow. "Better to let the police handle it, babe."

"I am," I said. "But you know I've spoken with Detective Frazier and so far he hasn't called me back with anything new. That's why I need a favor."

"What favor? You're making dangerous plans again aren't you?" Her eyes narrowed and I was sure she thought I was planning something like a stroll down the inside lane of I-75 at midnight.

"Of course not. Who deliberately makes plans to walk into danger?"

"You for one."

"Don't be silly. There's no danger involved. I need for you to stay with Whitney tonight while I check out the Harper's back pasture. That's all."

Sammi shook her head. She finally agreed, with what I was sure was the greatest reluctance. She arranged to show up at ten after Whitney went to sleep. And she promised to send out a search party if I didn't return in a few hours.

The Harper's back pasture—the one where she'd turned out Dawn Lady and the other mares in foal—was a forty-acre tract. It was set back from the highway and there were only two ways to get to it. The first way meant trekking directly through the Harper's yard past Scott and Brenda's bedroom window. They kept all four of their Australian Shepherds in the house at night, and the dogs had hearing like bats. The other route was only slightly more appealing. It involved an approach across the adjoining property, which was owned by a man who lived in Michigan most of the year. The land was a combination of pasture gone to weed, palmettos, and scrub pines sprouting wherever they could steal a bare spot of ground. The house was sizable, but badly in need of a makeover. The place had been for sale for about five years. No one had been interested as far as I knew.

Someone had dredged a small pond somewhere on the property, hauling off the dirt for fill. This meant alligators for sure, and probably water moccasins in the murky water. I shuddered.

I'd thought about these obstacles all afternoon. I was thinking about them now as I eased out of the Honda. The man from Michigan had left for his home state at the first sign of hot weather, so there was no one there to catch me skulking around. I pulled up the hood of my lightweight black jacket and took a plastic bucket out of the back seat. The bucket held about a quart of sweet feed.

From somewhere not too far off, an alligator grunted. I pulled a flashlight out of my jacket pocket and switched it on. I slid under the bottom strand of barbed wire on the pasture fence with my bucket in one hand and my flashlight in the other.

The moon was no more than a silvery blob behind a cloud. Fine for sneaking around, but not so fine for seeing what I was doing. I'd taped part of my flashlight the way they do on TV spy shows, and it was all I could do to make out vague shapes that might have been anything in the thin beam of light.

I was already sweating in the humid night air and wished I could take off the jacket, but it was part of my night disguise. I gritted my teeth and felt my way through the palmettos inch by inch, praying I wouldn't stumble over a root and cut myself on the sharp edges of the branches. Scratch marks on my arms could be hard to explain to my friends and family. So would a million mosquito bites, but so far the Off I'd drenched myself with seemed to be working, though it made me even hotter and stickier than I already was and produced a halo of scented air around me.

I pushed on, worrying that it was taking forever to get to the woven wire fence that separated this field from the Harper's pasture. The pond was around here somewhere, though I couldn't see it yet, and the last thing I needed was to race headlong over the banks in the dark. The alligators wouldn't mind, but I didn't intend to end up as 'gator chow.

The pond, with dredged up marl forming its banks, finally loomed as a lighter patch in the darkness. I saw it in time to keep from stepping over the edge, but I was still closer to the water than I'd ever planned to be. I waved the thin beam of my light across the surface, half expecting to see dozens of alligator eyes shining up like green marbles. There were only six eyes, so that meant three gators. Small comfort. I slowly backed away from the edge and began to skirt the pond.

I edged off to the left, toward the Harper's pasture, keeping every sense on alert. A long, dark shape on the ground nearly gave me a heart attack until I realized it was the trunk of a fallen pine tree and not the form of an alligator.

I took another step and was brought up short by a sound, a rustle in the tall grass between the fence line and the palmetto patch. I waited, straining to hear the rustle again. When it came, I pointed my feeble light in that direction, going weak with relief when I picked out the form of a fat possum waddling out of the underbrush. The light beam shot silver off its stiff, gray fur. The startled possum briefly aimed its snipey nose in my direction, then waddled away at double speed.

I started breathing again. Going by the weakness in my knees, I was definitely not cut out for undercover work.

The woven wire was invisible, but I saw the lighter colored fence posts in time to stop. As I'd hoped, Brenda and Scott's mares were close enough so I wouldn't have to get into the pasture with them if I could coax them to the fence.

"Over here, ladies." I shook my bucket gently, rattling the sweet feed in the bottom.

There wasn't a horse alive that didn't recognize the sound of feed rattling in a bucket and respond as though it hadn't eaten in a month. The nearest horse, an old bay mare I recognized as Brenda's first champion, swung her head up from the thick pangola grass. She pricked her ears in my direction and nickered softly.

"Quiet now. Come see what I've got for you, Mrs. T-Bird." My voice was meant to soothe, and the bay mare went for the bait.

Mrs. T-Bird leading the way, the horses marched single file in my direction. There were four mares, all of them with huge bellies impeding their progress. I panned the flashlight over their swollen bodies and frowned. Two more bays and a dappled palomino with a too-narrow front end. Where was Dawn Lady, a blaze-faced sorrel with four white socks?

I shook the bucket again, stepping away from the fence where the mares crowded against the wire stretching their necks out for a taste of the molasses coated grain. Another shape moved out from in front of a stand of pine trees and I made out the profile.

Dawn Lady. I'd recognize that elegant head anywhere. She nosed something on the ground, and a foal beside her in the grass pulled itself to its feet.

I caught my breath. So she'd already foaled, just as I'd suspected. The baby had to be at least a month old. When it reached the fence with its dam, I could see where the fuzzy foal hair around its eyes was already shedding. That didn't happen on day one. Brenda had lied about the foal's age, but why?

Taking a chance, I pulled the tape off the flashlight to give myself better light. The foal, a huge colt, was another magnificent baby out of Dawn Lady. It was colored sorrel like its mother, including the blaze face and high socks. I couldn't imagine any reason for the Harpers to hide a foal like this. Normally, full color photos of their best new babies were plastered across the fold-out page of the early spring issue of *The Equine Tale*.

The mares were milling around now, hoping for a bite of the feed. I knew I didn't have much time before the Harper's ever alert Australian Shepherds heard the commotion and sounded the alarm. I ran the flashlight beam back and forth over the well-built colt, trying to puzzle out why he'd been kept hidden.

It was luck more than anything else that made the colt drop to the ground and roll just as the beam went across his middle. The patch of white hair on his stomach was at least an inch and a half in diameter.

I swallowed hard; another crop-out. So Belle wasn't the only one producing spots this year. I'd seen something else, too. Now I knew why Rita had planned to report the Harpers to the ACHR. There was a hairless patch in front of the white spot. I knelt and shined the light on the colt's stomach to be sure. There was no mistaking the inflamed look of that hairless patch. It was a fresh wound, and it had to be causing the colt some discomfort. The white spot had originally been larger than an inch and a half across, but someone had deliberately burned the rest of the white area to leave a hairless scar.

I'd heard of people doing this kind of thing, yet I'd never quite believed anyone would actually try it. The colt, unlike Belle's filly, didn't have enough white or enough Spotted Horse characteristics to be papered with the SCHR, thereby reducing his value at least tenfold. The Harpers must have figured they could burn the white spot, leaving only a scar, and then register the colt as a Cattle Horse. The ACHR wouldn't suspect the scar was anything but an injury. Of course, an injury wouldn't prevent registration. It was obvious the Harpers were still in the process of burning the white off Dawn Lady's foal. It must have been too big a job to do all at once, so they were waiting for the first burn to finish healing before they took off the rest of the white, and then they'd present the foal as though it were newborn.

That wouldn't fool any of us in the horse club, but it was unlikely we'd guess the reason for the deception. Even if anyone suspected, there'd be no proof. We'd just think that Brenda wanted to brag about the foal's size, or that it had been injured or sick and she'd waited for it to recover. But somehow Rita had discovered the truth.

I slipped back across the pasture without letting the mares have the feed in my bucket. They'd fight over it and get hurt. I imagined they'd stand at the fence in disappointment for another ten minutes or so and then drift back under the trees, forgetting the whole episode.

Thankfully the dogs hadn't started a ruckus. I played it safe and re-taped the flashlight, but now I knew my way. It only took half as long to return to my car as it had taken to cross the field to the Harper's fence. I didn't encounter the possum or any other wildlife, except for an oversized frog, and I made a wide detour around the pond.

I was thankful to finally crawl back into my car. It wasn't cold out, but it was damp and the ever-present mosquitoes buzzed me in clouds. Out here, the car was the next best thing to home.

What next? Now I finally knew what Rita knew, yet surely that hadn't been enough to get her killed, at least not by the Harpers. But what if it was an accident? A scene formed in front of my eyes. My subconscious took over the driving as I watched act one roll across my mental screen. Brenda and Scott found out Rita knew about their foal. Maybe she'd foolishly called and told them she was reporting them. They came over to see her and possibly offer her a bribe to keep her mouth shut. They got into an argument when she refused. Scott, or maybe Brenda, had shoved Rita in anger and she'd hit her head. Or one of them had bashed her skull, maybe in self-defense.

I reached my driveway and turned in, letting the car roll to a stop in front of the door. I sat behind the wheel and stared into the blackness. No, the Harpers wouldn't have let Tinker get loose. They'd have known that Rita wouldn't put her show bridle on the horse to work her at home.

Not if they'd done it that way deliberately. Suppose they'd decided to make the killing look like an accident committed by someone who didn't know horses. Then they changed their mind and went for a loft accident. They—one or both of them—could have killed Rita.

I shook my head. Too fantastic and yet...the Harpers stood to lose big if Rita reported them and they were kicked out of the ACHR. After what seemed like hours, I trudged inside, gave Sammi a condensed version of my discovery, then showered before I fell into bed.

Chapter 21

Duty called. Groaning at the injustice of having to take Whitney and Brad to school when all I wanted to do was sleep, I crawled out from under the covers.

While I put together a breakfast of cereal and fruit, I tried to decide if the Harpers had been the killers. And when I wasn't trying to puzzle out the facts of Rita's murder, I was agonizing over how I could find the money to buy Kenneth's share of my home.

The phone rang before I finished eating. Angie's voice greeted me with a hello that seemed way too cheery, given my mood.

"Hi," I croaked in response. "Need help with the horses?"

"Thanks so much for all you've done, but we can manage." She sounded happier than at any time since I'd met her.

"Glad to help in any way I can."

"Sure," she said easily. "I wanted to ask you to stop by any time. I thought you could give us some advice about selling the horses."

"I'll come this morning, if that's okay." There was that notebook I'd wanted to peek at on Saturday, and I wanted to see

Tinker's stall again. Last week I'd been sure the stall had been latched when I put her back in. But now I was starting to doubt my own memory. Since I was fresh out of detecting ideas, a look at the crime scene was the best chance of jumpstarting my thoughts.

I rang off after Angie assured me they'd look forward to my visit. I dressed carefully, putting on my gray slacks, a loose gray blazer with wide pockets, and a red blouse that Sammi had given me for my birthday.

"You look nice, Mom," Whitney said.

"Thanks," I said absently, picking up my keys.

"I thought you were off work until Monday."

"I am. I'm visiting the Lorings, but that doesn't mean I have to wear my barn clothes."

"Are you going out with that guy again? I don't like him."

"Cut it out. Jared is very nice, though it happens we're not dating and I'm not going to see him. Not that it's any of your business."

Stan was at the stables when I pulled up. It looked like Angie had put him in charge of manure clearing. I took a quick look at Tinker's stall and rattled the latch. It was solid, the clip I'd applied still holding, and, as far as I knew, Tinker hadn't escaped on her own again. Had I imagined it being latched that day or was the stall open? My thoughts spun in useless loops.

Stan strode out of the tack room. "Glad you're here. I'm ready for a break."

"Need some help?"

"Thanks, but I'm done."

We headed to the house together. Stan inclined his head toward the garage apartment. "Angie tells me it was a big mistake letting Doug move out here to guard the house."

"That's Doug for you."

"He spends way too much time talking about absolutely nothing. And I'm not getting that much work out of him."

"Sorry," I said, shaking my head. "Rita always got her money's worth, but they fought a lot. If you threaten to cut his pay, he'll likely shape up."

"Probably, but I told him he has to get out by Wednesday."

"What are you going to do about someone to take care of the horses?"

"Nothing for now. Angie wants to sell them before we go back, probably to the Harpers. They've made what I suspect is a very low offer, but neither of us wants to stick around and do a lot of barn work while we wait for a better price. I'm turning into a regular ranchhand." He looked more like an overfed bank president than someone who engaged in manual labor, but I could understand him wanting to get back home to Pennsylvania.

I experienced a twinge of annoyance. If they'd already decided to sell to the Harpers, why had Angie asked me here to advise her?

We reached the back door and Stan motioned me into the kitchen. "Coffee?"

"Yes, thanks."

"There's a fresh pot on the stove, so help yourself. Would you mind if I took a few minutes to get cleaned up? Angie will be out in a minute."

"No problem." I reached for a cup from the drainboard. I stared out the window over the sink to watch a mockingbird and a crow engaging in bitter combat while I poured the coffee. I should have paid attention to my cup. Would have, if I weren't deliberately staging an accident. I overpoured, spilling coffee down the counter and onto the floor, barely missing my feet.

"Klutz," I said out loud in case anyone was listening. I pulled drawers open at random, finding silverware, kitchen bags, assorted nuts and bolts, and finally the dishcloths when I remembered which drawer they were in.

Rita's little notebook poked out from under a stack of neatly folded cloths, apparently undisturbed since I'd seen it last, the day after she was killed. I pulled the notebook out of the drawer and couldn't resist flipping through to see if Rita had written what she knew about the Harpers.

I couldn't tell from a quick look. There were notes in Rita's large handwriting about plans and events. Nearly all the pages were full and from what little I read, I could see Rita had made the book into a calendar with snippets of chores to be done randomly interspersed with comments about the weather, people she knew, and upcoming horse shows.

Down the hall, a door opened and closed. Stan and Angie would return any minute. I jammed the notebook into one of the oversized pockets of my blazer. After all, if Rita had been murdered the way I suspected, they'd want her killer brought to justice...except if they were the culprits. But hey, I was working for Rita, not the Lorings.

By the time they got to the kitchen, I'd wiped up the spilled coffee and settled at the kitchen table. I hadn't had time to add sugar and milk to my cup, and the black coffee tasted pretty gruesome.

Angie padded in barefoot. She was wearing jeans and a white tee shirt, and was still toweling her hair dry. She glanced at my cup. "Ready for a refill?"

"No, I'm fine." I turned away quickly. Good thing she hadn't noticed my bulging jacket pocket. I'd found out last night that I wasn't cut out to be a spy, and now I knew I wasn't meant to be a thief either.

Angie sat across from me. Her hair was nearly dry, but it was tousled, and she looked young and vulnerable. All at once I felt silly for having thought she might be a killer. But if she hadn't killed Rita, who had? I still figured Stan was capable of murder if he thought it would net him the money he needed to upgrade his lifestyle.

Stan came in and sat next to his wife. He grinned at me. "Is everything okay? You look tired."

"Stan." Angie slapped his hand. "Haven't I told you before it's not nice to comment negatively about a lady's looks."

"It's okay." I waved at her. "I *am* tired. But how are you doing?"

"Much better. I still miss Aunt Rita." She launched into an account of her plans for the horses—sell them to the Harpers. Rita's place—keep it for now. And their antique store—expand it.

Life was good for the Lorings, at Rita's expense. My mood shifted closer to depression as I listened and sipped my coffee. I didn't want Brenda Harper to buy Tinker from Angie. After all, she was Belle's foal. And I knew Rita wouldn't have wanted them to have her other horses, but Angie didn't seem to care.

The notebook weighed heavy in my pocket. I wondered if I could put it back or leave it somewhere in the house. I'd been foolish to think it contained a clue and foolish to decide I was justified in taking what didn't belong to me.

Before I could decide on a course of action, I saw Doug Reilly approaching the back door. He peered at us through the screen, his eyes shifting from side to side, his mouth twisting into an insolent grin.

I put my cup down and stood.

"Come in, Doug." Stan didn't look one tenth as friendly as he sounded.

Doug let the screen door bang shut behind him. "As long as I'll be here till Wednesday, I reckon I could work on that pasture fence. It'll cost you, though. Rita always paid extra for fence work."

Stan turned toward Doug. "We've hired a couple of men to finish the fence, so you won't be needed."

"Wouldn't hurt to have me show them what to do. I know this property pretty good. And, like I said yesterday, I can guard the place for you." Doug's confident expression was gone and now he reminded me of a weasel. He glanced hopefully at the coffeepot still on the stove, the end of his nose twitching.

"Thanks for the coffee." I picked up my purse. "I need to get going."

"You don't have to leave." Angie frowned. "Doug was on his way out."

"I have a ton of laundry waiting for me to work my magic. I hope the two of you will stop by my place before you leave."

"We'd like that. Call us, okay?" Angie gave me a quick hug.

"Of course." I included both of them in my good-bye wave.

Other than the conversation, the visit had been a wasted trip, except that I borrowed Rita's notebook. Stole Rita's notebook. I'd figure out a way to return it, after I made sure it didn't contain any clues.

Doug, his hopes for coffee and further employment dashed, clomped out of the kitchen behind me. When I yanked open my car door, my red clue notebook fell off the seat and smacked the ground at my feet. Doug smirked, watching as I tossed the notebook back into the car.

"Reckon the Harpers could use some help at their place?" he called before I could climb into the Honda.

"As it happens, Doug, I was out there yesterday. Looks like Brenda has more work than she can handle getting ready for the peak of the show season, and the mares are still foaling. And you know she has those boys to take care of."

He cocked an eyebrow. "She's that busy? I'll stop by and see her."

"You do that, Doug. You can even tell her I sent you." I smiled wickedly.

I sat down in my family room with Rita's notebook. Nothing about the Harpers other than that she was going to report them. Nothing about threats to her life. Not a clue I could take to the police. I shoved it back in my purse. Dumb idea, taking it.

I still needed to verify Maggie's alibi and check that the Harpers were actually home the morning Rita was killed. I wasn't sure how I'd go about checking on Maggie. But the Harpers had casually mentioned at the funeral that they'd been having their horses' hooves trimmed that day. I had to call the farrier anyway. I was having a special shoe put on Lena's hoof to take some of the strain off her injured leg.

My regular farrier had recently retired, and I still hadn't found anyone I liked as well. I dialed the Harper's farrier, John Allemann, and quickly outlined my situation.

"Brenda Harper recommended you," I said after introducing myself. Brenda certainly ought to know a good farrier.

"Yep, done her horses for about a year now...go out there every month. In fact I was there last week."

"That's right. Brenda said you were there Friday morning, a week ago." I reached for an apple from the bowl on the kitchen table. "The morning Rita Cameron died."

"I sure was."

"So Brenda was helping you with the horses that morning?" Brenda had said John was a gossipy sort. I didn't expect him to see anything strange about me asking so many questions.

"Brenda has so many horses I always show up about six in the morning. It takes me four or five hours to get through. So, like I said, there we were and all the time Rita was falling out of her loft."

"Both Brenda and Scott were there the whole time?" I tried to make it sound as though I were only mildly interested. John couldn't know that he might be their alibi.

"I think so. Usually Brenda holds the horses and Scott brings up the ones I need. So one or the other of them were around."

Sounded like a solid alibi to me. With a sigh, I said, "John, I have to go. Is Friday afternoon at 3:00 okay?"

"Sure. Thanks for giving me a chance with your horses."

Belatedly I played back my phone message. Kenneth wanted me to call him. Gee, surprise. I changed into work clothes and wandered out to the barn. I'd turned Belle and her new filly into the paddock connecting to their stall. They were standing together against the barn, and I made sure to give Belle a double helping of hay. I still had plenty of good hay up in the loft, but we were low on feed so I made a mental note to run by the feed store.

Sonny was standing quietly by the pasture gate, in the shade of an oak, but Lena was restless. She'd put her head down for a moment as if to graze, then after a mouthful or two, she'd swish her tail and trot up to Sonny before going back to her grazing. I recognized the signs. She was in season.

Whitney and I had made plans to breed Lena to a stud in Fort Myers that looked like he'd be a good cross with Lena. His foals were known for their calm temperaments. He was nineteen—fairly old for a stud—but he was new to the area and had a solid record for producing winning pleasure horses out west. Today was bad timing, but it wouldn't do to wait until too late in the year. The gestation period for horses is about eleven months. In South Florida, it's best to breed them early in the year so they foal during the mild winters instead of during the summer heat, rain, and insect season.

I called the Wallers, the stud's owners. They already had a stall ready for Lena, and I promised to bring her in the afternoon. Then I steeled myself and called Kenneth at his office.

"It's me," I said curtly when he came to the phone. "Returning your call."

"You can drop the attitude, this isn't about selling our house. Doreen wants to take Whitney to a ballet class tomorrow night. She can pick her up after school, Whitney can spend the night, and I'll get her to school the next morning."

I figured the likelihood of Whitney taking to ballet was about on a par with that of her deciding to run away to the South Pole. She was a tomboy and she'd already expressed her opinion of Kenneth's plan to replace horses and me with Doreen and dance. But if she wanted to go, I had no objections. "I guess your plan is fine if you can take Brad to school, too." I explained, and Kenneth reluctantly agreed.

I left a note for Whitney and headed out to hitch up the trailer. Lena was notoriously bad to load. At a show last year, three burly trainers had to lend their services to get her into the trailer after her last class.

Today was different. Maybe Lena sensed my dark thoughts and knew better than to defy me. Or maybe she was in the mood for romance and knew where I was taking her. She hesitated briefly at the sight of the trailer, lowering her head and snorting. I clicked to her and she broke into a fast walk, then leaped nimbly inside and buried her nose in the hay I'd already put in the feeder up front. I quickly shut and latched the door before she changed her mind.

As we rumbled down the driveway, Sonny loped along the fence line as far as he could, then stood in a corner neighing in anguish. I wished I could tell him Lena wasn't going to be gone forever, but I kind of understood exactly how he felt over losing his best friend.

The Wallers were a lovely, older couple with a few good horses. They had a trainer to do all the heavy work and the showing, while they sat back and enjoyed watching their horses win. They'd had to go out, so Seth Hames, their trainer, silently took delivery of Lena. He marched her into the nearest clean stall, unsnapped her lead and handed it to me.

Seth, who bore a strong resemblance to a grizzly in work shirt and jeans, was a man of few words. Other than commenting about my mare being lame, which I knew, all he said was, "Call you when she's ready. Ma'am."

"Tell Mrs. Waller I'll phone her." I assumed the grunt he sent my way was a yes.

Maybe if the Wallers had been home to invite me in for iced tea and horse talk, my mind would have stayed off the subject of Rita. Instead, when I passed the Harper's farm, thoughts of her death popped into my head. I looked across the road at my Great Aunt Dorothy's place. She was outside, working in her flower garden. On impulse, I hit the brakes and swung into her driveway. The empty trailer swayed and rattled in protest, but safely made the turn.

My aunt was wearing a faded housedress and a straw hat that might have once belonged to my grandmother. They were sisters, though Grandma was much older and had died about ten years ago. They'd lived here in the old wooden house that had been built by my great-grandparents. I often wondered how they'd managed to raise a family in the tiny four-room house.

When she saw me, Aunt Dorothy hauled her ample form to her feet and rubbed her lower back. She took off the hat to fan herself. "Hello there, stranger."

"I hope you don't mind me stopping in." A stab of guilt coursed through my middle. Lately it seemed I came by her place only to get oranges from the grove behind her house.

"Goodness no. Gives me an excuse to stop grubbing in the dirt." She washed her hands at the spigot, then wiped them dry on her dress, winking when she caught me watching. "I'll get us a drink and be right back." She motioned me onto the porch where I sat in a wooden rocker while she bustled inside. She brought out a pitcher of iced tea and two glasses that she placed on the table between our rockers. "Is this a social call? Must be, cause I'm sure you know I'm out of oranges this time of year."

"It's about Rita." I made a quick mental note to visit more often.

"That's right, it was you that found her, wasn't it? I've been on a church trip to Atlanta and missed her funeral. Guess I should have called you yesterday when I got back, though."

"That's okay. I was just wondering if you could tell me about Rita, anything you might know about her." I didn't expect Aunt Dorothy to have any clues, but I'd promised Rita I'd see justice done so she could rest in peace. I would not give up simply because I was a rotten detective.

She set her rocker into a gentle motion. "I knew Rita when she was a little girl. I was a friend of her grandparents. Growing up, Rita was prickly as a sandspur, but she never had it easy. Her parents died when she was only five."

I looked at her curiously. "I never knew that."

"She didn't talk much about those times. The thing is, the grandparents who raised her were as strict as they come. They meant well, but sometimes it seemed Rita couldn't do anything right. They were Bible quoting religious and they passed that on to Rita."

"I noticed." Rita had never tried to convert me, but she could barely get out a sentence that didn't have a Bible quote in it.

"Rita had a best friend growing up. Sue Ann was a lovely girl, but spoiled, a pampered little miss. She and Rita were tight as peas in a pod when they were together, and I always thought she'd be Rita's salvation from such a harsh life. Then Sue Ann moved north and got married before she was even out of high school, and I felt sorry for Rita. Once Sue Ann was gone, she seemed so solemn and lonely. After she got of school, Rita went up north for a while to visit with Sue Ann. Her whole life might have been different if her grandparents hadn't gotten sick and needed her at home, so she had to return. Took them a long time to die, though. Years. And they drained the life out of her."

Once again I was struck by how little I knew about Rita. We'd even shared a hotel room once when we attended an out of town show. Rita had brought along a box of magazines and her Bible. Spurning the Bible in the nightstand, she'd read her own, even marking the pages with a red pen. Whitney and I had settled for perusing the issues of *Horse Trainer Monthly* she'd brought along. Later Whitney had joked that Rita must have been writing the show results in her Bible.

Never once in all the years I'd known her had she mentioned her childhood or shared any kind of confidence. I wondered if it was hard for her to be raised so strictly while her friend was fussed over and privileged. It had to be; it had to have shaped her attitudes and turned her into the lonely person I'd discovered she was.

Aunt Dorothy plunked her empty glass down on the table. "I suppose this is gossip, but Rita's gone now, so it can't do any harm…long as you don't tell anyone." She leaned in closer. "There were some folks said Rita went up to Sue Ann's because she was pregnant and didn't want her grandparents to find out. They'd have disowned her the way they did Maggie." She'd lowered her voice almost to a whisper, though I was sure there were no lurkers in the bushes.

I choked and tea spurted all over my shirt. She might as well have said aliens carrying baskets of Mars rocks had landed on her front lawn last night.

Chapter 22

Aunt Dorothy thumped me on the back until I quit coughing, then she handed me a paper napkin.

"I never believed that tale, though rumors have a way of having at least some truth to them. But Rita being as religious as she was, she's the last person I'd have suspected of getting herself in trouble."

I twisted my hands together. Like Aunt Dorothy, I would never in a million years have believed Rita would have a child out of wedlock. But last year the minister of a big church in a neighboring state had run off with the choir director. So who knew?

"Now Rita's sister Maggie, you must know her, she's a year or two younger than Rita. Maggie didn't take to religion the way Rita did. She was a wild teen, out at all hours, ran with a rough crowd. Far as I know, she never went up north the way Rita did, but she did spend a summer or two with relatives in Tallahassee, to give the senior Camerons a break. Then her senior year the grandparents caught Maggie sneaking around with a boy from Arcadia and you could have heard the fireworks clear over to Fort Myers. That's why Rita inherited the bulk of the estate and they left Maggie nothing but a little piece of land and a four-room shotgun shack. And maybe that was a lesson for Rita, and reason enough for her to have a child up north and give it up. If that's what really happened."

"Maggie Cameron a wild teen? Big, solid, Maggie? Local dog groomer? Friend of Jeeves?"

Aunt Dorothy leaned over and patted me on the back. "See there, Leigh. You think your aunt is just a senile old biddy, but I know all about the old days. Of course, you won't repeat any of this gossip, will you?"

"I don't plan to spread it all over town, if that's what you mean." I reserved the right to discuss it with Sammi if need arose.

"And neither of them ever married, though Maggie did live with a fellow for a while. Goes to show you those childhood wounds run deep."

"Yeah, and those adult wounds aren't so pleasant, either."

She cocked her head. "What's troubling you, Leigh?"

I shot her a sharp glance, and she chuckled.

"You wouldn't have stopped by and asked about Rita if you didn't have something mighty important on your mind."

"I guess I am pretty obvious, aren't I?" I decided to tell her my suspicions about Rita's death.

When I finished, she looked at me steadily. I knew she was weighing the pros and cons and would give me an honest answer.

"I don't really believe the Harpers are capable of murder," I continued, "even if they stood to lose a lot of money, plus their reputations, if Rita reported them. But I wondered if you remembered whether either of them left their farm the morning Rita was killed."

"Goodness, girl, if you'd asked me that same day, I could have told you. But I guarantee you my memory isn't what it used to be as far as recent events go. Honey, I could tell you my first grade teacher's name, but last week...memory's already faded like a red shirt left on a clothesline all week."

"I guess you had no reason to notice," I said and sighed.

"I'm sure I was tending to my own business. Anyway, young lady, you should be telling this to the police." She shook her finger at me.

"I did. They haven't found evidence of anything suspicious. The detective acted like I was imagining things, but I know that stall door was closed and latched."

"Then maybe there isn't anything for them to find. But they should at least question people...her family, her closest friend."

"Angie—Rita's goddaughter—was questioned and her story checked out. As for the friend, you do mean Parker Fielding, don't you? I can't imagine why he'd want her dead if they were in love. Anyway, he was working the morning Rita was killed, so he has an alibi, too."

"Hmmpph. Maybe love isn't what it used to be back in my day." Aunt Dorothy crossed her arms over her chest.

She'd been married for about fifteen years, then her husband died of cancer. Apparently he was the only man for her because she never married again. I knew she disapproved of my divorce, though unlike my mother, she'd never come right out and said so. No matter how badly Kenneth treated me, I was supposed to stand by my man.

"You think Rita wasn't really in love?"

"Who's to say? It seemed surprising she'd want to change things so late in life."

I caught myself glancing over my shoulder as if Rita's ghost had come to haunt me for listening to gossip about her instead of getting busy finding the evidence that would allow the police to arrest her killer. If Rita had once found a little happiness outside the reach of her grandparents' wrath, I was glad for her, but sorry she couldn't have found someone who was available. And even more sorry if she'd had a child and been forced to give it up for adoption.

"Didn't seem much like love the day Parker Fielding and Rita were over here," Aunt Dorothy went on.

I sat up straight and stopped my rocker in mid-rock. "What day was that?"

"I told you I can't remember things. I'm falling apart like an old car...arthritis, creaky bones, age spots. In fact, if I *were* an old car, I'd already be in the junkyard propped up on cinderblocks with my wheels gone and half my engine missing. A few weeks back

Rita came out to look at that property across the road next to the Harper's place. That Parker fella was with her, and they stopped by to see if I had oranges; Rita had sold all hers. All they did was argue. He tried to keep his voice down, seemed embarrassed she was making a scene, but you know how loud she was."

"What were they arguing about?" This was the first I'd heard that Rita and Parker had problems. But then I hadn't known they were getting married either.

"Near as I could tell, he didn't want her to buy that property, said it was a bad investment and she'd have to spend too much clearing the pasture. He said she ought to at least consider the old Daughtry place on the other side of me."

I glanced to my right. The Daughtry place featured twenty acres of fenced pasture gone to weeds, a four-stall barn, and a sizeable cinderblock house badly in need of a makeover, including a new roof. The Daughtrys had moved to Colorado to be with family, and their place was still unsold.

"The Daughtrys let it get rundown, but Rita could easily afford repairs."

"True. It's a nice place and they don't want much for it. I'd buy it myself if I thought I could do the work getting it back into shape. But my forty acres is more than enough, what with hiring the crew to work the grove and all. Now Parker Fielding told Rita she ought to look at it. But Rita said she wanted to raise more cattle, not get a horse farm, said she needed eighty acres—not twenty—and besides *he* ought to know all about bad investments, he'd cost her enough. They ended up not even taking the last few oranges I had left. I reckon that's the last time I saw her."

Stan had said there was a problem with Rita's estate because of money not being found. Parker was an investment counselor. What if Rita had let Parker handle some of her money and he'd lost it? As far I could tell, that gave Rita more of a motive to kill Parker than the other way around, but maybe this was something the police could look into.

"What else is troubling you? And don't say there's nothing. You know, I used to work for the sheriff's department and I picked up a few of their tricks."

Aunt Dorothy had always had a way of worming the truth out

of me as if she were a detective cornering me in an interrogation room. I braided my fingers together and stared at the sagging porch boards. "Kenneth wants his share of the equity in my place and I'm trying to figure out a way to make him change his mind."

"Goodness, girl, you'd have a better chance trying to get the sun to stop shining. That man sure likes to have things his own way." Very kindly she did not remind me that she'd been the most vocal member of my family in trying to convince me to get my own divorce lawyer, if divorce was what I had to have.

"I know. I guess that's why I'm still worried about having to sell my horses and move to a condo." I made a face and Aunt Dorothy chuckled.

"Seems to me you're trying to solve the problem all wrong. Instead of wondering how to get Kenneth to back off, shouldn't you be trying to stay out of that condo you're so afraid of? More than one way to pluck a chicken, my daddy always said."

Sure, instead of the condo I could choose that trendy little starter home on Hansen. I hauled myself out of the rocker and squinted at the sky. Clear and sunny. "Thanks for listening, Aunt Dorothy. I promise I'll visit again soon."

"If you don't, I'll tell your mother. Don't forget you have an Aunt Dorothy." She squeezed my arm and I knew I'd keep my promise even if I had to crawl to get here. "And Leigh? I'll help you out any way I can. You just say the word."

"It's my mess, Aunt Dorothy. I have to do my own cleaning up." My father's words...he'd said them enough times.

Despite the background on Rita, I still didn't know who'd killed her. Parker had moved up a notch on the list, though. In fact, no one seemed to have a clue whether Parker and Rita had really been engaged. Parker had said so, but without *any* corroboration, I wasn't sure if I believed him. And Parker had used their engagement, plus what he claimed was Rita's intent to favor him in her will, to take over her estate on the day she died. But Rita wasn't around to confirm the engagement and, going by what I'd heard from the Lorings, Parker hadn't inherited so much as a keepsake. Odd. Closemouthed as she was about her personal life, you'd still have thought Rita would have told at least one person she was getting married.

I'd definitely have to take a closer look at Parker Fielding. I gritted my teeth in frustration. If the police would get off their butts and realize I was right about Rita, I wouldn't have to worry about him or anyone else. To Detective Frazier I was nothing more than another witness with a faulty memory. I wished I had a picture to confront him with. That would show him. That would—

I stopped in mid-thought. I realized I'd been driving without paying attention so I'd missed my turn for home, and now I was headed toward Del Canto, empty trailer swaying behind me.

Pictures. The police had taken tons of pictures of Rita's body and of the hay barn. But no pictures of the stables that I knew of. Someone else had been there with a camera, though.

I parked in a lot across from Paris Winslow's Realty. Because of the trailer, I took up more than my fair share of spaces, but I didn't plan to be there long.

Paris was in her office leafing through a model home magazine. The lime green and pink she'd had on when I'd seen her last had been replaced with bright orange and canary yellow. Marginally better outfit, except for her blouse, which sported a giant white collar that hung around her neck like a bib.

She motioned me in. "Sit yourself down. Coffee? Tea? Don't tell me…you're looking for another place and you want me to hook you up, right? Kenneth can do that and save you the commission, but of course, he's not as good as I am. And he sure didn't know what he was doing when he let you get away." She grinned and I grinned back, tension easing out of my muscles. Now I knew why she sold so much real estate.

"No to the coffee and tea. I'm not here for real estate either."

"My psychic abilities seem to have flown out the window."

"It's about pictures." I sat in a blueberry colored chair shaped like a star. Four of the points served for legs and the fifth was the back of the chair. Paris had apparently done her own office decorating. "Pictures you took for the newspaper the day Rita Cameron was killed."

"Took about a hundred." She nodded and fished around in the top drawer of her desk. "They only ran one of course, but I had to give them a choice. I don't have any of you, if that's what you're looking for."

"That's okay. I wanted to see the pictures, that's all."

"Take a look." She drew a thick manila envelope out of her desk drawer and handed it to me. Before I could open it, she said, "Sure about that real estate? I could find you a bigger piece of property so you could get more horses."

More horses. Right. If Kenneth had his way, then soon I wouldn't have *any* horses.

I flipped through the stack of pictures. "If it's no trouble," I said, "could you pull up a listing on the old Daughtry place south of town. I don't know the exact address, but it's on Queen's Highway." The listing search would give her something to do and prevent her from seeing which picture I was interested in.

While she tapped away at her computer keys, I found three shots of the interior of Rita's stable. Two of them showed the front of Tinker's stall and off to the side I could see Tinker in the washrack where I'd left her. The stall was closed and latched. My heart started thumping harder. I kept the two shots and picked out a dozen more, random views of Rita's pasture and driveway, and one with the arena and hay barn in the background.

"Do you mind if I borrow these for a few days?"

"Take whatever you want." She wiggled her fingers at me, but didn't look up. She frowned in concentration at her monitor, then a printer beside her desk clacked and whirred. She whipped a sheet of paper out of the printer and held it out to me. "The Daughtry place. Quite a steal if you ask me. It's rough, but livable. About twice as much acreage as you have now and they're not asking all that much more than your place is worth. Of course, the tradeoff is that your house is so much nicer, doesn't need any work, and it's closer to town."

I glanced at the paper to keep her happy. Raised both eyebrows. The property was what Kenneth would have called priced to move. I'd had no idea the Daughtry family was so eager to sell. I stood and handed her the envelope with the pictures I wasn't borrowing. "Thanks. I'll get your photos back to you in a few days."

"What about the property? I could pull up some other listings if you think this one involves too much work."

"Sorry, Paris. It's a nice place, but the only way I could afford it is if I could convince Kenneth to help out for Whitney's sake, and I don't see that happening."

"You're right about that. Between a slow real estate season and that high maintenance girlfriend of his—the one with the diamond fetish—I hear your ex will soon be a candidate for the bread line." Paris chuckled.

I stared at her, my hand in mid air still extended toward the door. Pieces of the Kenneth puzzle floated around in my mind.

Sell the horses. Might be dangerous. I want what I paid for that horse. I need my share of the equity in your place.

Daddy says they spent a fortune on the new house. Daddy says they can't afford a baby. Daddy says Doreen can have whatever she wants.

Then the biggest puzzle piece of all…Doreen wearing new diamonds when she showed up to see the filly. The pieces snapped into place so hard, I swayed on my feet.

Doreen, the woman I'd characterized as the type who'd name a Rottweiler "Fluffy," had turned out to be the woman who was taking Kenneth for every cent he had. I stood corrected. She'd still name the dog Fluffy, but it would be a Toy Poodle that would cuddle next to you in bed and when you turned your back, it would bite your head off. I wasn't stupid enough—not anymore—to believe Kenneth would stop at ballet lessons if Doreen wanted to "have more of a say in Whitney's activities."

I'd thought Kenneth was simply up to his usual control tactics and all along he was trying to dig up more money to keep his girlfriend happy. Blinking my way out of my temporary trance, I focused on Paris's puzzled face. "The Daughtry place is a little pricey for me, but I'll keep it in mind."

"I'll let you know if something else comes up."

I sighed. Even with the current real estate slump, affordable acreage wasn't easy to find. Jared's five acres had been the last parcel on the eastern side of town, which wasn't as expensive or as desirable as the south side. I held out little hope. Maybe I could find a way to board the horses. But boarding would cost even more than a higher payment on another place.

I felt like throwing myself down on the sidewalk and beating my fists against the concrete while I wailed that life wasn't fair.

Instead, I drove to the sheriff's department in a foul mood, which got even fouler when I discovered Art Frazier had the day off.

I left the pictures of the barn and a note of explanation with the receptionist. She assured me she'd get it to him. I wished she could assure me he'd figure out I'd been right all along.

Chapter 23

Whitney was at the barn admiring the filly. I took my time putting the truck and trailer away before I joined her.

"Mom, I got your note saying you were taking Lena to Fort Myers. Brenda Harper came by and she said Sonny's only fifteen hands and all the best youth horses are at least fifteen-two and we let Rita overcharge us. But I love him, Mom." she said fiercely.

"Tell that to your father. What was Brenda Harper doing here?"

"She was on her way home from the feed store and stopped to see the new filly. She was impressed."

"She should be," I said tonelessly.

"Hey, what's wrong?" Whitney jumped down off the stall boards where she'd been perched and came over to pat my shoulder.

"What do you mean?" I forced a smile.

"You look all hot and tired. And way sad." Her eyes filled with concern. "Are you still feeling bad about Rita?"

"No. I mean, yes. And I *am* hot and tired." I couldn't tell her that Rita was murdered and I didn't know who did it. And I still hadn't figured out how to get Kenneth to back off, but I couldn't because Doreen had proved to be a very expensive woman. "Hey, guess what? Your father phoned. He wants you to go to ballet class with Doreen tomorrow night."

"Yuck! What did you tell him?"

"I told him it was up to you."

"I don't want to hurt Doreen's feelings, but I can't see myself doing ballet. I don't know, though. She gets really whiney when she doesn't get what she wants." She looked at me to see if I'd tell her to be more respectful toward her impending stepmother. When I didn't, she danced around in front of the stalls, tried a pirouette with limited success, then stopped to hug me. "He can't make me go, can he?"

"I wouldn't know." Depended on how badly Doreen wanted to try befriending Whitney in dance class. But his chances of forcing me to sell Sonny and/or my place were getting better all the time.

"Well, I'll think about it. Can we go to the mall? You promised to take me to spend my birthday money and it's been ages."

"Sure, I wouldn't dream of breaking a promise to my favorite daughter."

"That's right. I'm your favorite." She stuck out her tongue and made a face at me. "You had a whole litter of little girls and you gave all the others away to some family that wanted to teach them ballet, but you kept the best one for yourself."

"Silly." I linked my arm through hers. I tried to cheer up. But Whitney's joke about giving away babies made me think of what Aunt Dorothy had said about Rita having a child she couldn't keep, and all at once I went what Whitney would call "way sad." But, determined to go through the motions for Whitney's sake, I pasted on a smile and grabbed my car keys. Putting put my suspicions about Rita on hold, off we went to Del Canto Place.

In the store nearest the entrance, Whitney pawed through acres of tiny tee shirts while I leaned against the wall. Eventually my shoulders tensed and I stretched, nearly stabbing someone with my elbow.

I turned and felt my eyes widen. "Sorry…Adam."

He studied my face. "You're not going to ask me what I'm doing here, are you?"

"Not this time." I shrugged and looked away from him.

"As it happens, I'm trying to find a gift for my father. I thought maybe a shirt, but now I'm not sure. Any suggestions?"

"What about a robe?" I crossed the aisle from junior girls to men and lifted a fleecy brown robe off a hanger.

"A robe? I can't recall my dad ever wearing a robe." Adam's parents lived in Miami. I'd met them last year, though it seemed more like a lifetime ago. I'd gotten the impression then that his father was the type who enjoyed hunting, fishing, and football.

"He usually wears a ragged pair of denim shorts and his Miami Dolphins tee shirt when he's lounging around the house."

"That's why a robe is a good gift. It's practical, yet it's something he wouldn't think to get for himself."

"The one item he didn't know he needed all these years until I gave it to him. Are you making this up?"

"I'll repeat the old cliché about it being the thought that counts."

"Now that's profound." He winked at me.

Whitney looked up from a clothes rack. A broad grin spread across her face. "Hi, Adam. These shirts are pretty gross, aren't they?"

Adam shook his head. "I took one look at the pink silk number with the grizzly bear on the front and knew it wasn't you." He bought the robe and then walked with Whitney and me to the music store.

Whitney, I noticed, carefully maneuvered herself so that Adam stayed between us. When we got to CD's Plus, she told me to stay with Adam while she did her own shopping.

I rolled my eyes, and Adam gently poked me in the ribs.

"Spending a few minutes with me won't kill you, will it, Leigh?"

"Guess not."

Whitney finally settled on a selection of CDs and a new boombox, since her old one was "skanky." Adam waited with me while she checked out.

I mentioned I was definitely not up to going home and cooking anything except possibly microwave waffles. Adam suggested sandwiches and accompanied us to the food court. As soon as I collapsed into a chair with my veggie wrap, Whitney spotted Brad Dakman at a table in the corner. Brad waved and pointed to the seat beside him.

"Mom? Can I sit with Brad?"

I didn't want to be alone with Adam. "Whitney…"

"Come on, Mom. I have to have *some* kind of social life."

Poor deprived thing. What was I thinking? She was already halfway to Brad's table, her bag from CD's Plus on the floor near my feet.

"She's growing up," Adam said.

"I'm not sure I like it, the way she's been lately." I sipped my iced tea. "I'm sorry for being rude the other night. Whitney didn't tell me she asked you to come over."

"Obviously. But don't apologize. She was so excited when she called and asked me if I wanted to watch the foal's birth, I couldn't turn her down. I didn't know you had company." He turned sideways and stretched his legs out.

"Just because we're both seeing someone else doesn't mean we can't still be friends." I studied my sandwich as carefully as though I supposed it might break into a million pieces at my touch. I knew I sounded trite and even silly. Besides, Adam may have been seeing someone, but I was exaggerating—fibbing—to say that I was.

I sighed. Of course Adam and I weren't going to start arguing every time we ran across each other in public, but we wouldn't exactly be close friends either…not anymore. Friends meant too much. I wasn't about to call Adam and risk having his new girlfriend pick up the phone. I felt a twinge of regret over what I'd lost, sorry that it hadn't worked out between us.

I glanced up and caught him watching me. His eyes had gone very dark. Whitney bounced back to our table and I was relieved to be able to turn my attention away from him.

She chattered non-stop all the way home, and I was glad for once because I didn't have to carry on a conversation at my end; all I had to do was nod occasionally and mumble agreement as telephone poles flashed by. I felt as though there was a giant energy drain somewhere in my body and I could hardly move.

Even when Whitney told me she planned to name the new filly Madonna, I nodded and said flatly, "That's nice."

The message light on the machine summoned me from across the room when we walked in. It was Jared. He wanted to know if we could set up a time to go out for the dinner we'd missed. I called him back, got his machine, and left a message that tomorrow night would be okay because Whitney was going to be with her father and for him to let me know.

Whitney tossed her gift bag on the couch. "Trouble on the dating front with that Jared guy?"

"Whitney, you're out of line." I wondered if Jared had gone over to Brenda's and bought a horse. I was sure he'd tell me when I saw him.

"Wow, someone's bitter."

"Never mind bitter. Do your homework and don't bother me for the rest of the evening unless there's a major emergency—meaning fire or other natural disasters." I put my hands on my hips.

Whitney's eyes went way big as she would have said.

There was only one more thing for me to do. I phoned Camilla Reed to see if she remembered exactly what time Parker Fielding had been at her house the day Rita died. Or to see if she was lying. And I could try to think up a discreet way to ask if she knew anything about a bad investment involving Rita and Parker, an impending marriage, a plan to change her will. Anything she could tell me without breaking a legal confidence.

The phone rang four times and then Camilla's perky message played back on her machine, "You have reached the office of Camilla Reed. I can't come to the phone right now, but if you leave a message, I will gladly return your call as soon as possible. Have a great day!"

"Camilla, Leigh McRae. Call me when you get a chance. I need to ask you something about Rita. It's important." Gently I returned the phone to its cradle. For the moment I'd done all I could.

Whatever had made me think I'd be able to sleep? I'd tossed and turned so much that I pulled even the fitted sheet off the bed during the night. It was wrapped around my legs in a tangled wad, like giant shackles. The phone had rung three times before eleven o'clock, but I hadn't answered. I was awake and staring at the ceiling when the alarm went off.

The idea about Rita giving up a child had finally taken shape and during the night I came up with answers that fit. Rita had gone north to visit her best friend. Rita had a goddaughter, Angie. Angie Loring looked something like Rita—tall and slender, same hair and eye color. And according to Angie, Rita had interfered in her life more than anyone would have expected of a godmother. Could Rita be Angie's birth mother? Could that be the secret Rita was going to tell her, the secret she needed to tell her in person? And what bearing could Rita's past have on her getting killed?

I crawled out of bed and dragged clothes randomly out of my closet. The snap on my jeans hung loose like it was about to come off. Always dressing in the height of fashion, I put on a belt that was the same shade of brown as my work boots. It would hide the loose snap well enough.

Whitney told me at breakfast that Sammi had called last night. "I told her you were resting. She said to call her back." She delicately took a bite of her toast. "And Camilla Reed called. She said you left a message for her."

"Camilla? I'll call her later. And who else?" I narrowed my eyes. "There was another call. I heard the phone."

"Oh, that. It was that guy with the J name." Her blue eyes went round and innocent.

"What did he want?"

"He said he'd call back. Don't get so huffy. I'm just trying to help you, Mother." She dusted toast crumbs off her hands, then smoothed down her black and green striped top and her little black skirt. "I know the world of dating is a maze for you."

"You are getting entirely out of hand, young lady." I put down my coffee cup and grabbed my car keys.

"I know. And Dad and Doreen will think so too, when I tell them I decided I don't want to go to ballet tonight."

"Whitney—"

"Don't worry. I'll tell him myself."

I dropped off Brad and Whitney, returned to the house, and

called Jared. No answer. Next I called Camilla at home. Again, no answer, so I figured she must be working at the banking center. I called there, thinking I could meet her for lunch.

"She didn't come in today," the operator said.

"Not in?" The news was so unexpected I almost forgot to say thank you and goodbye before I hung up. I mean, if she wasn't in her home office, where else would Camilla be in the middle of the week, unless she had a legal case?

I punched in her home number and got her message machine again. "Camilla, it's Leigh," I said. "I'm returning your call, but it seems we've gotten ourselves into a mean game of phone tag. I really need to speak with you about something important." I'd likely be out when she called, but we'd eventually get together.

I took the truck and headed for Cadbury's Feed and Seed. Cadbury's was east of town toward Arcadia. It was the only feed store in the county, except for the garden center, but nobody could afford the garden center. I only went there when I was totally out of feed and Cadbury's was closed.

The store was housed in an imitation log cabin connected to a huge metal warehouse. The log cabin part was where the supplies and tack along with a wide assortment of western show clothes were sold. The warehouse was for the feed, the seed, and three varieties of hay. I stopped when I first stepped inside and took a deep breath. I loved the smell of new leather and fresh hay and molasses coated feed all mixed together.

Gloria Stroud—cute, heavy-set, and good-natured—was working the register. She gave me a friendly wave. "Leigh, good to see you. Heard Belle gave you a terrific filly with a whole lot of white on her."

The equine gossip line was working as fast as ever. Good thing that unlike the Harpers, I hadn't wanted to keep the foal a secret. "Yes, come by and see our baby, Gloria. You'll love her."

"I'll do that." Gloria pushed her glasses up on the bridge of her nose and rang up the ten bags of sweet feed I ordered.

The door opened while I was filling out my check. I half turned to glance back, then stopped with my pen poised in mid-air.

Doug Reilly sauntered in smirking like he'd just cheated someone out of his last nickel. He saw me at the same time that

I saw him, and nodded curtly. He strutted up to the counter and held out an index card. "Okay if I pin this on the bulletin board, Gloria?"

"No problem, Doug. You know the rules...long as it's an ordinary ad and nothing illegal we'll post it for a month, but then you have to take it down or renew it."

Doug shoved the card under my nose. "I'm trying to find me a new job. Spent all afternoon yesterday at the Harpers trying to get Brenda to take me on. She's busy enough like you said, but the stingy little biddy said she couldn't afford help."

"I thought you were working for Rita Cameron's goddaughter." Gloria tucked a few stray pieces of hair back into her ponytail and took her glasses off, shoving them into her shirt pocket.

Doug hitched up his pants. "Angie Loring and her husband won't pay me what I'm worth. Course, they may see things different now." He nodded and looked around, obviously hoping for a bigger audience. He set his card next to the register.

"Why's that?" Gloria took my check and handed me the register receipt.

"I was there guarding the place for them, 'til they got uppity about my pay, so I quit. Wasn't *nobody* there yesterday afternoon when the house got robbed."

No wonder he'd walked in wearing a world class smirk. I was already turning to head for the door. I did an about face and stared at Doug. "What?"

"I'm surprised they didn't call and tell *you*, Ms. McRae. I thought you and the Lorings was pretty close." He paused to wipe his hand across the back of his mouth. "They was in Arcadia buying posts for the new pasture fence so they can fix it up before they sell. When they got back, the house was tore to pieces. Thieves took the TV and VCR, but that's about all. I hear they messed the house up like a tornado went through it, though."

I frowned, wondering why the thieves had made a mess and then only taken a few items. Could these be the same thieves Doug had run off last week? If so, they were either bold or desperate to come back so soon.

"Imagine if Rita were alive, what she'd say." Gloria shook her head. "My goodness, she always kept her floors clean as a hospital, though she had books and papers cluttering the place from here to Christmas. I didn't see anything about it in today's paper. There was a report about three other houses out that way got robbed last month, though. Reckon this latest one will make the evening news?"

Doug shrugged. "Only reason I know about it is Tina heard it on the radio and called to tell me what happened, but I figure it serves them right."

"Oh?" I jerked my chin up sharply. "It wasn't you who robbed the Lorings to make your point, was it, Doug?"

He snorted. "For your information, I have an alibi. I already told you I was at the Harper's farm all afternoon. And in case anything happened this morning that you might want to blame on me, I was at the unemployment office."

Yeah, no doubt claiming a check he wasn't entitled to. I climbed into the truck wishing I hadn't bought so much feed. I had to take it home and unload it. Unloading feed was no fun, but I supposed it kept me in shape. Each bag weighed fifty pounds and I'd bought ten of them. Whitney wasn't able to lift that kinds of weight, so it was my job, but at least I didn't have to spend money working out at a gym. I almost wished I were back at the office instead of stressing myself out trying to sort out alibis and motives.

Remembering that Sammi had told me Ray had originally been accused and had admitted he'd been out that way, I dialed her number from the barn office when I finished unloading.

"Hi, Sammi. I wanted to ask you something about Ray."

"Ray who?" Her voice was muffled and she sniffled into the receiver.

"Ray your boyfriend."

"He isn't. Not now and not ever again." This time there were sounds of sobbing coming over the line.

Chapter 24

"What's wrong?" Alarm pitched my voice high.

"Ray and Junior Ray got arrested for burglary. See, all along I thought he didn't do it because he was with me when those three places got robbed, but it turns out that sometimes Ray stole and sometimes it was Junior Ray and sometimes it was both of them together. Then the cops found a fingerprint and got a search warrant. They found all this stolen stuff in a shed on Ray's property, and they came over to my house to get him. Leigh, it was awful, they were wearing *guns*. Then Jeeves got excited and accidentally banged into one of the cops and for a while I thought they'd arrest me or shoot Jeeves and they read his rights to him just like on TV—"

"They read rights to Jeeves?" I pictured the sheepdog footcuffed and tossed into the back of an animal control truck.

"No, they read rights to *Ray*. And they put handcuffs on him—on Ray, not Jeeves. Junior Ray's in jail, too, and I'm never going to speak to either of them again, even though when the cops said they wanted to question them about robbing the Lorings, he swore he didn't do it. Like it would make a difference even if he wasn't lying to me."

"Whoa, Sammi, slow down. When was this? The arrest, I mean?" I'd started getting an adrenaline rush that made me so woozy I had to sit on the desk.

"Last night. But Ray lied to me, so I dumped him for good."

"You did the right thing, Sammi. Why didn't you call me?"

"I did, last night, but Whitney said you were already in bed. Anyway, I guess I was feeling pretty sorry for myself and I was afraid you'd say you told me so, even though you never do."

Sammi and I had made a pact years ago. We'd had a rough patch in high school when we'd disliked each other's boyfriends—with justification, it turned out. After an argument that featured about a hundred I-told-you-so's flying back and forth like spears, we ended up not speaking for almost a month. After we made up, we resolved to be friends forever, friends who would be supportive and never again repeat the awful phrase.

But I remembered the flippant remarks I'd made about Ray. I'd been such a jerk. "Do you want me to come over?"

"No. I have a job assignment this afternoon, but call me tomorrow, okay?" She sniffled again, then blew her nose.

"I promise," I said softly. "I'll come over and make you tea and my special pound cake and I'll treat you like a queen. But I have to ask you something...do you remember having an appointment for Jeeves at Maggie's the day Rita died?"

"I canceled because I got the new job and had to pick up my uniforms. Remember, you had to take him for me the next day?"

"I remember, I just wanted to make sure you didn't go out there at all." I hung up, but I left my hand on the phone while I considered. If Maggie had killed Rita, she couldn't have planned the crime in advance. She would have had no way of knowing both her appointments—Sammi and Vivian Rheinhardt—were going to cancel. But she still could have gone over to see Rita about something, and if they'd gotten into an argument, the killing could have been an accident.

Detective Frazier and his partner drove up before I could formulate any new theories. It didn't matter. At the rate I was going, all the suspects would be dead and gone before I made any headway.

"This is Stephanie Groves," Frazier said, in response to my greeting at the door. "My partner."

"We'd like to ask you a few questions." Detective Groves' voice was flat and her face expressionless as if she were a mannequin with only the barest outlines of features. I wished she'd act human and let me know what was going on because an icy cold feeling had begun creeping up my spine.

"Of course." I smiled, doing my best to hide my growing concern. "Would you like something to drink?" They declined and I motioned them into the family room where I settled myself in my chair. In unison, the detectives sat across from me on the couch.

"This is about Rita Cameron's death." Groves finally put on an expression, authoritative and yet somehow sad. "Art says you spoke with him last week about your suspicions."

"I thought the police had pretty much ruled her death an accident."

"That was the consensus until this morning when we took a closer look at the pictures and the note you left us." She shook her head. "Seems Ms. Camilla Reed also had an accident this morning. One accident's a tragedy, but two gives me a very bad feeling."

"Camilla? What accident?" I put my hand to my throat and felt my pulse thumping like a drum under my fingers.

The two officers exchanged glances. "I'm sorry, but Ms. Reed was found dead in her car this morning...in a canal," Frazier said.

"Oh, no!" I closed my eyes, which only made me feel dizzy until I opened them again.

"At first, it seemed like a normal car accident, but when the coroner took a closer look, it was apparent she didn't have the type of injuries you'd expect from an accident like that. When we checked her home, we saw she'd left a note on her calendar that she was going to see Parker Fielding. Her car was found a couple of miles from Fielding's place, headed back toward town, as though she'd been to see him and was on her way home."

"She was going to see Parker? Why?"

"We hoped you might be able to tell us," Frazier said. "We found a message from you on her answering machine. You said it was important you speak with her about Rita. Since you've been so determined to prove Ms. Cameron was murdered, we thought you might know something."

"I called to ask about Parker. Camilla does—did—accounting work for Parker and she said he was with her the morning Rita was killed."

Detective Groves eyed me critically, and I felt my face grow hot. I knew she understood that I'd wanted to verify Parker's alibi and I'd been meddling in police work.

"Camilla called me last night, returning a message I'd left, but I was in bed. I called her back this morning and wasn't able to reach her." I'd forever regret not taking her call last night. What if she'd told me something, something I could have used to prevent her death? "Have you talked to Parker? He can probably clear this up more quickly than I can."

"We'll do that as soon as we find him," Groves said. "When we do, we're going to ask him exactly where he was this morning and the morning Rita Cameron was killed. And what happened to money he was investing for Ms. Cameron."

"I thought the police checked his alibi and cleared him." I frowned an accusation in Frazier's direction.

Two pairs of eyes fixed themselves on my face and I bit my lip almost hard enough to draw blood. Camilla had provided his alibi. And now Camilla was dead. I didn't know why she'd lied to the police, but that lie, as well as whatever she knew about Rita's and Parker's finances, had probably cost her her life.

My stomach clenched. I suddenly thought of Parker, of that faint limp I'd noticed the day after Rita's death. I'd believed him when he said he'd tripped, but now I realized the injury was more likely the result of Rita trying to fight him off. I related my suspicions to the detectives. "The only thing is," I said after they'd finished beaming me twin you're-a-little-late looks, "I can't imagine why he'd want to kill Camilla, too."

"Ms. Reed most likely knew something about the money we suspect he embezzled. After all, she was Ms. Cameron's lawyer." Groves abruptly stood and Frazier was a second behind her. "If you think of anything else that might help, give us a call."

"Sure." I walked them to the door. I thought about Aunt Dorothy saying Parker and Rita had argued and that there seemed to be a dispute over money. I wouldn't hide this from the police, but I wanted to see Aunt Dorothy first so the police visit wouldn't be a shock when they went by to question her.

I shivered. First Rita, and now Camilla. I definitely did *not* want to be alone for the rest of the day in my empty house as long as Parker was on the loose. And he'd been so nice to me. I'd helped him with the horses back when he thought he'd inherited Rita's estate.

I grabbed my clue notebook out of my room. My "clue notebook" was silly because it was mostly empty. Besides I was sure the police had solved the crime and would arrest Parker any moment, but I thought that if I went over it one more time, I'd see something about the case, something I'd missed that might help them put him away.

The city park would do. Both the view and the presence of passersby would be soothing. I checked the horses before leaving. They were dozing quietly, Belle and baby in their stall and Sonny in the pasture. I envied them their peace.

I buzzed into town five miles over the limit and left the Honda near the entrance to the park. I chose a bench in front of a stand of coconut palms. It was cooler near the trees, but hot weather was predicted for the afternoon and even the shade wouldn't help once the sun was high. I hoped the cops caught up to Parker before noon, otherwise I needed to find an air-conditioned spot to do my thinking.

I fanned myself with my notebook as I watched the activity around me. To my left, a group of dog walkers maneuvered their charges away from the path and onto the grass. Two camera-toting tourists snapped pictures of the boats. I turned and glanced toward the harbor. Adam's boat was in its berth near the end of the dock. He'd recently painted it and the black lettering "Harbor Queen" had been outlined in a gold color that made it stand out against the blinding white of the hull. On a whim, I wandered over to take a closer look.

Then I wished I hadn't. On days when he didn't take the boat out, Adam usually worked with a friend who did construction. I certainly hadn't expected to find him on the boat, popping up from below deck with a fishing rod in his hand and a surprised expression on his face.

"Leigh."

"I, uh, was in the park and came over to see the new paint job. I didn't think you were here. Sorry, I'll leave."

"Not avoiding me, are you?"

"No, I don't want to bother you while you're working."

"I'm not working today, other than trying to find out why the line keeps snagging on this reel." He stepped onto the deck and indicated the ladder with a wave of his free hand. "Come aboard. I ripped out a couple of cabinets and put in some more seating. See what you think."

Why not? It wasn't like we hated each other post breakup.

I admired the new seats while Adam fixed a pitcher of iced tea. "Apple pie?"

"No thanks." I shook my head listlessly.

We sat across from each other at the tiny galley table. Adam took a gulp of his tea and eyed me over his glass. "What's up? I haven't seen you looking this wilted since the day after Rita Cameron died."

Okay, I hadn't really come over to look at his paint. I was human. These days he wasn't my first choice for a confidant, but Adam was always a good listener and Sammi wouldn't be home until sometime this evening.

"I've changed my mind about that apple pie, if you don't mind."

While Adam was getting the pie, I tossed my notebook onto the table. I rested my head in my hands and sighed deeply. I still felt shaky. It could have been me Parker decided to kill to keep me from talking instead of Camilla. Not that I knew anything, but he might have decided that I did.

"I've been such an idiot."

Adam put my pie down in front of me. "What's wrong?"

"It's Rita. She was murdered and I knew it, but I couldn't figure out who the killer was in time."

"Murder?" Adam sat heavily in his chair. "Are you sure?"

"The police just left my house. They finally decided I was right. But it's too late for Camilla Reed. They're pretty sure Parker Fielding killed her *and* Rita, and now they're out looking for him."

"Camilla Reed's dead? That woman who's worked so hard with her law practice?" Adam put both his hands over mine. "No wonder you like you've been through a salad shredder."

"Hey, thanks. And to think I spent an hour getting ready this morning." I explained my original suspicions and how I'd left pictures with the police.

"But why—"

I interrupted to explain about the embezzled money. "The police still don't know why he killed Camilla. But she did work for both of them, so there was some kind of money connection. I've been such a dope, running around with my stupid notebook and thinking I was gathering evidence, while all along everything was right in front of my face. He wanted the money, he thought Rita had changed her will to favor him, and he wasn't about to wait until she died a natural death. Besides, I heard from Aunt Dorothy there's a possibility he made a bad investment for her… and the police mentioned embezzlement. Maybe he was afraid she'd dump him and change her will back to favor Angie. Except she'd never changed it to begin with and Angie inherited most of it."

Adam dumped another spoonful of sugar into his tea. Stirred. Sipped. Put his glass down. "Don't be so hard on yourself. After all, he fooled me, too. I've seen Parker Fielding around town. He looks like a dignified old southern colonel. Are the police sure he's the killer? What about Rita's hired hand?"

"What about him?" I picked at my pie.

"I've heard he and Rita argued a lot."

"That's not much of a motive. And why would Doug want to kill Camilla?"

"Don't know. So maybe it was Maggie Cameron."

"But she had no way of knowing whether she was inheriting. What was her motive?"

"Guess the police are right and it was Parker. And what's this about a clue notebook?"

"Take a look." I flipped open the notebook; it was embarrassingly almost blank. Adam and I read the first line together. *Gather clues.* Brilliant.

"So much for that idea. Well, your heart was in the right place."

"Wait," I said. "I have Rita's notebook. I've already looked through it, but maybe you'll see something I missed."

I dug in my purse and dragged out a second notebook, the same size and shade of red as mine. "The last time I was over to see Angie and Stan Loring, I borrowed it when they were out of the room."

"You stole Rita's notebook?" Adam looked like he was about to remind me of the Ten Commandments.

"I'll give it back when I'm through." I shrugged. "I wanted to see what she'd written about the Harpers and about Angie. Why should they mind if it helps to catch her killer?" I opened Rita's notebook to the first page and read her list of tasks to be done. The first was to place a call to Angie; she'd put a star by that entry. The rest was nothing I didn't already know, including the plan to report the Harpers to the ACHR and a note that Maggie needed a loan to build her new dog kennel and grooming shop. Rita had starred that one, too. I held the notebook sideways and shook it hoping for a loose page to fall out.

Nothing. I'd taken the notebook for nothing, and now I was going to have to either confess to the Lorings or find a way to put it back without them seeing.

"I'm surprised there's nothing much in there about Angie. She told me Rita wasn't happy she quit her job to work with Stan." But what if the old gossip were true? And if Angie were Rita's *daughter*, Rita might not want to criticize her in writing. I started to tell Adam the rumor about Rita having had a child, but held back for some reason. Now that the mystery was solved, it wouldn't matter. I'd keep her secret the same way she had, even if it meant Angie would never know the truth.

"Stop beating yourself up. Let the police arrest Parker Fielding. After all, if you hadn't figured out Rita was murdered, the police might be inclined to dismiss Camilla's death as an accident."

"I'll do my best to give myself a break today. Speaking of crime, did I tell you about Rita's house getting broken into yesterday?"

"No, but I heard on the news about Ray Afton and his son

getting arrested for burglary."

"Yeah, Ray and Junior Ray, Del Canto Crime Wave. I don't know what Sammi was thinking. Probably the same thing I was thinking when I married Kenneth." Kenneth would have a stroke if he knew I were comparing him to Ray Afton.

Adam raised an eyebrow, but he wisely didn't comment. I yawned. There was no need now to double check Maggie's alibi as I'd planned. The killer was identified. And not by me. Hey, so I wasn't cut out to be a detective. At least now everyone knew the truth about Rita's death.

I finished my pie, thanked Adam, and left to spend an hour or so at the library browsing through women's magazines. I guessed I was supposed to get domestically motivated from stuffing my mind with recipes and home decor articles.

Didn't work. The pile of magazines slid to the floor and I pulled my lips into a tight line. I kept thinking about Camilla and blaming myself for not taking her call last night.

I left the library and walked down the block to a diner where there was a TV hanging on the wall. While I was drinking the iced tea I'd ordered, the news came on and there was a brief bulletin about Parker being brought in for questioning in the deaths of wealthy local horsewoman Rita Cameron and her attorney, Camilla Reed, but no details. I let out my breath in a big sigh. I felt sad and relieved all at the same time, glad he wasn't on the loose, but still kicking myself for not being able to save Camilla.

I left the diner and picked Whitney up at school instead of letting her ride the schoolbus home. When she finally got through a mass of waiting students and into the car, I headed toward town instead of home.

"We have to tell your dad you're not going to ballet," I said, when she questioned me.

She made a face. "I hope he doesn't threaten to send me to dance military camp or something."

"He won't. Military camps cost money and I hear he doesn't have so much of that lately." I screeched the Honda to a halt in front of Kenneth's office.

For once Mona led us straight back to Kenneth without telling us he shouldn't be disturbed. Whitney clasped her hands in front of her and stood in the doorway.

"You're here early. I was going to drive out and pick you up after work."

"Dad, I don't want to go to dance class. I'm going home with Mom."

Kenneth's face reddened ever so slightly. "It isn't fair to disappoint Doreen like this." He ramped into a ten minute tantrum, blustering and waving his arms while he complained about Whitney's defiance. Then he turned to me. "You put her up to this."

"No." I felt strangely composed for the first time since Rita's death. "Whitney made her own decision. Kenneth, you can try to control us by forcing us to move and sell the horses, but you're not going to be able to push my buttons anymore. And Whitney's at an age where she can choose her own activities without being forced into toe shoes."

"Now where did that come from? I didn't say one word about control or button pushing."

Whitney slipped her hand into my mine and squeezed hard. I squeezed back, letting her know I appreciated the support.

"Don't pretend you have no idea what I'm talking about. And by the way, in case you haven't heard the news, Rita's death was a murder committed by Parker Fielding. Just like I said all along, horses and horse activities aren't dangerous. A person could fall and hit their head dancing." Okay, not likely unless they were a really bad dancer. But still.

All that speech got me was a repeat performance of the tantrum and a stare that could have melted steel. I shrugged. Somehow the ties that bound me to Kenneth had finally started to unravel. And the vague stirrings of a plan were forming in my mind, a plan for independence and a place to keep the horses.

Chapter 25

I took Whitney to the mall to pick out a birthday gift for a friend, then out for pizza. By the time we got home, the trees were dark outlines against the amethyst sky to the east, and to the west, the last rays of the setting sun had painted the sky a deep gold-orange streaked with pink. Sonny Joe neighed as soon as he saw my car. Poor deluded animal must think I had Lena crammed in the trunk along with the magazines the Lorings had given me that I'd never bothered to unload.

We fed the horses before we went to the house. When we got inside, I talked to Whitney about Parker having killed Rita and Camilla. I didn't say that I'd suspected something all along and had been running in circles trying to find clues but had accomplished nothing except to worry myself sick. What little girl needs to know her mother isn't the brightest crayon in the box?

"Poor Rita. And she was going to marry him, Mom?"

"That's what he said. No one knows for sure. And he killed Camilla because she knew something about Rita."

Her eyes went wide. "What if Parker Fielding thought Rita told you something about him and he killed you, too?"

I took a shaky breath. "Well, he didn't. Don't worry. I'm not in any danger unless the police let Parker escape."

"At least it's over. Mom, didn't you think Daddy seemed distracted about something when we were in his office?" With the quick recovery typical of youth, she'd turned her thoughts from murder to domestic woes. "He didn't even get as mad as I thought he would when I said I wasn't coming over tonight."

"He probably lost a sale." Or Doreen had asked for another diamond bracelet and he was still in shock. "But don't count on him backing off about the ballet lessons."

She made a face. "I'm going back out to the barn to see Madonna. And, Mom? I want to ride Sonny tomorrow. Even if Daddy's going to make us sell our horses, I've decided I want to spend as much time with them as I can before they have to go."

"We aren't selling them." Not if my plan worked.

I kicked off my shoes, then remembered I hadn't bothered to catch up with Jared. My turn. I dialed his number, got his voice mail again, and left a long message of apology. I excused my bad manners by telling him how I'd been preoccupied over Rita's death, which had turned out to be murder as I'd suspected all along. Even though he'd probably heard the news, I said Parker had been brought in for questioning and Camilla had been killed and now I was going to be home all evening reading Rita's old horse magazines and drinking herbal tea, so it was a good time to call. His machine finally ran out of space.

I went outside to get the magazines out of the Honda's trunk. My hand on the lid, I frowned, staring at the boxes. One of them had tipped on its side, spilling its contents. I really ought to stop being such a procrastinator. A quick shrug, then I started cramming everything back in the box. In addition to magazines there were sheets of folded newspapers with political articles circled, loose pages from last year's calendar, Rita's Bible, and another notebook.

My heart skipped a beat. This notebook was blue, but otherwise exactly like the other one I now realized I'd left on Adam's boat. I'd had no idea the boxes contained anything other than magazines. Apparently, neither had the Lorings.

It was too dark to read out here by the light of the car trunk. I carried the notebook and the Bible inside; the notebook so I could see if she'd left a clue about Parker that I could give to the police and the Bible because it seemed disrespectful to leave it outside. Besides, it was something Angie would want and I'd take special care of it until I returned it to her.

I fixed myself a cup of peppermint tea and curled up in Greenie with the notebook, expecting to read more lists of chores. I didn't know what I was looking for…maybe Rita had spelled out what she intended as far as Parker.

Nothing jumped out at me. The first few pages were about Angie and how disappointed Rita was that she'd married Stan instead of that nice doctor she used to date. The rest of the notebook was blank. I double-checked, then made myself another cup of tea. Rita's Bible was on the end table and I took it back to the chair with me. I might be able to find a comforting psalm or prayer to help me stop feeling so guilty.

When I opened the Bible, a sheet of folded paper fell out from the between the pages dividing the Old Testament from the New. The handwriting was Rita's, the same as the writing on the bill of sale for Sonny Joe. My heart thumping harder, I scanned the page.

Before I finished reading, a chill rippled down my back. Now I was sure I knew who killed Rita and why. And it wasn't Parker Fielding. No wonder someone had broken into Rita's house.

Ray had told Sammi he wasn't the one who robbed the Lorings and this time he hadn't lied, I was sure of it. The burglar had to be Maggie. Maggie would have known Rita kept notebooks where she might have written something incriminating, something that would bring a killer to justice. Maggie must have known she *had* to have this paper. I read over it once more, making sure I hadn't missed something.

Maggie was here Monday. Wants me to give her money for a new grooming shop and kennel. She doesn't understand most of my money is tied up in land and animals and other investments. Besides, she's worked her business for years and if it hasn't paid off, what makes her think it will help to expand? No call for her to get ugly with me the way she did. I said I'd expect an apology or I was taking her out of my will.

I carefully folded the incriminating paper and put it back in the Bible. Maggie had most likely known Camilla was Rita's lawyer. As soon as Camilla took care of the new will, Maggie wouldn't get a thing. Her grooming and kennel business would go under without the money. She had to kill Rita to get her inheritence and she had to do it before the will was changed. But somehow she'd found out Camilla already knew Rita's wishes. Camilla had never made a secret of her love for money. Could she have tried to blackmail Maggie? Could she have threatened to file the new will if Maggie didn't give her a portion of her inheritance? Maggie would have had to kill Camilla or face a lifetime of blackmail.

Cursing myself for being so dense, I tucked the Bible under my arm and ran to the car, where I locked the Bible and the papers in the trunk.

Thank God, Maggie didn't have a clue I was on to her. I took a deep breath, counted to five, and my thinking cleared.

I had to get Whitney in from the barn and keep her safe by my side. And I needed my purse and my shoes before I went anywhere, and it wouldn't hurt to call Detective Frazier to tell him I'd found something important and was on my way.

I scurried back inside and grabbed the nearest phone, the one in the family room next to the couch. The dial tone hummed reassuringly. I called the barn office and Whitney answered.

"Road trip, sweets. We're leaving in about five minutes."

"Oh, Mom. I was just petting Madonna. She nibbled feed off my hand."

"Sorry. I'll tell you everything on the way to town."

Big, self-pitying sigh. Then, "Pick me up in front of the barn when you're ready, okay?" She hung up, no doubt to go back to mooning over her filly for a few more minutes.

It wouldn't take me long to speak to someone at the sheriff's office. But my finger had only punched in the nine when Heidi trotted into the room and sat in front of me. Her dark eyes studied me sadly. She whimpered, then rolled over and put all four paws in the air. Dead dog. I'd forgotten to feed her.

I chewed on my lower lip. There was no telling when I'd be finished with the cops. Animals first. It would take only a minute to pour food in her bowl. I snapped my fingers and Heidi's pitiful expression turned hopeful.

"Okay, sweetie. Dinner time."

She trotted behind me to the kitchen and I fixed her a big bowl of kibble and gave her fresh water. While she was eating, I went back to the family room and reached for the phone. Then I paused, thinking I'd heard something outside. Whitney must have gotten tired of waiting for her driver to arrive and decided to meet me at the house.

Before I could yell for her to hurry, a soft scraping sounded near the window as if someone had rubbed a piece of metal against the stucco. The hair on the back of my neck stood up.

Heidi bounded into the room. She stared toward the front door, her ears pricked and her tail wagging like a signaling flag. She'd heard the sound, too. Heidi was the type of dog who'd bark to alert me to a stranger, but I'd never known her to bark at someone she'd already met. This was no stranger. This had to be Whitney teasing me. Smiling, I tiptoed to the window and peered out. Too dark to see and I couldn't get the right angle to see if she was still next to the outside wall. I was tempted to jump out and say boo, but I'd give her a few minutes, make my phone call, then sneak around the other side of the house and come up behind her.

With a half-suppressed chuckle, I went back and picked up the phone. This time I heard nothing. I frowned. What in the world? I shook the receiver a couple of times and when that didn't help, I dropped it. My heart thudded hard and fast.

The scraping on the side of the house sounded again, and I heard a horse moving in the pasture. Sonny Joe was agitated, trotting the fence. Something had gotten him stirred up. Whether he knew it or not, he was alerting me. Someone was outside and this time I was sure it wasn't Whitney.

The phone was dead and someone had to have made it that way. Heidi knew and liked Maggie. She hadn't barked. Maggie was here. After Maggie had failed to find Rita's papers at the house, she must have realized I had them. I remembered I'd stupidly told her Angie and Stan had given me some of Rita's things.

To heck with waltzing outside where Maggie lurked in the bushes to bash me over the head. God, what if she'd already gone to the barn and discovered Whitney?

I found my keys and jammed them in my pocket. There were all manner of knives and heavy frying pans in the kitchen. Any one was them would make a handy weapon. On the other hand, they wouldn't be much good if Maggie had a knife of her own or even a gun. I'd be better off to find my daughter and get away from here without Maggie catching me. I was not going to wait in the house, helpless, while she broke in and killed me. That had to be her plan or she wouldn't have cut the phone line.

At least if I were outside, I'd have a chance to get to Whitney and make sure she was safe. I glanced around, saw only one shoe, and didn't bother with a search for the other. I slipped barefoot out the front door and shut it as quietly as I could, telling myself the loud click of the latch catching couldn't be heard by anyone except me. I would make a mad dash for the car, race to the barn to get Whitney, then we'd tear out of here before Maggie realized I'd gotten past her in the darkness.

I sprinted, making it the finish line for the race of my life. But before I was twenty feet away from the house a shape loomed out of the shadows on my right. Human, but too dark to make out details. I caught a glimpse out of the corner of my vision and put on a burst of speed.

She grabbed me before I could twist away. I screamed as if I were in the clutches of King Kong, and a second later a hand clamped over my mouth. Then a powerful arm wrapped around my body. Her grip kept me from screaming again or pulling away. I struggled, trying to break free, but she was like a steel octopus with a couple of extra arms. All the while I wondered if she'd gone to the barn first.

I tried to stomp her feet, and she moved them, catlike, out of range. I was barefoot anyway. Fat chance I'd stand of inflicting any damage. I wanted to bite her hand, but it was pressed too tightly against my face for me to open my mouth.

I struggled harder, hoping I could free my arms. She was cutting off my breath and the fear of suffocation only increased my panic. A couple of times we went down, and I scratched my knees on the shells in the driveway. My keys were still in my pocket. I thought if I could reach them, I could use them to jab her, but I couldn't get my hands close to my pocket.

My breath came in sick little gasps as sweat rolled down my body in rivers. I sagged toward the ground. I had to use my will to hold myself together. If I couldn't break free, Maggie was going to kill me...and Whitney.

Behind me, her face close to my neck, Maggie breathed hard. I sucked in a breath of my own and got a whiff of the doggie cologne. Her arms tightened around me. I tried to drop to the ground so I could twist loose, but she held me up and pulled me backward.

She had the strength—a lot more strength than I'd imagined—to drag me across the driveway and into the barn as though I were a mere inconvenience and not a dead weight. Without bothering to speak or flick on the light, she yanked open the door to the feed room and shoved. I was propelled across the floor, ending up on top of the bags of feed I'd so carefully stacked this morning. The door slammed and the padlock clicked shut before I could move.

"Maggie, what are you doing?" I yelled. "Let me out."

Footsteps sounded in the aisle, the gate opened and closed, and then I was alone in the barn. I held very still in the dark, straining to hear something, anything that might give me a clue as to Whitney's location. Sonny had stopped trotting, though he was still being very vocal about the disturbance. Belle and her filly were in their stall and not making a sound, and I imagined the cats were asleep in the loft, not that the animals would be any help.

"Whitney?" I called, barely above a whisper.

"Right here, Mom." Something moved in the corner next to me and I jumped. She was on the floor hiding behind the stacked feed bags.

"Oh, thank God, I was so afraid she'd hurt you." I dropped to my knees and pulled her to me in a hug. "But why are you hiding in here? Now we're both locked in."

"I jumped off the stall and hurt my ankle. So I came in here to look for the leg wraps 'cause I knew that's what you'd do—put on a leg wrap and some ice. But then I heard Sonny and I knew somebody was out there. I remembered what you said about Parker Fielding, how he was a killer, so I turned off the feed room light in case he escaped and came after us. When I heard you scream, I hid." She buried her face against my shoulder and sobbed. "I'm really scared. And I wish we were in the office instead of in here with all the roaches."

I helped her get on top of the feed and then pulled myself up to sit beside her, tucking my legs up under me to get my feet off the floor. This was a feed room. Feed attracted mice and rats, but the cats did a good job of keeping them under control. There was one thing the cats didn't keep under control. Roaches loved tropical living. They loved the warmth, the humidity, the constant supply of food.

Out here in the barn with all its nooks and crannies and its delicious smelling feed room, the roaches had not only set up camp, they'd invited all of their friends and relatives and set up an entire country of their own. The insects were wide and dark, with probing antennae, fast moving legs, and wings that could propel them through the air like miniature rockets.

They rustled in the dark, scuttling around in the stack of empty feed bags in the corner. I gritted my teeth and wrapped my arms around Whitney.

They're just roaches, I said to myself. Nothing at all compared to the killer out there.

Something brushed against the back of my neck and it was all I could do to keep from leaping across the room. Shuddering, I pulled myself into a tight ball.

Get a grip, I ordered myself. This isn't *Fear Factor*, this is real. There are a lot more important things to worry about than roaches…such as Maggie Cameron and how she's going to add a couple more victims to a growing list if you don't figure out a way to stop her.

Chapter 26

I couldn't huddle on top of the feed with my daughter waiting for Maggie to come back and finish us off. Where was she? Why had she locked me in the feed room? But I knew the answer. She needed to find the journal entry, the one that said Rita intended to cut her out of the will. If she couldn't locate it, she'd need me alive to tell her where I'd put Rita's things.

There had to be something I could use for a weapon. My eyes had adjusted to the blackness so I could make out the shadowy forms of feed bags. Unfortunately, feed and feed bags were the only things in the room. I held my breath and listened, trying to hear if she was returning. Beside me Whitney's sobbing had quieted to an occasional sniffle, but her fingers were gripping my arm so tightly I knew I'd have a row of bruises in the morning. If I lived that long.

"How's the ankle?" I said.

"It hurts really bad. I think it's broken."

"Hang in there, baby. I'll think of a way out of this mess." I pried Whitney's fingers loose from my arm and stood. I turned in a complete circle, hoping to find something I'd overlooked.

Hopeless.

Then in the faint light I made out the jar on a shelf. It was the peanut butter I used to disguise worm pills I fed to the cats. I snatched up the jar. Maggie had said she had a deadly allergy to peanuts. All I had to do was dig out a big glob of Jif. When she came back in, I'd be waiting in front of the door. I'd shove a handful of peanut butter in her face. That should be enough to disable her until we could get away. Hopefully it wouldn't kill her, but if it did…well she'd already murdered two people and Whitney and I were likely numbers three and four if I didn't act.

I sucked in a deep breath and was assaulted with the odors of horse barn, feed, and something else. I frowned, trying to remember why it seemed so familiar. There was an odor of soap all over me, a musky kind of soap, the designer dog cologne I'd smelled at Maggie's shop. No surprise there. She'd held me in her octopus grip all the way from the house to the barn. I brought my arm up to my nose. Maggie's dog cologne smelled musky, but her shop—and Maggie—also smelled like the coconut scented flea spray she used.

A chill shot up my spine. I didn't smell coconut. And if the odor wasn't Maggie's dog cologne, then what was it? I knew I should recognize that scent.

Closing my eyes, I sniffed one more time. Something lit up in my odor detection center. The scent was cologne. Men's cologne.

It was the same scent Jared had worn the day we went to the horse club meeting. I was positive, because I'd thought at the time he smelled oddly like Jeeves. When I ran out of the house, everything had happened too fast and since I knew she had a motive, I'd assumed the assailant was Maggie. Once I made that assumption, I didn't allow for anything else. But now that I had time to think, I couldn't remember soft breasts against my back when the attacker dragged me along.

I dropped the Jif jar and watched it roll into a corner. It was useless, too small for me to use to bash Jared over the head. There was nothing I could do except wait for him to come back and hope for a miracle.

Why was he doing this, anyway? What possible motive could he have to kill Rita and Camilla and now me? I thought back to the day I'd discovered her body. Jared had come to the barn to wait with me in Rita's office. I remembered him looking shocked, and then he recovered. Nothing suspicious about his behavior. He'd even helped me in the barn. He'd put away the saddle and bridle, opening the tack room and lifting them onto a wooden rack.

I caught my breath. His fingerprints would be all over the saddle. If the police had believed my story and investigated, he'd have the perfect explanation. But how had he known where the tackroom was in the first place, since he supposedly had never been to Rita's? But he'd know if he were the one who'd removed the saddle and bridle from their racks to begin with.

I pictured him when he'd first come in and leaned against the door. Periwinkle blue eyes like Maggie's. Hair an unusual shade of chestnut with cherry cola highlights. I remembered now. It was the same color as Maggie's hair before she went gray. Maggie and Rita were sisters. Rita's child could have inherited Maggie's coloring, the same way Whitney and Sammi had the same color hair.

I didn't know. But I was sure of one thing. If the killer was Jared and he didn't yet know Whitney was here, then I had to keep him from finding her. I'd said in last night's message that Whitney was going to be at her father's tonight. I hadn't, I was almost sure, said in my newest message that she'd changed her mind.

I whirled to face the feed bags. "Whitney? You've got to hide."

"Where? There's nothing in here except feed and a couple of wall shelves."

"Under the feed, of course." This morning I'd regretted buying so much feed when I had to unload it. Now I wished I had twice as much.

Without protest, Whitney curled up on the floor behind the full bags of feed, and I took bags from the front row and stacked them around her before I gently put a final bag on top of her.

"You okay?"

"I can still breathe."

"I'm going to get out of here when the door opens. No matter what happens, you stay put and don't make a sound. When it's clear, get the police."

"I will, Mom. I'll hobble for help if it takes me all night."

Sonny snorted an alert before I could tell her how much I loved her. I scanned the room one more time. The empty feed bags held no promise, but the full ones weighed fifty pounds apiece. As a weapon, a bag of feed didn't show a lot of promise, but it was my only option. I picked up a bag from the side, making sure Whitney was still hidden.

I moved to the door, holding the feed against me with both arms. A roach zipped across my foot and I didn't move. The metal barn gate clanged open. Footsteps, quick and confident, sounded in the aisle. The padlock rattled and I clenched my hands tighter, slowly lifting the feed bag as high as my trembling shoulders.

The door opened. I swung the full bag, landing it in the middle of the figure in the doorway. The figure fell back with an *oomph*, and I shot out of the room, streaking for the end of the barn.

I hadn't counted on him having such quick reflexes. He lunged and hooked my left ankle with one hand, yanking me down on the hard packed dirt of the barn floor. My head thunked against one of the stallboards as I fell, dazing me so I couldn't even fight as he tossed me back into the feed room.

I sat huddled near the door, rubbing my head, as I faced a silhouette holding a flashlight. He jerked the light up, shining it directly into my eyes so I couldn't see. But now I knew who he was. The scent of cologne drifted toward me in the damp night air, and though I couldn't make out details, I recognized the general outline.

"Jared."

The hand holding the flashlight lowered itself a few inches. "I didn't want to involve you, Leigh. But I had no choice."

"Why are you after *me*?" My mouth was powder dry, my voice raspy.

"Come up slow. No more nasty tricks with bags of feed."

I pulled myself up from the floor, forcing myself to go slowly. The last thing I wanted was for him to turn on the light and find Whitney. I wondered if he had a gun and, as though he'd read my mind, he switched the flashlight to his left hand and pulled a gun out of his jacket pocket with his right.

"Come out of there. Move." He motioned, backing up at the

same time.

I joined him in the barn aisle, leaving the feed room door hanging open. "What do you want?"

"Turn around, Leigh."

I turned and he poked me in the back with the flashlight. Hard enough to stagger me. If I lived until tomorrow, I'd have a bruise over my left kidney to match the ones on my arm and my knees. I thought he wanted to go to the house, but instead he directed me into the barn office. Too close. Way too close to a little girl who might be tempted to try to save her mother.

He backed me into a corner, then he perched on the edge of the desk and stared at me. I stared back, mostly focusing on the gun. A lot of good my staring would do if he pulled the trigger.

"All I want," he said smoothly, "is Rita's notebook and any other papers that came from her house."

"What notebook?" My response was automatic.

"The notebook she used to keep lists and journal entries. Don't deny you have it. I turned Rita's house upside down searching and it's not there."

"Rita's house? I thought that burglars—the Aftons—broke in." I didn't, not anymore, but I'd say anything to buy time.

"So did everyone else when they saw I'd taken the TV and VCR."

Ray and Junior Ray had been arrested and were still in jail. Like everyone else, I'd assumed at the time they'd robbed Rita's house because they'd committed the other burglaries. And that assumption had worked out fine for Jared.

"Leigh, the notebook."

"What makes you think I have it?"

"Doug Reilly. I crossed paths with him this morning at the gas station and he was running off at the mouth about how bad the world treats him. This time he actually said something useful, said you'd been to see Angie Loring and you acted upset, and then he saw you leave with a notebook that looked a lot like one Rita used to have."

Clumsy me. I'd dropped my stupid clue notebook practically on Doug's feet the last time I was at Angie's. Of course he had no way of knowing one notebook from the other. And then, to really seal my fate, I'd left Jared a message telling him about all the magazines Angie had given me. Talk about running off at the mouth. It couldn't have taken too much thought for him to figure that if what he wanted wasn't in the notebook, it might be in the box with the magazines.

There was no use denying I had the notebook. Two of them, actually, as well as Rita's Bible. But she'd written nothing about Jared. I still had no clue what he was looking for. And every reason to keep Rita's things out of his reach.

"Well? And before you make the wrong decision about giving me what I'm after, I'll just say I've got all the leverage in the world. Your daughter is coming home from her father's tomorrow, isn't she?"

Chapter 27

"You wouldn't," I rasped through dry lips. What if he'd gone to the barn first? What if he'd decided to search the feed room? What if I hadn't left that message telling him Whitney was going to Kenneth's? Sweat trickled down my forehead, dripping past my eyes.

"I'm not negotiating. Rita wouldn't acknowledge me or give Maggie what she should have had all these years from her grandparents' estate. I don't expect you to believe me, but I didn't mean to kill her. After she was dead, I had to make sure no one ever found out about me or they might add things up and realize she went out of that loft with a little help. Then it'd be just a matter of time until they got around to me."

"What could Rita possibly know about you? You were there to buy horses."

A slow grin spread across his face. "Take a good look and see if you can figure it out."

I already had. As if she were standing here beside me, I could hear Aunt Dorothy's voice saying, "There was a rumor Rita left town and had a baby."

"She wouldn't acknowledge me," he said again. His face twisted and for a second I pitied him. "My parents adopted my sisters when I was in college. After that, I might as well have been the family cat. When I found out Rita was worth millions, I came down to establish my claim to the family fortune. She refused to give me anything, said she was making a new will and specifically excluding me."

"You killed your own mother over money?" The pity I'd felt a second ago gave way to revulsion.

A puzzled expression flickered across his features before he threw back his head and laughed. "You think Rita was my *mother*?"

"Wasn't she?"

"Rita, the religious fanatic who thought the sun rose and set on the Bible? You have to be joking."

"Then what, who…" I trailed off. Maggie. Maggie with the purply eyes and the cola colored hair. "Maggie got sent away one summer…and then her grandparents wrote her out of the will."

"Bingo. Half their estate should have belonged to her. She would have kept me, but they wouldn't let her, said she'd never get a dime if she brought shame on the family. They left her damn little as it was."

"So you felt resentful that Maggie gave you up."

"Cut the psychological crap. All I ever wanted was mine—and Maggie's—share of what was rightfully ours. Rita acted like I was dirt." His gun hand trembled, the barrel wavered toward the floor, then back up to point at my chest. "She said she wasn't going to be scared by a worthless piece of humanity like me."

I couldn't help but wince. Harsh words for her sister's only child. I could understand his hurt and anger. But not his justification for murder. "Then you pushed her or something and she hit her head. You could have told the police it was an accident."

"Like they'd believe me." He waved the gun around like a wand and I cringed. "The notebook and any other papers you got from Rita. Anything that might mention me and my connection to the Cameron family. Hand them over."

I had to get him out of the barn and off the property so he wouldn't find Whitney. But once I gave him what I had, he'd have no reason to keep me alive.

Maybe, just maybe, when Detectives Frazier and Groves spoke to Parker and figured out he wasn't the killer, they would come back tonight to ask more questions. Sure and if I were really lucky, they might figure out who killed me.

Jared slammed his fist—thankfully not the one holding the gun—against the desk. "Give me the notebook."

"You killed Camilla, too." It was a statement of fact.

"She knew Rita was going to change her will and leave Maggie out. Thanks to your meddling, the police hadn't closed the case. I had to get Camilla out of the way before they questioned her and made me a suspect."

I stole a glance at my watch. Only a few minutes had passed since Jared pushed me into the office. "Rita didn't mention you in her notebooks."

"Don't play me like an idiot. Let's stop wasting time and tend to business."

"Business?" *Please, God, I promise I'll stop making jokes about Doreen's bedazzled shirts and I'll go quietly when Kenneth buys her a private jet studded with diamonds and forces me to move to a condo.* "And what do I get out of this little transaction? You'll shove me out a loft the way you did Rita?" I inched slowly forward. It had occurred to me that since he was going to kill me anyway, I might as well try to jump him. There was a chance in a million it would work. "That's why you came back to Rita's that day. The notebook. You didn't have time to find it after you killed her." *Very good, Leigh. Fine job of detecting, but way too late.* I inched forward.

He caught the movement and stepped back. "Don't try it. It would be a shame for you to die in a barn fire."

A barn fire? My legs turned to noodles so I could hardly stand. He was truly a monster. Thank God he had no idea Whitney was a few feet away.

I hung my head in pretend surrender. "You can't kill me," I said, not trying to disguise the tremor in my voice. "Then the police will know Parker isn't the real killer and they'll find out it was you."

"I have that all worked out. The police questioned Parker

earlier this afternoon, but they didn't have enough solid evidence to charge him, so they turned him loose. I'm going to provide them with all the evidence they need. I'm going to reconnect your phone line so you can call him and ask him to come over here. Then I'm going to arrange another accident. By the time I'm finished, the police will conclude he murdered you, but got caught in his own trap. Or maybe I'll make it a murder-suicide. No matter."

It mattered to me. My mind reeled. I'd assumed Parker was in jail or I'd never have come home by myself. Sammi would have been glad to let me stay with her and Jeeves for a few days and Whitney could have gone to Kenneth's.

My shoulders slumped. "All right, I have no choice. Let's go up to the house and I'll give you Rita's notebook."

"The house? Don't get cute. I searched your house while you were locked in the feed room. No notebook to be found. Would you like to rethink your answer?"

That's what I got for leaving the door unlocked, though he'd have broken in if I hadn't. I thought fast. "Uhm, I think it's in my car." It wasn't; there was nothing in the car except for Rita's Bible and my own pathetic little clue notebook, the one with mostly empty pages. Maybe I'd better start calling it my clueless notebook.

"The keys." Jared pointed to the desk.

I fished the keys out of my pocket and dropped them on top of the desk. He snatched them up and stepped to one side, motioning me toward the door.

I trudged out of the barn trying to look completely defeated. Every step away from the feed room was a step away from Whitney. Until Jared got Parker over here and then he might set the barn on fire. I'd told Whitney to stay put. She'd stay in the feed room until it was too late. I had to make a break for it, even though he'd probably shoot me in the back when I did.

It was still pitch black outside except for where he shone the flashlight beam. I took a slightly wayward path toward the car, hoping his light wouldn't pick up the hole near the driveway. I was sure I knew exactly where it was. I should—I'd tripped in it enough times.

I saw the hole at the last second before I would have stepped into it, and I put in an extra long stride. Jared didn't. He fell sprawling, the breath whooshing out of him, at the same instant that I took off running.

I didn't head for the house. The outside lights as well as all the inside ones were blazing. I'd stand out as an easy target.

Going down the driveway on foot didn't seem like a good option either. Jared would get in the car and run me down before I could go a hundred yards. Besides, the shells in the driveway were gouging cruelly into my bare feet at every stride. I turned off the driveway onto the grass and found myself at the pasture gate. I unlatched and swung it open in one movement. At least I was off the brutal, cutting marl even if I still had no way to escape. All I could hope for was to lead him away from Whitney long enough for her to get out of the barn.

Sonny Joe trotted forward, stopping short in front of me and extending his head. I grabbed his halter and held him, slipping off my belt with my other hand. Behind me I heard my car start. Jared would be here in seconds, picking me out with the car lights.

I looped my belt through the ring on Sonny's halter. Then I grabbed a fistful of his mane and jumped, hooking one leg over his back. Sonny, bless his gentle heart, stood like a stone while I scrambled to a sitting position. The car was coming across the yard now, the lights swinging in our direction like a search beam.

I pulled the belt, using it as a rein to turn Sonny away from the gate and into the pasture. Jared drove through the gate, bumping across the grass in my direction. I kicked Sonny into a trot, waiting until the car was in an uneven spot where the wheels couldn't easily grip, before I tugged my horse back around facing the car almost head on. I leaned low over Sonny's neck and kicked him hard.

He rocketed into a gallop. The car, not as agile as a horse, jolted to a stop as we raced past. Once out of the pasture Sonny turned automatically to the right, heading toward the road.

There wasn't a car in sight in either direction when we got to the highway. I knew better than to race along the side of the road toward town. Jared would ram us with the Honda before we'd gone half a mile. Instead, I used my voice to slow Sonny until we crossed the pavement, then I kicked him back into a gallop straight at the woods on the opposite side of the road.

Pine branches whipped my face and slapped my legs and arms. Ignoring the stinging needles, I held on tight. Eventually Sonny slowed to a trot to keep his footing in the palmettos. My legs, feeling like stretched out elastic, nearly lost their grip on his smooth sides, and at every stride a jolt shot up my back. At one point, Sonny tripped over a log and nearly went to his knees. I somehow managed to hang on and coax him to a walk.

There was no way Jared could follow us through palmettos—it would be like trying to drive over a boot camp obstacle course. I intended to keep going until I reached the highway on the other side of the woods that led straight into town. Of course Jared would know that. He'd likely be waiting for me on the other side, but I couldn't wander around in the woods forever. If I were lucky, I could get past him in the dark. He wouldn't know exactly where I'd come out, even though the options were limited. Meanwhile, Whitney could escape. He might get me, but she'd be safe.

Sonny kept up a steady walk. Not fast—there were too many obstacles in the blackness for that—but we were covering the miles. My legs trembled, my back ached, and I realized I had at least one cut on the bottom of each foot. I nudged Sonny into as fast a walk as I dared.

Eventually light began to show through the trees in front of us. Town. I had no clue how long we'd been in the woods. Sonny sped up on his own as the trees thinned, no doubt sensing an end to our midnight ride. I had to struggle to hold him back. It wouldn't do to burst out of the woods into Jared's waiting arms.

We finally reached the edge of the trees where I pulled Sonny to a stop. There was a shallow, but wide, ditch in front of us, then another highway. Across the road were three houses, spaced so close together it seemed that anyone inhabiting them would be able to lean out a window and touch the wall of the next house. A street light in front of the middle house lit up half the street.

I waited, hardly daring to breathe, and examined every shadow, imagining it was Jared. Three shrubs looked big enough for him to hide behind. Cars in the driveways provided even more cover.

After a few minutes, Sonny grew restless and tried to move forward, so I patted his damp neck to calm him. A dog barked from somewhere in the direction of the harbor, and the horse snorted and pawed the ground.

If Jared were anywhere around, he couldn't fail to hear. I hardly dared to breathe as I waited, straining to hear another sound. More minutes crawled by and I convinced myself that Jared couldn't be close or he'd have come after us already. Besides, Sonny was growing impatient and I didn't blame him. Biting gnats gathered around my face and Sonny swished his tail steadily while he bobbed his head up and down.

I finally nudged him across the road, intending to cut through back yards as much as I could until we got to the police station in the center of town. It was a great plan. But we weren't quite off the pavement when Jared leaped out from behind a car.

Sonny hit the brakes and snorted.

I pitched forward and got a face full of mane. Somehow I managed to right myself and keep from slipping off completely.

"Hold it." Jared held the gun in front of him.

Anger surged through me. No. I wouldn't let him take me home where he might find my daughter. I took my only chance, kicking Sonny hard with both heels and gripping his mane so tightly my hands ached. His hooves slipped and he scrambled for an instant on the pavement, and then he was on the grass, gaining traction and accelerating. Jared stood his ground, his expression showing his surprise. At almost the last second, he raised the gun. There was an explosion of sound and something jabbed my shoulder, but I held on while Sonny kept going…right where I'd guided him.

Sonny tried to turn aside. But, as though I was holding him to a fence at a show, I gripped with what little strength was left in my legs and wouldn't let him. He slammed into Jared, galloping over the top of him before he could fire another round.

My quivering leg muscles finally gave out. In slow motion, I slid sideways, tumbling off Sonny's back and hitting the ground on my right side. My head slammed against the ground and I fought to stay conscious. I had to get Jared's gun away from him.

I struggled to sit up and made it on the third try. Something warm and sticky ran down my left arm and dripped off my fingertips. I looked around wildly, searching for Jared. Then I saw him. He was lying on his back in one of the driveways. His gun was a few feet away from his outstretched hand, and he wasn't moving.

A porch light came on, a door opened, and a scrawny man wearing jockey shorts and a tee shirt leaped off the porch of the house on my left. He raced up and squatted to peer into my face. "Darlin', are you all right?"

I swayed, struggling to keep from toppling over, and said, "Don't call me, darlin'."

Chapter 28

The ambulance braked to a stop. Gentle hands picked me up and put me inside. Soon an IV dripped something into a vein in my arm and a dimly seen figure stuck a needle attached to a syringe into the IV tubing.

In the emergency room a white-coated woman bent over me and asked my name and address. I think I gave the correct information. I must have, because when I woke again, I was in bed in a hospital room with bright sunlight pouring through a window and Whitney and Sammi sitting beside me.

"Hi," I croaked, after a few seconds.

"Oh, Mom." Whitney hugged me, careful not to bump my bandaged left arm.

"Baby, are you okay? How's your ankle?"

"I'm fine, Mom. It's a sprain, not a break, and I'm fine."

"What about Sonny Joe?" The last I remembered he was galloping loose in the darkness, heading away from town in the direction of I-75.

"The police found him grazing on the playground at the elementary school. Pat Ansley came and got him with her trailer."

"And what about…Jared?" Too late it had occurred to me that maybe I should have asked about him before I asked about Sonny.

Whitney and Sammi exchanged glances. "I'm afraid Jared didn't make it," Sammi said in a half-whisper.

"Jared's dead?" I sat up halfway, then sank deeper into my pillow.

"He apparently had a very fragile skull." Sammi's expression was filled with sympathy, but I knew it wasn't meant for Jared.

"Sonny didn't kill him. I mean, he ran over the top of him and caused him to hit his head, but I *made* him do it. Jared killed Rita and Camilla, too." As if that were justification. The thought registered that now *I* was a killer. Sort of.

"We know, Mom." Whitney patted my arm. "Try to rest."

"What about Heidi? The little non-watch dog."

"She's fine. Don't blame her. Jared made friends with her the night Madonna was born. Remember?"

"Oh, yeah. In that case she's forgiven for not barking a warning." I shifted position and pressed a button on a little console placed conveniently close to my right hand. This raised the head of my bed. My left arm hurt, but not too badly. I looked around the room. There were at least ten flower arrangements on the dresser. I raised an eyebrow and looked at Whitney.

"They're mostly from your friends in the horse club," she said. "Daddy and Doreen sent the pink roses. Aunt Dorothy sent the gold lilies, and Brenda and Scott sent that little purple vase with the white carnations."

In a few days Brenda and Scott would be sorry they'd sprung for flowers. They'd be hopping mad at me after I rang them up and told them I knew all about their crop-out colt. I'd say I wouldn't report them as long as they quit trying to eradicate the white spot. Brenda would screech and squawk and accuse me of being another Rita, but I'd stand firm.

"So did the doctor tell you any horrible news about my condition that she's keeping from me?" I asked, not looking at her.

Sammi laughed. "The bullet grazed your shoulder and you

have a cracked rib and a concussion."

"I guess I won't be in here too long," I said hopefully.

"You can probably go home tomorrow. I'll pick you up and stay for a few days to look after you and Whitney."

"Sammi, I'm so sorry. I was supposed to be the one taking care of you after your breakup."

"I'll take a rain check. I'm afraid your house is quite a mess right now, so Whitney and I are going to spend the rest of the day putting it back together. Or at least I am. Whitney will do whatever she can from a pair of crutches."

"Jared ransacked the house looking for that awful notebook I wish I'd never seen."

"If you'd never seen the notebook, then Jared would have gotten to it first. The notebook and Rita's Bible."

"Rita's Bible?" I frowned. "Then Maggie would have been blamed for killing Rita."

"But they would have gotten to Jared sooner or later. The police found the Bible and Rita's notes about her fight with Maggie when they searched your car. You obviously didn't read the family record page where Rita had recorded Angie's birth as well as Jared's. And there was another paper tucked between the pages. Jared had been harassing and threatening Rita. And Parker had been embezzling money from Rita, pretending he'd made a bad investment. She'd decided to cut Maggie out…because of Jared. She'd asked Angie to come for a visit so she could tell her everything."

"Some detective I am. I'd have had the whole case solved the first week if I'd bothered to unload my car and go through the things the Lorings gave me." I pretended to slap the side of my head with my good hand. "Detective Procrastination at your service. Or maybe Detective Clueless."

"Don't be so hard on yourself. All your poking around got me worried about you last night. After I heard Parker had been released, I tried to call you to be sure you were okay and I couldn't get through."

"Jared cut my phone line."

"I know that now. But after I rang you a bunch of times and couldn't get through, I got worried and drove over to check. Of course, you were already gone when I got there. Adam pulled up right behind me. I don't mind telling you we went into a complete panic when we saw the house torn apart and the front door standing open. Then Whitney heard us and came out of hiding. When she told us what happened, we called the police on Adam's cell phone."

"Why was Adam there?"

"He came over for the same reason I did…he couldn't reach you by phone and got worried." Sammi squeezed my hand. "We've got to go, but we'll be back this evening."

Whitney kissed my cheek. "I love you, Mom."

Tears stung my eyes and I turned my face toward the window. I couldn't wait to go home. I wanted to hide in the safety of my room for probably the rest of my life. It would take about that long to get over killing Jared, even if I didn't mean to and it was self-defense. I knew the bad feeling would always lie curled somewhere inside me.

Despite the bustle of the busy hospital unit, I dozed off. Someone brought a plastic lunch tray, and I forced down half a cup of chicken soup. Then I turned on the TV. I winced and reached to change the channel when I saw that the news was on. I hesitated when the camera swung in for a close up of Angie standing next to Maggie out at Rita's barn. They had their arms around each other. I wondered what had led to their becoming friends.

The interviewer brought out the fact that according to notes found in her Bible, Rita had intended to write Maggie out of her will, but Angie intended for Maggie to get half the estate. Angie had been much more generous to Maggie than I'd ever imagined she'd be. The reason for that became clear when Angie referred to Rita as "my birth mother" and called Maggie her dear aunt. So she knew. Maybe she'd known all along.

Now I understood what Jared had been using to try to blackmail Rita. And I understood a lot more. After their grandparents had disowned Maggie and forced her to give up her child, Rita hadn't dared let them know about her own pregnancy. They'd gone to their graves never knowing that Rita had "sinned." She'd inherited their estate while Maggie had gotten almost nothing. Maggie must have known, though. It was likely she'd promised to keep Rita's secret in exchange for an occasional handout and an eventual big payout. I was sorry Rita had died, but I was glad Maggie was finally going to get something.

Poor Maggie. Despite the fact that he was a killer, Jared was still her son.

I flicked off the TV. I'd no sooner lowered the head of my bed back to "resting, do not disturb" then I heard a sound outside my door. I looked up, expecting a nursing assistant to come in to pick up the tray.

"Not you," I said when I saw that the figure in the doorway was not a hospital employee. I glanced down at the front of my stylish hospital gown.

Adam sauntered into the room carrying a basket of fruit. He put the fruit on the dresser next to the flowers, and pulled a chair close to the head of the bed. "What kind of a greeting is that for a friend?"

"Sorry. It's only that I feel so ashamed, stupid, and all the rest."

"I don't think you're stupid. Sammi told me everything last night while we were waiting in the ER. Even the part about Kenneth saying you have to give up your horses. For whatever it's worth, Leigh, I'd never do that to you and Whitney."

"Did she tell you I was a terrible detective? Rita's Bible that held clues about Jared has been in a box of books in my car since the day after she was killed."

"So? The last time I checked, I didn't see any detective training certificates on your wall. And when it came down to the end, you figured things out and you did what you had to do to save Whitney and yourself."

Something about the way he was looking at me, made me suspicious. "Uhmm, did Sammi tell you anything else?"

He shot me an impish grin. "Nothing much. Except that she's sure you're still not over me and sure I'm still in love with you and she thinks we're both acting silly to pretend otherwise."

I rolled my eyes. "Great. Good old Sammi. I'm going to kill her when I feel up to it. Well, not kill her. No point in making a habit of killing people. For your information, I'm sure I don't care all that much about you. Almost positive."

"Hey, thanks. Nice room," Adam said looking around. "Very, you know...soothing. A soothing kind of place where you can heal."

I nodded. "It is. I feel very soothed." Slowly, watching his eyes, I reached out and took his hand, hanging on as though it were a lifeline.

"You know, I think it's only fair to tell you," he said after a few moments.

I dropped his hand. "Tell me what?"

"I'm not seeing anyone right now."

"You mean you broke up with...the redhead? The one I saw you with the day Rita was killed." I didn't know what else to call her. He'd never mentioned her name.

"The redhead, as you call her, was part of a group I took out on the boat. She was only in town for two days, and you happened to see us together the day we went out for coffee. Perfectly innocent."

"And you happened to see me with Kenneth telling him I was not going to sell my place and move into the model home he'd picked out for me. Perfectly innocent."

"Glad to hear it."

Some hard part of me—okay, a *stubborn* part—cracked. When I could speak, I said, "Adam, I think it's only fair I tell you something, too."

"What's that?"

"I have to sell my place. I'm giving Kenneth his equity in the property and every cent he paid toward the purchase of Sonny Joe. Even though we bought Sonny for Whitney and I didn't do anything wrong to let him pay for half, I'm not going to let him keep trying to control my life."

"Are you sure?" We were holding hands again and this time I didn't know who'd initiated the move. "I can't see you giving up your horses. Maybe I can help."

"No," I said quickly. "You can't. But I'm going to speak to my Aunt Dorothy. There's a place next door to her for sale. She's talked about buying it, but the property is more than she can handle. I think we can work something out." I was sure we could. She'd promised to help and only my pride had stood in my way.

But it wouldn't be a one way deal. I'd help in her house and her garden, even manage the grove for her if she wanted me to, and I'd pay her back every cent.

I felt better now. I'd only hide in my room feeling bad for about ten years now. Or maybe not quite that long. After all, Whitney and Adam needed me.

I wondered if Heidi and George would get along. But, hey, with Adam holding my hand and whispering something about us belonging together, the last thing I needed to worry about was my dog's social life. I closed my eyes and let Adam feed me grapes from the fruit basket he'd brought me. And promised myself I'd never get involved in a murder investigation again.

Breinigsville, PA USA
03 January 2009
230135BV00001B/148/P